ON THE ORIGIN OF SPECIES

Count Lambert nodded, then said, "There has been a lot of talk about witchcraft lately, Sir Conrad. Do you think...?"

"No, my lord, I don't. So-called 'witches' are just a bunch of crazy old ladies. If they ate properly, most of them wouldn't be senile."

"But everyone knows about witches!"

"Tell me, my lord, why is it that every witch you hear about is a poor miserable old hag? If they really had magical powers, wouldn't they make themselves into beautiful wealthy young women?"

"You have a point there. I'll keep an eye out for beautiful young grandmothers who are rich."

By Leo Frankowski
Published by Ballantine Books:

THE ADVENTURES OF CONRAD STARGARD
Book One: The Cross-Time Engineer
Book Two: The High-Tech Knight
Book Three: The Radiant Warrior
Book Four: The Flying Warlord*

COPERNICK'S REBELLION

*Forthcoming

THE
RADIANT
WARRIOR

**Book Three in the Adventures of
Conrad Stargard**

Leo Frankowski

A Del Rey Book

BALLANTINE BOOKS ● NEW YORK

A Del Rey Book
Published by Ballantine Books

Copyright © 1989 by Leo A. Frankowski

Library of Congress Catalog Card Number: 89-90700

ISBN 0-345-32764-0

Printed in the United States of America

First Edition: July 1989

Cover Art by Barclay Shaw

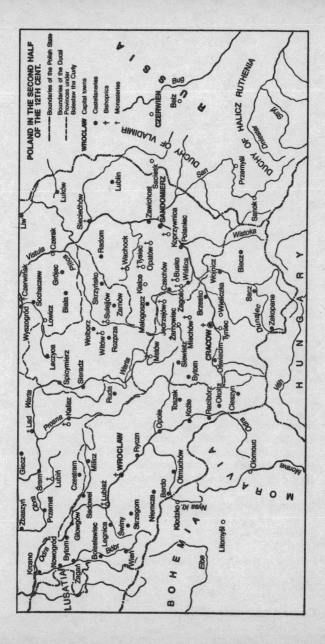

POLAND IN THE SECOND HALF OF THE 12TH CENT.

———— Boundaries of the Polish State
– – – Boundaries of the Ducal
– · – · – Provinces under Bolesław the Curly

WROCŁAW   Capital towns
●   Castellaneries
✝   Bishoprics
†   Monasteries

Prologue

SHE UNLOADED the temporal canister, glanced quickly at her new subordinate, loaded it with her last superior, and sent it two and a half million years uptime. One contact every fifty years and that for only a few seconds. Life this far back was a bitch.

The new arrival was biosculpted into a male version of herself, a type twenty-seven protohuman. He was barely four feet tall, skinny and with dark brown skin. He was also naked, since clothing wouldn't be invented for millions of years.

She switched off his stasis field.

He looked up at the stalactites hanging above him from the cave roof. Confused, he looked over at her.

"Surprise! You son of a bitch!" she shouted. "Welcome to two and a half million B.C.! Welcome to a hundred years of dodging leopards and eating grubs and shivering up in a tree all night, you bastard, because it's all your fault!"

"What? Where am I?"

"The where is eastern Africa, you lucky boy, but the fun part is the when! You're in the Anthropological Corps now and you get to do the exciting work of tracking protohuman migration patterns!"

"This must be some sort of a joke! And you are the rudest and the ugliest woman I've ever seen!"

"Watch your language, buster! I'm your boss and will be for the next fifty years. And if you think *I'm* ugly, just wait until you see yourself in a mirror, not that we have one."

"What is going on here? None of this makes sense! I was in twentieth-century Poland, doing my paperwork, when the monitors came in and I woke up here. And I look like you?"

"Yeah, minus the floppy tits, ugly."

"But . . . why?"

"Your file says it's a punishment detail for gross incompetence. You completely failed to brief a new subordinate on security procedures! She left the wrong door open. And the Owner's own cousin, who had never heard of time travel, got transported back to Poland's thirteenth century, ten years before the Mongol invasions. Then the Owner himself found his cousin in the battle lines during the invasion. The man had been there for ten years before he was discovered! There was nothing they could do about it without violating causality. When you screw up, you don't fart around!"

"But . . . without notification, without trial?"

"You mess with the Owner's family, you're in deep shit, boy!"

"Well . . . what are you doing here, then?"

"You don't recognize me? I suppose I should be crushed, you bastard, but I'm not. I'm the woman that you failed to brief, you shithead! I've been in this lousy pest hole for fifty years because of you, and now I've got fifty more to get you back for it!"

"Surely, madam, there's no reason to be vindictive about it. After all, if we're both in the same boat—"

"A boat wouldn't be this bad, bastard! We are in the middle of a bloody wilderness with nothing to eat but carrion and grubs! There's nothing to do but wander around after a tribe with less brains than a bunch of morons, and nobody to talk to that has a vocabulary of over forty words except each other.

"Hell yes, I'm vindictive! And I'm going to stay that way for the next fifty years!"

He rolled over and groaned.

She looked at him. "Well, in fifty years, my replacement will be the dolt at the thirteenth-century portal who should have caught your screw-up. Then you get to be *his* boss. It gives you something to look forward to."

He groaned again.

Chapter One

▲▲▲▲▲▲▲▲▲▲▲▲▲▲▲

FROM THE DIARY OF PIOTR KULCZYNSKI

My name is Piotr Kulczynski. I am an accountant. I was taught my craft by the lord I serve, Sir Conrad Stargard.

He is a good lord, and well loved by his people, for he is a giant in mind, body, and soul.

His learning is renowned above that of all other men, and scarce half a day passes when he does not create some useful device or demonstrate some new technique or sing some new song. He has built great mills and efficient factories for his lord Count Lambert and on his own lands, gifted to him by that count, he has thrown up huge buildings in but a few months. Our Church of Christ the Carpenter at Three Walls is reputed to be the biggest in Poland. Sir Conrad says that soon we will be making iron and steel in vast quantities, as well as a sort of mortar called cement.

He is vastly tall, and must bend his head to pass through any normal doorway. For his buildings at Three Walls, he decreed that the doors be tall enough to let him pass with his helmet on. He claims that the next generation of children will be, some of them, as tall as he, because they will be eating properly. The carpenters built as he required, but they laughed that any children of his size must be of his get.

His prowess in battle is above that of all others, and but three days agone he defeated one of the greatest champions in Poland, the Crossman Sir Adolf, in Trial by

Combat. He not only destroyed that Knight of the Cross easily, he actually played with the man while he did it, first throwing away his shield and then his sword, winning the fight with his bare hands to show that God was truly on his side.

And he is a saintly man, kind to those in need and always ready to help the poor, the aged, the oppressed. The very Trial I mentioned was caused when, out of pity for a gross of Pruthenian slaves, he beat seven Crossmen in fair combat, killing five and wounding a sixth almost to the death, then saving that man's life with his surgical skill. He met that caravan of slaves when he was traveling a great distance to ransom a casual acquaintance with a vast sum, to keep that man from being hung.

And he has been blessed by God. At the Trial, after he had defeated his opponent so easily, he was foully attacked by four other Crossmen. With my own eyes, I saw four golden arrows fall from the sky, killing the men who would have harmed the Lord's Anointed.

Yet he is my enemy.

Never would I do harm to my lord, nor even think evil of him, for evil is far from all his words and deeds. But since I was a small child I have loved Krystyana.

Before I dared profess my love to her, she was chosen by Count Lambert to be one of his ladies-in-waiting. I could do nothing while she warmed Count Lambert's bed, and those of his knights, for she went to this task willingly. Yet I was consoled, for it is the custom of that lord, once one of his ladies was with child, to marry her to one of the commoners of his village. My father promised to talk to Count Lambert and to Krystyana's parents when the time was right, and I thought that one day within the year I would have my love by my side.

But then Sir Conrad came to Okoitz. He came from someplace to the east, though from exactly where is a mystery, for a priest laid a geas on him that he may not speak of his origins.

I was among those to whom he taught mathematics, and he paid the priest to teach us our letters. He gave me a responsible position, keeping the books of his inn, his brass works, and now the city he was building at Three Walls. This made me a man of some substance, which bolstered my claim to Krystyana's hand.

Then Count Lambert sent my love, along with four others, with Sir Conrad to the vast lands awarded him.

Sir Conrad gave all five ladies positions of considerable importance, and it is his custom that no woman may be forced into marriage, nor even strongly encouraged, but that each may marry the man of her own choosing, or even not marry at all.

My love Krystyana has never looked kindly on me. Even when our positions force us to work together—for she manages the kitchens that feed Sir Conrad's nine hundred people, and I must account for every penny spent—she treats me coldly.

Long have I been convinced that could she but lay by my side for a single night, her love would come to me. Yet I see no way that this could happen.

Today at Count Lambert's town of Okoitz, Annastashia—one of Sir Conrad's five ladies—was married to that fine young knight Sir Vladimir. It was a beautiful ceremony, with Sir Conrad giving the bride away and all the ladies crying. But Krystyana's thoughts were plain on her face, and I knew that she would not be content to marry anyone less than a true belted knight, and that knight, Sir Conrad.

So I wait while hope dwindles.

FROM THE DIARY OF CONRAD SCHWARTZ

The evening after my Trial by Combat, I was annoyed to discover that my loyal carpenters were so convinced that I would lose and be killed that they had made a beautiful coffin for me, and that my loving masons had cut me a fine tombstone. Now they wanted me to tell them what to do with the damn things! I ranted for a while about their lack of faith. Then I rejected my first three thoughts about where these things should be stuffed, deciding that the man who had lost the fight didn't deserve any special favors from me.

The coffin was really a nicely carved rectangular chest, without anything overtly morbid about it, so I told them to carry it back to Three Walls. I'd use it for storing clothes.

We threw away the stone, and much later I found it used as an outdoor table, with my name still carved on it. I should have smashed the damn thing.

I was also miffed to discover that most of my workers had bet against me when I fought Sir Adolf. One of them explained that it was the sensible thing to do. After all, if I won, they knew that their futures were secure, but if I lost, they would each need every penny just to survive! It still left a bad taste in my mouth.

I was able to talk to the Bishop of Wroclaw just before he returned to his cathedral. He was actually in the saddle when he granted me an audience.

"Your excellency, I now have a city of over nine hundred souls without a full-time priest. But I don't want just any priest. I want a man who is capable of running an entire school system. Is it possible for me to get such a scholar?"

"That's interesting, my son, for not three days ago I got a letter from an excellent young scholar looking for just such a position. I shall write him immediately on my return to Wroclaw. Yes. It will be nice having an intelligent Italian in the diocese."

He gave me his ring to kiss, and rode off before I could reply. I had to wait for someone to come all the way from Italy? That could take a year!

Sir Stefan and his father, the baron, were leaving at the same time. There was a lot of bad blood between us, starting last winter over a disagreement about working hours. Since then, a number of other things had caused friction between us, and the man had become my avowed enemy. Everything I did seemed to fan his hatred, and I had just about given up trying to get him off my back. As he left, he bit his thumb at me in insult.

"It's not over, Conrad!" he shouted.

* * *

Christmas at Okoitz was as raucous as it had been the year before. With my people there as well as Count Lambert's and the workers from the cloth mill, the church was no longer big enough to hold us all. They cleared the dyeing vats, washing tubs, and other equipment out of the first floor of the cloth factory, and we held the affair there.

Along with Count Lambert and myself, Sir Vladimir, his two brothers, two of his sisters and all of their husbands and wives, plus his parents sat at the high table along with the priest and the priest's beautiful wife. Added to these were my four remaining ladies and Count Lambert's current six (he was trying to cut down). Thus twenty-four nobles were available for the peasants and workers to take out a year's aggressions on. You'd think that the pranks would have been spread around a bit more, but Count Lambert and I still caught the brunt of it.

At least this year I knew what to expect, and could psych myself up to play the clown before I had to do it. They selected a King of Misrule by passing out bread rolls with a bean in one of them. As luck would have it, the bean came to one of my topmen, the men who climbed to the tops of the huge trees to cut them off so that the trees could be felled. The topmen were all extroverted Yahoos, and I had not been polite to them lately.

The Queen of Misrule fell to one of the clothworkers, a remarkably attractive young woman who at least looked the part.

I won't bore you with the buffoonery that went on. Count Lambert and I left as soon as possible and retired to his chambers.

"Gad! I swear it gets worse every year!" Count Lambert said as he took off the yard-long codpiece he had been forced to wear. He filled two silver goblets from the silver pitcher on the sideboard and handed one to me.

"I can't see how next year could possibly get rowdier, my lord." I took off the pointed wizard's hat I'd been given and took a long pull. The drink was what I needed, though in fact it was wretched stuff. The lack of glass bottles and decent corks ruined medieval wine pretty quick. Most of it was drunk in the year after the grapes were squeezed, and nobody ever considered recording the vintage; wine didn't last long enough to age.

"Just wait. On some matters a peasant can be very creative. But there's nothing to be done. Custom is custom." He sat down on a chest next to a table and motioned me to the one opposite. A chessboard was already set up.

"Still, my lord, it marks the end of quite a year." I picked up a pawn from each side, shook them in my cupped hands and concealed one in each fist, offering them to him.

"It has been that. Think! A year ago today was the first time I'd met you. One might say it's our anniversary. A year ago yesterday you killed that brigand, Sir Rheinburg, who had been infesting my lands and killing my people. And three days ago you killed Sir Adolf right here on my tourney field. Counting your battle with the Crossmen on my trail, that makes three fights in one year!" He had chosen black and was moving his pieces out in the Dragon variation that I had made the mistake of showing him.

"More than that, my lord, depending on what you call a fight. By the time I got here, I had been involved in four separate acts of violence." There wasn't much I could do about his opening but make the standard replies.

Seeing his eyebrow raise at "four," I said, "There was my first run-in with Sir Adolf where he bashed me in the head. Then one night on the river at Cracow, Tadaos the boatman killed three thieves who were trying to murder him. You know about the irate creditor on your trail, and the fight with Sir Rheinburg's band of hoodlums. The fight with the whoremasters' guild in Cieszyn took out three of the thugs, and against those child molesters, Sir Vladimir and I killed or maimed six out of the seven Crossmen.

"I guess I can't count the incident at the ferry at Cracow last summer, since it started when I got a rock on

the side of my head and it was over before I got my wits
back. The rabies victim wasn't a fight. He had me so
scared that I killed him out of fright. It was simple
murder." The opening was over, and Count Lambert was
moving from a Sicilian defense into a strong center position.

"That last thing you mentioned, this 'rabies victim,'
was a *vampire*. They must be killed. You did right, Sir
Conrad. But think, in about a year you have been in
what?—say ten bits of action. You forgot your brawl
with Sir Stefan. Do you realize that I haven't had the
chance to draw my sword in earnest in four years? And I
must spend a third of my time on the road."

"True, my lord, but you always travel in the company
of a dozen armored knights." Now what the devil was I
going to do about that damn bishop?

"Dog's blood, but you're right! From now on I'll
travel in simple garb and I'll travel alone! Let the rest
follow an hour behind! That ought to get some action
going."

"My lord, I was just talking idly, trying to get your
mind off your chess. I never meant to get you killed!" I
was being forced into the corners where I couldn't ma-
neuver.

"Well, damn the chess! I know! I'll fill two saddlebags
with silver, and try to hide the fact. Word will spread like
a covey of scared rabbits!" He took my queen's bishop.

"Please, my lord. Your life is important to me." I
slaughtered his knight in return.

"Well, thank you. A touching sentiment. But a man
must keep his hand in, musn't he?" He took my knight
with his pawn! Now why the hell?... Oh no!

It was best not to let this run too long. "You never
told me how your beehives were doing, my lord." I castled, but I knew it was too late.

"What? Oh, wonderful! Twenty-nine of your hives
caught themselves bees. We only harvested six of them,
but think! From what you said, that means there must be
twenty-nine wild hives out there. Add that to the
twenty-three I left, and that means fifty-two new hives

next year, for a total of seventy-five! And every man of mine will have at least a gross of hives next summer! In a few years, we'll have honey pouring out of our noses!" He continued his merciless attack.

That last simile bothered me because like most engineers, my mental imagery is entirely too graphic. I see things while people are talking. The image formed was of honey coming out of Count Lambert's nose and being licked up as soon as it filtered through his thick moustache. Sometimes I wish I was a dull person.

"I wish my own had done as well. By the time I got to my lands last summer, it was a bit late in the season. My gross of beehives only got me eight colonies." I made a try at forking his king and rook, but he saw it and blocked.

"A pity! Shall I harvest one more of mine and send it to you?" He pushed an innocent-looking pawn.

"Thank you, my lord, but no. You know my customs. I always eat the same as my workers. Split between nine hundred people, the harvest of one hive would come to about one honey cake each. In a few years, we'll have enough to make mead." I was forced to trade a bishop for two pawns.

"Mead! I've heard of that. My grandfather was said to have loved it. But who could afford to drink it now, honey being as rare as it is? I doubt if anyone still knows the way of making it. Do you know?" He took my queen's rook, hardly glancing at the board.

"It happens that I've made several barrels of the stuff. It's simple enough, and in truth, my lord, it was better than what we're drinking. I'll show your people how when the time comes."

In modern Poland, the making of alcohol in any form is illegal without a state license. In America, where I went to college, any adult may make wine or beer, up to two hundred gallons a year, which is a lot. One of my dorm brothers was over twenty-one, and—purely in the interest of studying ancient technology—we had produced seven plastic garbage containers of the stuff, mead being the cheapest palatable drink that is easily made. I recall that it was under two dollars a gallon, buying honey wholesale and making mead of twelve percent alcohol.

"Sir Conrad, I know that I have said this too many times before, and that you have always proved me wrong. But what if you should die? What if no one else remembers how to make it?"

My position was untenable. I saw a forced mate in five moves, and Count Lambert would probably see a shorter one. I tipped my king over, acknowledging defeat. Count Lambert started to reset the board for another game, turning the board so that I would play black.

"As you wish, my lord. You dilute the honey with water at the ratio of three-to-one if you want a sweet wine, or from four-to-one even to six-to-one if you want a dry wine for hot summer afternoons. Boil it for a little while and skim off the foam that comes up.

"Add spices if you want to. You might have some fun playing with them. Lemons are good, but I don't think you can get them here. You might try substituting a few handfuls of rose hips. Or try apples. In fact, substituting apple juice for the water, and using less honey makes a fine drink. All of that is to your own taste. Making any wine is an art form.

"The only important point is to use wine yeast, not beer yeast. That is to say, have a merchant bring you some very new wine up from Hungary. Tell him you want it still bubbling when it gets here. Put a little of the dregs into the mead after it has cooled.

"It's fit to drink in a few weeks, and it will last a long time if you keep the air away from it. After that, always save some of the dregs from the last batch to start the new one. Start out with new barrels, and keep it far away from a beer brewery or a bakery."

Once I had a glass works going, I could make a vapor lock easily enough. These people didn't have a decent cork, anyway. The nearest cork trees were in Spain, and I doubt if the Spaniards knew what to do with them. A siphon? The nearest rubber tree was in the Amazon valley!

"That's all? Not nearly as hard as the way you told us of making steel! You've taught us so much. Your mills, the factories, your excellent hunt! Did I tell you that I have thought on a way to do one of your 'Mongol hunts' on all of my lands, and thus clear them of the wolves and bears that have been killing my people?"

"No, my lord, you hadn't." Count Lambert had gotten entirely too good at the modern far-flung sort of chess-style. This time I threw an old-fashioned Stonewall attack at him.

"Well, you remember that the problems were that my lands are many days' walk across, and if the peasants acting as beaters had to be out more than one day, we would have difficulty sheltering them at night, for the hunt must take place in the late fall, when the game is the fattest and the furs are good.

"Also, no one knew how we could keep the wolves from sneaking out in the dark.

"The solution is simple. Not one big hunt, but a lot of smaller ones! I shall divide my lands into many smaller 'hunting districts.' Each of these will be of such a size that a man can walk from the border to the center in less than a day." He replied to the Stonewall in the standard manner. He hadn't forgotten a thing!

"Interesting, my lord, but what stops the animals from crossing from one district to another between hunts? You could have one district cleaned out, and then have it reinfested before you cleared out the next." I fianchettoed my queen's bishop.

"Not if we do all of them on the same day! I think I have peasants enough to do it, and if the nobles tire of the sport, why, the commoners can help with the killing as well. Also, I think that many knights from the surrounding counties might well come if invited." He was pushing in at my center again.

"It sounds good to me, my lord. You can count on my support." I castled king's side.

"More than that, Sir Conrad. I was counting on your leadership. I want you to organize the thing."

"Well, if you wish, my lord. But are you sure that I'm

the best man for the job? I really don't know much about hunting. I don't know the borders of your lands at all. And I don't know which of your knights and barons own which sections of your lands. I don't even know who the surrounding counts are, except for your brother."

"It could be a very remunerative position, Sir Conrad. As Master of the Hunt, you could claim a certain portion of the take for yourself. All the deer skins, for example."

"Thank you, my lord. But I repeat, I'll do it if you want me to, but I don't think I'm the best man for it."

"I've already *said* that I want you to!"

I sighed. When Count Lambert wants something, he gets it. Best to bow to the inevitable. "As you wish, my lord, and thank you. Would you object if I appointed a deputy to assist me?"

"Not in the least. Who did you have in mind?"

"I think I'll ask Sir Miesko first. If he's not interested, then perhaps Sir Vladimir."

"Excellent. Let me know when everything's settled. No hurry on anything. Work all winter if you need to."

"Thank you, my lord. On another subject, the second mill, the one that is to thresh and grind grain. I can't help noticing that work is slowing down. Do you know why that is?" I was being smashed back into the corners again.

"In fact I do. I ordered it slowed down because I haven't figured out yet what to do with my lawbreakers if there is no grain to grind. As it is, if there are no law-breakers, my peasants must take turns at the hand-operated mill. After all, the grain must be ground and everybody knows it. This keeps them all on the lookout for any infraction. It also gives me a form of punishment that everyone knows is not cruel, but simply tedious. Few men would turn in a neighbor for a whipping, but for a few days at the stone? Why, that's treated with humor.

"As a result, I have very little real crime and my people all love me. But without their having to grind grain, what am I to do?"

"I see, my lord. So you need a job that is unpleasant but necessary, and must be done year around by a few men."

"Yes. You have a thought?"

"Perhaps, my lord. Did you know that right here, we are sitting on top of one of the world's major coal deposits?"

"Coal? Right here?"

"Many layers of coal, my lord. They stretch almost all the way from Cracow to Wroclaw. I don't know how far down the first big seam is around here, but it's one of the thickest in the world, more than two dozen yards thick in most places. I would guess that it's at least eight dozen yards down. But most farmers would find working in a mine to be unpleasant."

"Yes, I can see it! It might work! Slaving all day in the cold and dark and wet! They *are* cold, wet, and dark, aren't they?"

"Most assuredly, my lord."

"Yes, that would solve the problem nicely. Only, what would we do with all the coal?"

"Well, heat your houses with it, for starters! Later on, I'll show you lots of things you can do with it."

"Now, Sir Conrad, I know that won't work. I know a man who tried to burn coal in his firepit. It stank up his house so badly that they all had to run out into the snow! That house stank for years!"

"In an open firepit, you're right my lord. It takes a special kind of a stove. I hope to be making potbellied stoves by next summer, at a price that a peasant can afford. They'll burn anything."

"Excellent! It's getting to be a long walk for firewood, and the peasants will see the need for coal. You will be able to show my people the way of digging this mine?" He took my rook and knight in rapid succession. All I got out of it was his bishop.

"Of course, my lord."

"Then it's settled. I'll have work speeded up on the grain mill. It should be done by spring, so have your plans ready right after spring planting.

"Another thing I wanted to discuss with you. I like that blacksmith you sent me. I don't think he's as good as Ilya, but he doesn't make me mad enough to kill twice

a day. What say I trade you, Ilya for the new man?" I
lost my queen.

"Fine by me, my lord, if both men are willing."

"They are. It was them that brought the matter up to
me. They also both wanted to leave Ilya's wife here, but
I don't see how we can allow that. The Church would
not be pleased, and it's never been too happy with me."

"The Church is not pleased because you are separated
from *your* wife, my lord. Why can't you grant the same
privilege to Ilya?"

"Why? Because I'm a nobleman and he's a commoner, that's why! The commons don't have the brains
or the ability to regulate their own lives properly. That's
why they serve us, and why we serve them. I may not be
the pillar of marital fidelity, but my wife has not taken
another husband and I have not taken another wife.
What these smiths are proposing is nothing less than that
the one should step into the bed of the other! That is
clearly against the laws of the Church. Without the influ-
ence of the Church and Christian morality, we'd have
nothing but chaos on our hands! The Church must be
maintained and its laws enforced!"

"I suppose you're right, my lord. Well, what's a few
more mouths to feed?" I lost my last knight and my position was terrible. I knocked over my king. I had lost two
out of two. Damn. When we first started playing, a year
ago, I'd won the first two dozen games.

"Good. Then shall we go make an appearance at the
festivities?"

They started the gift-giving when we returned. The
gambling pot I'd won in the course of surviving my Trial
by Combat had a fair amount of jewelry in it, which
made gift-giving pretty simple. I started with those
nobles least important to me, Sir Vladimir's sister and
her husband who had come down from Gneizno. I'd
never met them before and would likely never see them
again, so a small gift was appropriate. I took out a sack
of my least valuable jewelry, poured it on a tray and
asked each to choose what he or she wanted. They were
delighted.

As I went up my guest list, I periodically noted when

the pile was growing small and added another sack of jewels, a step up from the first batch, but nobody knew that but me. My own ladies were near the end, and after Annastashia took her choice, I added to it the purse of silver I had denied her a few days before.

"I hear you've been acting properly, daughter!" I said, and the crowd cheered. The rumor was out that she had thrown Sir Vladimir out of her bed once I'd adopted her and she was no longer a peasant wench.

I'd saved Count Lambert's priest, Father John, and his magnificent French wife until the end. Lady Francine was easily the most beautiful woman I had seen in this century. She chose a heavy gold pendant and chain with some sort of green stone in it. It might have been an emerald, but who could tell? It was polished smooth and glassy, since the cutting of facets hadn't been invented yet.

"Father John, last year I was ignorant of local customs and didn't realize that I owed you a gift, so the best I could do at the time was a poor one. This year, I notice that your altar furnishings could use some improvement. Would this be acceptable?"

I held up one of the stranger things I'd found in my booty from the Crossmen, a large and ornate glass goblet. The crowd's reaction surprised me. Gold and silver jewelry they had taken in their stride, but a piece of glass got a chorus of "oohs" and "aahs."

Father John stood up. "Last year I gave you some of my carvings. This Christmas I hadn't expected to see you alive! The truth is that I have nothing to give you in return!" The crowd laughed.

"Well, you won't get off that light!" I said. "We've just built a big church at Three Walls that is bare of all carving. I'll take it out in trade!" The crowd was in a good mood.

The other nobles distributed their gifts. I collected quite a lot of nicely embroidered garments, and Sir Vladimir and his brothers had clubbed up to buy me a magnificent gold-handled dagger, with all sorts of stone and inlay work.

Count Lambert's gift to me was to publicly appoint me his Master of the Hunt, a job that I didn't want. I tried to take it with good grace.

After most of the gift-giving was over, I stood up again. "I'm going back to Three Walls after the wedding. I won't be here for Twelfth Night, when one gifts the members of the opposite class, so I have to give my gifts to the residents of Okoitz early. Bring it in!" Four men rolled in two heavy barrels.

"Last year, Ilya promised to make each of you a set of door hinges. Then I kept him busy all year long working on my projects, and now I'm stealing him from you!" Ilya looked surprised. This was the first he'd heard of my approval of his permanent move to Three Walls. "In those barrels is a set of brass hinges and a brass door latch for every commoner's door in Okoitz—no longer will you close your doors by lifting them into place!" That brought down the house!

When the noise stopped, I said, "What's more, I'm going to be rude enough to hint at what I want for my present! You remember all those seeds I gave you last Christmas? Well, I want them back!

"If you can't do that, then give me about a quarter of your new seeds! And I'd like you to loan me the packages they came in, so I'll know what's what!" They all laughed and cheered again, so I expected that we'd have watermelon next year.

As things were winding down and I was leaving, Count Lambert half jokingly said, "You gave the priest that magnificent goblet and I only got this gold chain?"

I was dumbstruck. That chain weighed half a kilo! It was probably worth eight thousand American dollars!

"I didn't realize that you wanted the goblet, my lord. But I'll make you a promise. In four years, I'll gift you with a hundred glass goblets, and enough glassware so that every man below you, commoners and all, can toast you with it!"

It was his turn to be dumbstruck.

Chapter Two

THE NEXT day we had a beautiful wedding. Everything went off nicely, the church was packed and I gave the bride to a beaming Sir Vladimir.

As father of the bride, I paid for the wedding feast, which also was held in the cloth factory for lack of anything else large enough. Lambert gave me a good price on the food and drink, since if it wasn't for the wedding, he would have had to put on a feast that day anyway. It was the Christmas season.

The honeymoon trip wasn't then a local custom, so the next morning we went back toward Three Walls, Sir Vladimir and his new wife included. We got as far as Sir Miesko's, where they were ready for us.

After the workers were settled into the copious hay of Sir Miesko's biggest barn, we sat down to dinner in the manor. At his suggestion, since seven more places were available once Sir Miesko's family and my party were seated, I invited in my bailiff, my two foremen and their wives, and my accountant, Piotr.

These people were awestruck at the honor done them, and scarcely said a word as supper started, although Piotr kept glancing at Krystyana, who was sitting across from him. The poor kid was still smitten.

I told Sir Miesko about Count Lambert's plan for the Great Hunt. I also told him that I really didn't want to get much involved with it, but that Count Lambert had insisted. "What I'm building up to is that I would like you to do the job for me. Would you like to be my deputy? Count Lambert said that we could take as our portion pretty much whatever we wanted. Do you think you might be interested?"

"I might. Even a small share of the take from all of Count Lambert's lands would be vast! Consider what was harvested from your lands alone! But there are details to be considered . . ."

We were soon into a deep conversation, with Lady Richeza and Krystyana sitting between us. These two fine and understanding women looked at each other, got up, and sat back down once Sir Miesko and I had scooted close together. The conversation never broke and not a word was said about the new table arrangement.

The deal we made was that Sir Miesko would take complete charge of the project in all but name. He would divide the county into eight or nine hunting districts, and appoint a district master for each. The district masters would be responsible for building an enclosure if something suitable wasn't already available, seeing that everything was properly arranged and feeding the people participating. In return for this they would get all the deer skins taken in their district.

Peasants participating would divide one-quarter of the meat between them, and the nobles there would get another quarter. The landowners would get half the meat, proportioned according to their areas. Sir Miesko would get all the furs taken, except for the wolf skins, which were to be mine. I also got any aurochs captured, to be delivered live to me. They were an endangered species and I meant to domesticate them.

"Sir Conrad, you're taking the short end of the stick!" Sir Miesko said. It's interesting that he used an expression that has lasted to modern times. The local custom among these largely illiterate people was to account for debts by cutting notches into a stick. If I lent you three pigs, we would cut three notches into a stick of wood. Then we would split the stick about in half, down the middle of the notches, so we each had a record. When the sticks were put back together again, it would be obvious if either of us had done further whittling! Wood never splits evenly, and as the lender, the creditor, I got the larger stick of wood and became the stickholder. You, as the borrower, got the short end of the stick.

"I'm satisfied with the deal as it stands."

"Be that as it may, Sir Conrad, wolf skins aren't worth much. Half the time they're burned along with the rest of the animal! The other furs will be worth a thousand times as much."

"Fine. You'll be doing all the work and bearing all the expenses. I'm happy just to get the whole project off my shoulders. Just remember to stress that all the females and young of useful species, along with one-sixth of the males, are to be spared."

"That much is obvious, once you've explained it. But you've been given a gift and I've taken it from you."

"I said I was happy. Just try not to get me in trouble, okay?"

"Rest assured of that. But I don't think my trouble or expenses will be large. I need only write a few dozen letters. It will cost me nothing to send them since every landowner in the county, or at least their men, comes by here monthly to deliver food for your city at Three Walls."

"What? I thought that *you* were providing our food."

"I am. You asked me to keep you supplied and we agreed on prices. Surely you don't think that the hundred farmers I have here could feed the almost thousand folk you have in your valley! I mentioned your needs and your prices to my fellow noblemen, and they have delivered their surplus grains here, for pickup by your people.

"I have paid the others precisely what I have charged you, so I have made no immoral profit. I have charged them reasonable rates for fodder for their pack animals and storage in my barns, but surely you can't complain about that."

I was surprised, but I didn't have a legitimate bitch. I was getting what I had agreed on.

"No, no, Sir Miesko, I have no complaint. I simply had never thought it out. I owe you thanks for supplying my needs without bothering me with details. I hope this will be a precedent for the Great Hunt."

While we were talking, the party went on around us. Sir Miesko's wife, Lady Richeza, is the most gracious woman imaginable. Warm and caring, she was working my awkward subordinates into the conversation. By the time I was back into it, they were all talking boisterously about recent events. Soon she summoned her musicians and we were all dancing.

I noticed that little Piotr Kulcyznski asked Krystyana to dance a waltz, and she turned him down. He soon went outside, and Lady Richeza followed. As things were breaking up, she came to me. "That poor boy truly loves Krystyana."

"I know. It hurts me to see his pain. But she won't even look at him! That little kid is brilliant! With a proper education he'd be a Nobel prize winner."

"And what is that?"

"Where I come from, there is a yearly set of prizes given to those who are judged to have made the greatest contributions to an understanding of the world around us, and the greatest contributions to literature, medicine, and peace. To win one of these is a greater honor than to, say, be the chief administrator of the United Nations. It also pays well. With training, I think Piotr could win the prize in mathematics."

"Yours must be a wondrous land."

"There is much good about it, but also much bad. This land has much to be said for it."

"Yet you came here."

"It wasn't exactly voluntary. Still, I can't say that I regret it. I think I've found a home here."

"A home with Krystyana?"

"No. Please understand that I like Krystyana. She's a fine girl, an intelligent girl and competent at whatever she sets her mind to. And—I hope you aren't offended by my saying this—she's a wonderful bed partner. But, dammit, she's fifteen and I'm thirty-one! I've had seventeen years of formal schooling and she's had about three months! There's too big a gap between us to consider marriage. Marriage shoud be a thing between equals. Krystyana and Piotr and I would all be better off if they would get together."

"Do they know your feelings about this?"

"I think so. I've tried to be obvious about it."

"But you haven't actually *talked* with them about it," she said.

"No, I guess I haven't. Sometimes it's hard . . ."

"Would you object if I talked to them?"

"Object? I'd be forever grateful!"

"Then I will see what I can do."

She tried, but nothing came of it.

The next day we were back in Three Walls, and the day after was a normal working day. The country folk knocked off work for two weeks around Christmas, but the people at Three Walls had mostly been recruited from a city. City folk worked whenever work was available, and there was plenty for us to do.

Winter is the best time of the year for logging, the wood is drier and the logs are easier to move around on the snow. Also, the tops of the fir trees were about the only fodder the outdoor animals were going to get. Besides the six dozen bucks left over from the fall's hunt, we had a thousand sheep in the valley. All of them ewes.

I got a lot of ribbing about that, the gist of which was that I didn't know that rams were needed to make little sheep, but I didn't care. I happened to remember that sheep have a five-month gestation period. Any ewe you buy in December is pregnant if she's going to be. And sheep are sexually mature in six months. Next year we'd have plenty of rams. I think.

Well, I had one ram in another, much smaller herd. If he fell over dead from exhaustion next breeding season, I'd have to buy some more in a hurry.

We kept the sawmill going all winter, with sixty women walking back and forth on that huge teeter-totter. The main wooden buildings were up, but we needed lumber for furnishings, shipping containers, barrels, and so on.

Some construction went on as well. The coke ovens were dry-laid sandstone, so there wasn't any worry about mortar freezing. But putting in foundations was difficult.

The big problem was the lack of decent artificial light. By Christmas, we were down to about six hours of daylight. Most Americans don't realize just how far north Europe is. Southern Poland is farther north than Lake Superior, and our seacoast is farther north than the shores of Hudson Bay. A high latitude means a large yearly variation in the length of the day.

Mining went on continuously, of course: it was always dark down there. It was also fairly warm in the mine, and coal mining came to be the job everybody was trying to get. I hoped that Count Lambert wouldn't hear about it.

But even when the weather was good, which wasn't all that often, we were lucky to spend seven hours a day working.

Well, if you can't spend, invest!

I set up a school for the adults. A school for the children was already being taught by two of Lady Richeza's women, so once the children's school was out, the adults took over. Most of my people couldn't read, write, or do simple arithmetic.

By spring they could. That's not quite the accomplishment that it sounds, because Polish is an easier language to learn than English. Polish is absolutely phonetic in its spelling, rather than nearly random as English is. Every letter has a distinct sound, and there are no silent letters. You spell it exactly as you speak it. Learning to spell in English gave me nightmares.

Many Americans who write use spellchecking programs in their personal computers, since the English-speaking peoples can rarely spell their own language. When I got back to Poland after my college days, none of my Polish friends would believe me when I told them this. They thought that I was telling an ethnic joke!

But we had enough people around who could teach arithmetic and reading. Aside from monitoring things, teaching a course in first aid, and tutoring Piotr in math,

I had a fair amount of time to myself, which was wonderful.

I could close the door of my new office, sit down on my new armchair, put my feet up on my nice new desk and do some serious thinking. Mostly about standards. The weights and measures of the Middle Ages were a vast agglomeration of random events. Length was measured in feet, yards, cubits, spans, hands, fingers, miles, and days. Not only was there no agreed-on relationship between those units, but the size of the unit varied from place to place. A Cieszyn yard was not equal to a Cracow yard which was not equal to a Wroclaw yard.

It even varied from commodity to commodity. Fine velvets, for example, were sold by the Troy yard, which was shorter than all of the above. And these weren't minor differences of a few percent. The Wroclaw yard was half again longer than the Cracow yard.

Weights were in even worse shape. Cheese, wheat, and oats were all sold by the quarter, for example. A quarter of what, you ask? Why a quarter of cheese, wheat, or oats! There was no "whole" or "half." But a quarter of wheat was more than five times larger than a quarter of cheese, which was maybe a hundred kilos. And a quarter of oats was bigger than both of the others put together. And of course a quarter in one city was not equal to a quarter anyplace else.

Well, a pint of milk weighed a pound, but milk is the stupidest standard possible. The specific gravity of milk varies by at least five percent, with the richest milk being the lightest. It spoils quickly, so there is no possibility of having a standard jar of milk somewhere. Yet this didn't seem to bother anybody but me. Of course, if a merchant sold short weight, he might get hung, but you never got any complaints out of him after that.

The Church had been working on calendar reform for a century, and things in Poland were not really absurd. At least we all agreed on which day was Sunday and what year it was. From what a merchant friend, Boris Novacek, tells me, in Italy it is possible to leave Venice in 1232, get to Florence in 1233, then go to Milan in 1231.

Some people started the new year on Christmas, some a week later, and some on March first. For them, December really was the tenth month.

Well, we had a standard yard. Given my own choice, I would have preferred to use a meter, but my liege lord had specifically ordered me to use his yard, the distance from his fingertip to his turned-away nose. This was shorter than a meter and slightly longer than the American yard.

And we had a base-twelve numbering system. This was something that was sort of done to me at first, but I soon saw the advantages of the duodecimal system. Since twelve has more factors than ten, you run into infinitely repeating decimals less often. It often takes fewer digits to express large numbers and math just becomes easier to do.

Since last winter, I had been carefully copying down every constant I could remember, and already I had several pages of them. The distance from the Earth to the Moon and to the Sun. The specific gravity of aluminum and how many centimeters to the American yard and all sorts of things. An engineer needs thousands of numbers, and much of what I did not remember, I could interpolate.

Playing with numbers and all the constants, I was delighted to discover that a thousand (that is to say, 1728 in base ten) of our yards was almost exactly equal to an American mile! The American mile is almost equal to the old Roman mile, which was still somewhat in use.

So, a dozen yards was a dozyard. Twelve dozyards was a twelmile and twelve of these was a mile.

Going down, one twelfth of a yard was a twelyard. Divide that by twelve and you had a dozmil, and a mil was about half a millimeter.

Another nice accident that happened was that a cubic yard of cold water weighed slightly under an American ton, and a thousandth of that, or one cubic twelyard, weighed just over an American pound. This gave us a standard of weight and volume. We had a ton, a pound, and a pint, which was the volume of a pound of cold water.

In a few days, I came up with a complete set of weights and measures, all based either on our yard, or in the case of my electrical standards, on Avogadro's number. Our amp was actually related to the number of electrons flowing.

The medieval day was divided into twelve hours, as was the night. But the day was measured from sunrise to sunset. This meant that an hour on Midsummer's day was three times longer than an hour on Christmas day. This made paying people by the hour a little silly. In fact, most men were hired by the day, and were paid half as much in the winter as they were in the summer.

We obviously needed a clock, but when I set out to build one, I was annoyed to discover that I couldn't remember how an escapement worked.

A grandfather clock has a weight which drives a series of gears that turn the hands. The speed of this turning is controlled, slowed down, by a pendulum. The escapement connects the pendulum to the gear train. It must also impart a little energy to the pendulum to make up for friction losses. I couldn't sketch one that I could convince myself would work.

I was hard to live with for three days and then designed a new one. On the fast end of the gear train, I put a large drum with a zigzag groove running around it. A small wheel attached to the pendulum ran back and forth in the groove.

The gears facing the way they have to, this meant that our pendulum didn't swing from side to side. It swung forward and back. Also, it didn't go tic-toc-tic. It went fump-fump-fump. But nobody here had ever seen a grandfather clock, so I didn't hear any Polak jokes.

I also came up with a new system of time. Staying with the base-twelve standard, we had a twelve-hour day, rather than the usual twenty-four hour day. The clock was reset occasionally so that zero happened at dawn. This was at the nine o'clock position of a modern clock. At the equinoxes, three was at noon, with the fat hand pointing up, and six was at sunset. Midnight was nine, with the fat hand pointing down.

There were four hands on the face, each moving twelve times faster than the one before. After the fat hand, which showed hours, there was a longer arrow for dozminutes, a wiggly hand that showed minutes, and a thin straight hand for twelminutes. Or, you could say that the fat hand went around once a day and the skinny hand went around once a minute. Just remember that our hour was a hundred-twenty modern minutes long, and our minute was as long as fifty modern seconds.

When I got it built, using parts I had made at the brass works, I assembled them in the coffin the carpenters had made for me. I hadn't bothered trying to make anything small, and that coffin was a nice piece of furniture, even though I got sick of looking at it in my bedroom. I had a built in closet and a chest of drawers, anyway.

It took about a week of TLC ("Tender, Loving Care" in the colorful slang of American engineers) to get it working reasonably well, and it never was accurate to more than one percent, but it was good enough. It had to be oiled daily (goose grease seemed to work best) and the weight raised just as often, but what the heck.

I set the clock up by the south wall of the dining room, so the fat hand, which had a little sun on it, moved about with the position of the sun. People seemed to have very little difficulty reading it, or picking up the concept of standard time. I simply said that we would start work when the fat hand was here, eat dinner when it was there, and stop work when it was over there. Krystyana made sure that the kitchen staff served our meals according to the clock, and that was that. There are advantages to being a medieval lord. No committees!

Our system of measuring angles naturally followed from this clock. Imagining a horizontal line drawn through the axle of the hands, you called out an angle as though it was a time of day as shown by the fat hand. A three o'clock angle was a right angle, and all angles were measured clockwise rather than counterclockwise, as is the modern way of doing it.

I also designed a calendar, with four thirteen-week quarters and no months at all. New Year's Day happened on the winter solstice, and wasn't a day of the week. That is to say, it went Saturday, New Year's Day, Sunday. On leap years, there were two New Year's Days. This meant that the calendar for every year was the same, and should reduce confusion considerably. But I tabled it because I decided that I couldn't get away with it.

I could get away with designing a system of weights and measures because there were so many of them that one more didn't make much difference. I could design a new clock because nobody had ever seen a clock before, not in Poland, anyway. But the Church had spent centuries fumbling with the calendar and it would take someone with a lot more weight than I had to push a new system through. Maybe once I beat the Mongols.

Toward the end of January, I made my monthly visit to Okoitz. It was part of my contract with Count Lambert.

I got there early in the morning, since my mount, Anna, can travel farther in half an hour than a peasant family can walk in two days.

There was a commotion in the bailey when I got there, and Count Lambert waved me over to one of the peasant's rooms on the outer wall. "Some trouble here, Sir Conrad. Perhaps you should look at it."

An entire family was lying in the bailey on the usual straw mattresses. They were all dead, with not a mark on them. A man, his wife, and four children lay peacefully as if asleep, their bodies cold and stiff. A fire had burned itself out, but these huts had straw roofs and the walls weren't all that well-sealed. I didn't see how it would be possible to asphyxiate in there. It hadn't been particularly cold, so I doubt they had all frozen to death.

Food poisoning? I'd seen a woman get ptomaine once, and there had been nothing peaceful about it. There had been vomit all over the place!

Some disease? That had to be it, but I'd never heard of a disease where the person didn't even know he was dying.

I came out and said, "I'm mystified, my lord. All I can imagine is some disease. Once these people are taken care of, have sulfur burned in there. Burn all their food stores, on the off chance that they somehow poisoned themselves. In fact, I'd suggest that you have all their belongings burned.

"And fire up your sauna. After they're buried, and get that done today, everyone who has touched the bodies should clean themselves thoroughly. But all that is simply a precaution. I really don't know what killed them." Since I had touched the corpses, I stooped and washed my hands with snow.

"It shall be as you say, Sir Conrad." Count Lambert nodded to one of his men, who went off to make arrangements. "There has been a lot of talk about witchcraft lately. Do you think . . . ?"

"No, my lord, I don't. Any so-called 'witches' around are just a bunch of crazy old ladies. If they would eat properly, most of them wouldn't be senile."

"But everyone knows about witches!"

"Tell me, my lord, why is it that every witch you hear about is a poor miserable old hag? If they really had magical powers, wouldn't they make themselves into beautiful wealthy young women?"

"You have a point there. I'll keep an eye out for beautiful young grandmothers who are rich."

"Do that, my lord. Who were these people?"

"You don't recognize them? That's Janina's family."

Janina was one of the girls that I took with me to Three Walls from Okoitz. She was running the store there and was a close friend.

"My God. It'll be rough telling her. Her whole family."

"Not quite. Her little sister—Kotcha, I think she's called—had supper and spent the night with one of the other families. The poor child is in a very bad state."

I remembered the kid now. Last winter she had become a good friend of Anna's, and together they had hauled logs in the snow. "Perhaps she should come back with me to Three Walls, my lord. She could live with Janina."

"A good thought. We will ask the child about it after the funeral."

I never did find out what killed those people.

Interlude One

I HIT the STOP button.

"So what killed them, Tom?"

"I don't know. I can check it out if you wish."

He turned on a keyboard and began typing.

"With all our technology, why hasn't somebody developed some decent artificial-intelligence programs? It can't be all that difficult. Then you wouldn't have to use that silly keyboard," I said.

"Such programs have been developed. I've just forbidden their use. Machine intelligence is dehumanizing to the people that use it. I like people and I want to live in a human world."

"Aren't you exaggerating a bit?"

"I don't think so. The ballet they put on last night. Did you enjoy it?"

"Sure. It was great. What does that have to do with computers?"

"Everything. That whole show could have been simulated by a computer and displayed in one of our tanks to a degree of accuracy such that you couldn't tell if it was real or not. Would it have been the same?"

"Hmm . . . No, somehow I don't think so, but I'm not sure why."

"Well I am. What makes ballet or any other art form worthwhile is the fact that it is done by people. When you watched the dancers, you were putting yourself in their place, imagining what they were thinking and feeling. A recording or transmission of that performance would not have been as good, because you would have been farther removed from the people doing it. A mere computer display of the same show would have been absolutely worthless."

"But if you didn't know—"

"Maybe you could have been fooled. But you would have been angry when you found out. Back to that dead family. It was an onion mold got them. Toxin 8771 from mold 15395, extinct in 1462. The really deadly ones don't last very long. Killing your host, or the people who cultivate your host, is bad ecology and not good for your own survival."

He hit the START button.

Chapter Three

MY MONTHLY two-day visits to Okoitz were used to supervise the construction there, but just then there wasn't much to do. The cloth factory was shut down until spring. Without glass or a decent light, the only way you could work indoors was next to an open window, a little rough in this weather. At that, you could only get in six hours a day in good weather.

I checked out the wet mill that sawed wood, worked hammers, and did all sorts of work. There were thousands of tons of water in there, and if it froze, the mill would be wrecked. I checked each of the tanks, but everything was still liquid. The walls of the mill were a half a yard thick at the thinnest, and that much wood is a good insulator even if it is wet. The windmill kept turning even when it wasn't in use, and my calculations had shown that the energy imparted should keep the water warm enough even in the worst weather. But theoretical calculations are often a long ways from reality! I was relieved.

Work was progressing on the grain mill, but it was simpler than the wet mill we'd built last summer, and Vitold, the carpenter, needed no help from me.

Quite a bit of logging was going on, mostly to clear land for pasturing more sheep. Count Lambert had been buying wool to keep his mill running, and he thought that this was stupid. They were using the steel saws I'd shown the smiths in Cieszyn how to make, but they didn't need my help.

So I took a sauna to make sure that I wasn't carrying

anything communicable, and then looked up Kotcha.

I sort of fell into the position of Janina's sister's foster parent. Janina was living in my household, and in fact I slept with her some of the time, so I suppose that the relationship was a natural one. Kotcha was silent through the mass and funeral ceremony. The world can be very brutal when you're nine years old. After her family was in the ground, she wanted to talk to Anna.

My mount was not an ordinary horse. She was a bioengineered creation from some advanced civilization somewhere. Or maybe I should say somewhen, because Anna said they were in the distant past and they used time machines, which she didn't understand. She couldn't talk, of course, but she could spell things out. She was intelligent in an odd sort of way, and she was a full member of my household. She even got paid like everybody else, not that she spends much of it. Most adults wouldn't believe any of this, but a nine-year-old girl has no such difficulty. They were good friends.

"Kotcha, do you think that you would like to come to Three Walls with Anna and me?"

"Where would I live?"

"Why, in my household, with your sister and me and Anna."

"Anna lives in your house?"

"Some of the time, and it's more of an apartment than a house. Anna has a stall in the barn, too, but most of the time she sleeps in the living room."

"Could I sleep with Anna?"

"If you want to. Or you could sleep with your sister or even have a room of your own, except when we have company over. I bet you'd take good care of Anna. She gets a good grooming in the barn, but I've always felt that she deserves special care."

Anna nodded her head, Yes. Then she tapped her right forehoof and scratched the ground with her left. We had this code worked out.

"You want something that you want to pay for," I said to Anna. "You mean you want to hire Kotcha?"

Yes.

"Well, what do you think, Kotcha? Do you want the job?"

"Yes!"

"Good. Does a penny a week sound all right to both of you?"

Yes and "Yes."

"Then the two of you have a deal, and you might as well start now. Give Anna a good rubdown. If you need anything, I'll be at the castle. Remember that you're in my household now, Kotcha. You can always come to me with problems."

Giving her something to do was probably the best thing for the kid. Physical activity is usually the best therapy for someone whose problems have no real solution. Nothing in the world could bring her family back, and the best thing to do was to forget.

At the same time, it was sort of funny. Lord! It was strange enough when my handmaids got handmaids. Now my mount had a private rubdown girl!

Back at the castle, I asked Count Lambert if I could take off early, since there wasn't much for me to do.

He had other ideas. He handed me a cup of wine and sat me down. "Sir Conrad, last summer you talked of various flying machines, and how most of them were too complicated for us to assay to build. But my mind has been turning over that 'hot air balloon' you mentioned. I see no reason why we couldn't make one.

"I have bolts of good linen cloth, plenty of rope, and most of that barrel of linseed oil left. There is a pile of wicker for the basket you mentioned, and I've a big, light brass serving-tray that would do to hold the fire. My wife bought it but I never use it. What say you?"

Lord. Another fad coming up. I could see it. Now that every knight in Poland was flying kites, Count Lambert had to upstage them all with a hot air balloon. But kites at least were safe. There's no telling where a balloon will come down. A man could drown, if he didn't fall out.

"My lord, this sort of thing is dangerous. You can't

control a hot air balloon. You go wherever the winds blow you, and the winds up there can be pretty fierce! You could end up in the Baltic Sea!"

"Well, what of it? You're the one who's been taking all the chances lately. Didn't we decide that last month?"

"Count Lambert, your support has meant everything to me and my projects. Without it, I might never get things going well enough to fight the Mongols in eight years."

"That's touching but no longer true. It might have been, a year ago, but now you have the support of Duke Henryk. I suspect that if I died, he just might give all my lands to you, and let my wife go hang in our lands in Hungary. Isn't it enough for me to say that I *want* this balloon?"

I exhaled. When Count Lambert wanted something, he got it. To try going against him was pissing into the wind. "As you wish, my lord. You want me to design a hot air balloon?"

"Of course! What have I been saying? Just a small one, enough to take me alone high above the hills and trees!"

"Even that will be quite large, my lord."

"What of it? You'll find I've had a drawing board of the sort you favor built and set up in your old room, along with a supply of parchment, pens, lamps, and that sort of thing. I'll send a wench to call you to supper. Pick one to your liking for tonight, but you might want to try out Natasha. She's nicely skilled. Well? Be off with you!"

I went to my room and got to work. I obviously wouldn't be allowed to leave Okoitz until I had completed a set of drawings.

I spent a few hours doing arithmetic and decided that if I could heat a sphere of air fourteen yards in diameter to fifty degrees warmer than ambient, I could lift about five hundred pounds. Was it reasonable to expect a warming of fifty degrees Celsius? Would Count Lambert plus an undefined balloon made with unspecified and unweighed materials weigh less than five hundred pounds?

I hadn't the foggiest idea. I wasn't even certain about the specific gravity of air. Nobody had ever asked me to design a balloon before.

All I could do was to make a number of reasonable-sounding engineering approximations, which my colorful American friends called WAGs: Wild Ass Guesses.

I was called to supper by an attractive and cheerful young lady who announced that she was Natasha. Again bowing to the inevitable, I asked her to join me for supper.

Once seated with Count Lambert and another lady, I was told that Kotcha was in the kitchen, and what did I want done with her?

I told Count Lambert that she was joining my household, and it seemed right that she should eat at the same table as I did. He nodded benignly. Perhaps he was glad to be getting out of having to provide for her, which he would have done if I hadn't wanted to take her, or perhaps he realized that I was quite capable of making an issue of not hurting a girl's feelings.

But in any event the ragged little nine-year-old was soon sitting wide-eyed between me and Count Lambert. He soon had his arm around her. People in the thirteenth century touched a lot more than those in the twentieth. It was a fatherly caress—Count Lambert wasn't interested in a lady sexually until she was filled out.

It was a pleasant meal. Even though there were only five of us at the table, four wenches were serving and three musicians playing. Almost everything in medieval Poland was expensive except for people. You could have as many servants as you could afford to feed. A peasant considered getting a job as a servant to be a wonderful thing. The work was easy and they fed and clothed you well, for almost no nobleman wanted ragged or starving people around.

Count Lambert got his maids by exercising a variant of his *droit du seigneuy*. Separated from his wife, he asked the prettiest girls in his town to be handmaidens. This was a euphemism, since they were usually pregnant in six months. He then found each of them an acceptable husband, paid for the wedding expenses and a small dowry, and went to church regularly, with everybody happy with him.

Musicians didn't have the high status they enjoy in the modern world. They were playing quietly in the background, ignored while the conversation went on: Muzak. I was talking. "You understand that I've never designed a hot air balloon before, my lord? I can't promise that the first one will work. We'll have to build one and see how it goes."

"Reasonable, Sir Conrad. But you've had a chance to think on it. Tell me what the first one will be like."

"It's a cloth bag, made of the same thin material that we made kites from. It's like a ball on the top and a cone on the bottom," I said, gesticulating. "It is the custom of my people to make them brightly colored, but that's up to you. It should be fourteen yards across at the widest and twenty yards high. It must be strongly made, but kept as light as possible.

"To launch it, I think if you found three big trees in your forest that grew in a triangle, and cut the tops off, they could serve to support the balloon until the air inside is warm. It should be launched only in a dead calm, the sort that often happens in the gray dawn."

"That seems easy enough. I'll have it done. You will have drawings of this before you leave, won't you?"

"Yes, my lord. Would it be too much to ask if you tethered the balloon for safety? Tied it to a tree with a long rope?"

"Well at first, of course. After that, we'll see."

"Count Lambert, I say again that there is no controlling these things. You don't know where you'll come down. Do you really want to fall into Frederick the Second's outhouse?"

"Ha! That would *stuper* his *mundi*, wouldn't it!"

I gritted my teeth, but there was nothing else that I could do.

I had Kotcha put up with a couple of Count Lambert's ladies—they were only five years older than her—and intended to get in an hour of drawing before I sacked out. Such things "*gang aft agley*" at Okoitz. Natasha was all she was cracked up to be. Lord, what an enthusiastic young lady! We went to bed early and I really didn't get much sleep. Good, though.

I started drawing the next morning, but to make an accurate drawing, with dimensions, of a single panel required an awful lot of math. And it all had to be done long hand, without a calculator of tables or anything but my skull and a goose quill pen.

Halfway through, I found that I was doing everything in decimal rather than the duodecimal arithmetic that I had taught everybody else. I have always had the darndest time thinking in duodecimal, and going over this diary, sometimes I'm not sure myself when I was talking in base-twelve and when in base-ten. So far as the balloon was concerned, I completed the calculations in base-ten and then translated the whole thing into base-twelve.

And there were all the detail drawings. How to do a tent stitch, how to fasten the ropes to the basket, the importance of carrying sandbags. I wasn't done until noon the next day.

Natasha stayed with me, eager to run errands but happy if ignored. I began to realize that there was a good mind in that pretty little head.

After dinner, I explained my drawings to Count Lambert, because he couldn't read.

"Excellent, Sir Conrad! I think we can make short work of it. You seem to have taken a fancy to my Natasha. Would you believe that not a week ago, she sported a maidenhead?"

"That's hard to believe, my lord. She's remarkably ...adept."

"Isn't she though. But I can certify it since I relieved her of that liability myself. She has a pure natural talent. See here. I've kept you half a day past our agreed time. What say I give her to you in compensation?"

"You're going to *give* her to me?"

"If you wish. As I said, she's only been here a week.

There's months and months of use in her yet."

She'd probably be a lot happier and healthier at Three Walls than at Okoitz, anyway. "I'll take her, my lord."

So I headed back to Three Walls with Kotcha riding in front of me, Natasha riding sidesaddle at my back, and my huge wolf skin cape thrown around all three of us. Anna didn't even notice the extra weight.

Once home at Three Walls, I had the unpleasant job of telling Janina about the death of her family. That cast a pall over the household for several days. But life continues and these people were used to death. They saw so much of it.

Kotcha took her job as Anna's servant quite seriously, and sometimes it was hard to get her out of the stables and into school.

Natasha, well, Natasha was remarkable. Natalia was my secretary, but handling our records, the bank, and the payroll took up most of her time. Natasha became my personal assistant, not that I'd realized that I needed any such person.

But she was quite capable of sitting for hours, sewing or knitting, without making a sound or intruding on what was going on. Then if I needed an errand run, which was fairly often in these telephoneless times, she was eager to drop everything and run it. And she always did a competent job. There was nothing stupid about her. Just absolutely . . . compliant.

It was so easy to take her for granted that sometimes I even forgot she was in the room. I occasionally neglected to dismiss her for the night. In fact, once I was in bed with Yawalda and actually in the middle of the sex act when I realized that there was another person in the room, at which point there was nothing to do but invite her in.

All told, a strange, interesting, and remarkably comfortable young woman.

And a far cry from Krystyana, who was getting increasingly feisty.

FROM THE DIARY OF PIOTR KULCZYNSKI

Sir Conrad had drawn up a table of organization for his people at Three Walls. This was a chart showing who worked for who, which made it child's play to know who to go to for a given thing. This chart was mounted on the wall in the dining room, where all could see it. Further, the name of every adult in the city was written on little pieces of wood that could be moved around on the chart. It took a while for us to grasp the significance of this. Here was a place where a man could rise! Another of his gifts to us.

It also defined the status and pay of each person, and I was surprised to discover myself near the top, directly below Sir Conrad himself, and an equal to the foremen and my love Krystyana. I was now paid three pence a day, an excellent sum, since my food, my lodging, my work clothes, my horse and expenses were all paid in addition to this. My net was easily five times what my father made, and I had naught to spend it at but the inn, which I did.

The Pink Dragon Inn was a remarkable place and all of Sir Conrad's planning. The common room was bright and clean and always full of good cheer, with good beer at reasonable prices. The waitresses were all very pretty and immodestly clad, with tall heeled shoes and fishnet stockings. They wore a hat with rabbit ears and a sort of loincloth with a rabbit's tail. And that was all. When it was cold outside, the innkeeper kept the fires high in the two big fireplaces to keep the waitresses warm but unclothed. Their bodies and breasts were bare. This had the effect of attracting the men, though most of the ladies stayed away, for fear of the competition.

Most of the people at Three Walls were from Cieszyn, except for the Pruthenians, and they were still children. The people of Sir Conrad's household were mainly from Okoitz, my hometown, but they rarely came to the inn. I usually drank with Ilya, the blacksmith foreman.

"Aren't you supposed to be with your family, Ilya?" It

is pleasant to talk as an equal with someone you once worked for. It gives a real feeling of progress. "I distinctly remember that you promised to spend half an hour a day with them when Sir Conrad allowed you space in the bachelors' quarters."

"I spent all night with her Sunday last. That's four of these new hours, so I'm good for the week. If you don't like it, I'll stuff one of your ledger books up your arse."

"But my wishes hardly matter. What if your wife doesn't like it?"

"Then I'll stuff one of them up her arse! Look. I never wanted to get married, but Count Lambert told me to do it. You know the man! Could *you* argue with him?"

"That's hardly the question. It's—"

"Count Lambert doesn't like *his* wife, so she stays in Hungary and he beds down half the girls in Silesia! But me? All I ever wanted was to be left alone! So I get saddled with a silly woman and a clutch of bawling brats! Sir Conrad doesn't want to marry, so does anybody force him to the altar with that snip of a girl you want? He's a bigshot nobleman, so of course not!"

"And I pray that never happens."

"More the fool, you! You have a silly little boy's attitude about things! You think you can marry your princess and live happily ever after! That happens in fireside stories, but it doesn't happen in life. In the first place, she'll never have you. She's set on getting herself a full belted knight, just like her friend Annastashia did. In the second, if you did get her, she'd make your life miserable, the same way every woman has made every man miserable since Adam was stupid enough to want an afternoon snack."

"There can be true love, my friend. Consider..." But I saw that he was no longer listening. He was staring over my right shoulder. I turned to see what it was about, and was shocked. No one else in the place would know her except Ilya and me, for we were the only ones here from Okoitz. But the absolutely beautiful and nearly naked serving wench tending the table behind us was Francine, the wife of the priest, Father John, at Okoitz!

"What do we do?" I whispered to Ilya. It was hard taking my eyes off her.

"I don't think we do anything, except maybe change tables so she waits on us!" He whispered back, not even looking at me. "It's none of our business. What she does and what the priest does are up to them."

"But what would Sir Conrad say?"

"What he says is up to him. Would you want her blood on your hands? This could come to that!"

She was back at the bar now, but I said, "Doesn't the inn require that every waitress be a true intact virgin? But she's been married for years!"

"I know nothing. I see nothing. I hear nothing," Ilya chanted.

Soon our waitress went off-duty for the night, so Francine tended our table. I didn't know what to say, and so was silent. Ilya pretended that he had never seen her before, and slipped a few silver pence into her loin-cloth. She acted as though she didn't recognize him, although of course she must have. They had lived in the same village for years! She gave him a hug in thank you, while he sat there, her magnificent breasts on either side of his hairy cheeks. I was dumbstruck.

She gave me a squeeze as well, even though I had not tipped her, and then went to her other tables.

Ilya refused to discuss the subject.

We stayed until closing, and then both came back the next night, to find Francine again tending our table. I'm sure that neither one of us mentioned anything to any-body, but I think somebody must have, for there was an air of foreboding about the inn that night, like a storm about to break or a battle about to be joined.

She was calling herself Mary now, but there was no mistaking her or her thick French accent. It was near closing when Francine's husband hurried into the inn.

He was in his usual clerical garb, but it was covered with snow, for it was a foul night. He was bare-headed and must have been long without his hat, for his hair and eyebrows were thick with rime.

His eyes were red, as with madness or as with one who has not slept for many days. A frightening sight! It was hard to believe that he was the quiet man who had taught me my letters.

Ilya and I froze, but the other twenty or so patrons paid little mind, at first.

"Woman, come home!"

"No!"

"You are my wife!" Father John grabbed her by the hand. She pulled herself away.

"Get away from me! I'm *not* your wife!"

I saw Father John draw a knife. "Woman!"

By this time, every man in the place was on his feet, and would have gone to her aid, had there been but time. But it all happened so quickly!

Being much smaller than the others, and behind many of them, I could not see what happened. I only heard the scream, the crash, and the dull sound of the body falling to the floor.

Chapter Four

▲∧∧∧∧∧∧∧∧∧∧∧∧∧∧∧∧▲

FROM THE DIARY OF CONRAD SCHWARTZ

Krystyana and the innkeeper's wife were shaking me awake. There was trouble at the inn.

I called for Sir Vladimir, Tadaos, and Anna. Whatever was wrong, I wanted some force behind me. As Sir Vladimir was just changing guard with Tadaos, they were both up and in armor, so I didn't bother with mine. They were ready before I was, and the four of us, followed by a crowd of gawkers, went across the snow to the inn, with Krystyana and Annastashia guarding the closed gate.

The innkeeper had let no one else leave and had touched nothing. Francine was crumpled in a corner, nearly naked. I was shocked to see her. I hadn't known that she had left Okoitz. And how could a married woman get a job as a waitress at the inn? Yet she was in that uniform, what there was of it. She stared at me, but I couldn't read her eyes.

The body was stretched out on the floor, facedown. The clerical garb was obvious, as was the trickle of blood pooling beneath the head. I turned to the innkeeper. "What the hell happened?"

"Well, my lord, the short of it was that he came in, there was some shouting, and she tried to get away. He pulled a knife and she hit him on the head with a stool. I was surprised that it killed him, but it did. I would have smashed him one myself, only I never had the chance."

I nodded, and turned the body over. The forehead

was caved in and the face was streaked with blood. It was a few moments before I recognized Count Lambert's priest.

I sat down at a table, still not quite awake. Being lord also meant that you had to be the cop, as well as the judge, the jury, and sometimes even the executioner. I noticed that Natalia had come along.

"Natalia, get everyone's name and then send them home. Lady Francine, come over here. We must talk. Somebody get us some beer." Coffee would have been more welcome, but there wasn't anything available with caffeine in it.

The place was soon cleared and the body was taken to the church. It was closing time anyway. Francine walked unsteadily over. Her long black hair was disheveled and her face was streaked with tears. They were running down her cheeks and falling to her bare breasts.

"My lady, what is this all about?" I asked.

At my gesture Natalia started taking notes on birch bark. Later, if it was needed, she would make a good copy on parchment, which was expensive.

"About? I suppose it's about my being a murderer." She spoke with a thick French accent. Her huge eyes were still gushing tears. Her tiny nipples were wet and dripping. I gave her my handkerchief.

"Murder? I'm not sure of that. They say that you tried to get away and he drew a weapon. That's not murder. That's manslaughter at the worse. I'm still not convinced that a crime has been committed.

"For starters, what are you doing here? And what are you doing as a waitress?"

She tried to dry her tears, but they kept coming. She even wiped her chin and chest.

"I came here to earn money. It takes money to travel and France is a long ways away. It is well known that a woman can make more as one of your waitresses than at any other trade, even the most sordid." Even in her emotional state, she was still rational. There was good metal under that lovely exterior.

"But a waitress must be a virgin. The innkeeper's wife should have checked it."

"She did. I qualify." She was somehow half proud and half ashamed at saying this. She was starting to get herself under control.

"But you've been married for years!"

"Have I been? Some would not say so!" You could see the anger that had been locked inside.

"You mean you never ... ?"

"I mean *he couldn't*!" The tears started again.

What a horrible situation! I tried to imagine what it must have been like for them, him with a stunningly beautiful woman by his side every night for years, and physically unable to satisfy her yearnings. Her knowing always that any of a thousand men would be eager to take her, but being a public figure in a small town, unable to act freely.

And all the while the act, the hypocrisy of pretending to be stalwart pillars of the community. It would have driven a stronger man than me to madness. "So you left him. Did you tell him where you were going?"

"We fought."

"You fought. Did he hit you?"

"We shouted and screamed. He wasn't man enough to hit me. I said that I was going back to France, and I am. But the only merchant caravan was going east. They stopped at Sir Miesko's, and I ended up here."

My decision was obvious. "I'm afraid that you will be staying here for a while. I don't think that a crime has been committed. You merely defended yourself, and I don't think that blow was meant to kill. I don't think that Father John had the right to force you back, because I don't think that he was your husband. A marriage must be consummated.

"On the other hand, a man is dead and Count Lambert has the right to high justice. I'll inform him of how matters stand and see what he says. Frankly, I can't imagine him harming you. It isn't in his character. But until I have his decision, you must stay at Three Walls.

You will not be restrained, but you may not go beyond the gate either."

"May I continue working?"

"If you want to. Or I could find room for you somewhere. You could join my household if you liked."

There was no jail at Three Walls. In fact there were very few jails in medieval Poland. Jailing someone was not considered punishment, since many would enjoy the chance to sit around, not have to work, and still be fed. A person might be restrained when a trial could not be held immediately and the person might be dangerous or try to run away. I couldn't see either of those situations happening here.

"I'll work. In a few months I'll have passage money home."

"As you wish. You go to sleep now. I'll go to Okoitz tomorrow. I'll inform you of Count Lambert's decision as soon as possible." Waitresses bunked together at our inns. She wouldn't be alone.

"Thank you, my lord."

She got up and walked away. She was still a bit unsteady, but her bare back was straight.

I liked the way she said "my lord."

The next morning, I called in each of the witnesses and got essentially the same story from every one of them. The innkeeper had told the simple truth. Natasha kept notes, and while her handwriting was not as attractive as Natalia's, there was no problem with accuracy or legibility. I kicked her up from level one to level two in status and pay. It was still a notch below the other main girls, but the differential left her something to work for.

Before noon, I got to Okoitz, where I found out that the main floor of the cloth factory had been turned into a balloon factory.

Count Lambert was lord of over a hundred knights, but most of them were home for the winter. He had more than that number of young, female clothworkers for his factory, but they were gone also, and would be replaced in the spring with a mostly fresh batch. But besides these, he had eight dozen peasant families locally, which were pressed into service to make his balloon.

When I got there, the wicker basket had been completed and the brass platter was installed. This had been a beautifully embossed tray two yards across, the sort of thing that might be used to bring out some fancy dish at a big feast. Now it had a thousand holes punched in it, to let the air flow through the fire better.

Had I known how attractive the platter was, I would have had another fire grid made, and taken that one in trade. But such is life, with its many lost opportunities.

Inside, three dozen ladies of all ages were sewing the long cloth panels together. They sat in a great circle of trestle tables, with the finished top of the balloon crumpled in the center. Count Lambert had elected to have his balloon colored red-and-white, the colors of the Piast family and later those of Poland.

I found Count Lambert in the castle.

"Sir Conrad, you are here early this month. I hadn't expected you for another week at least."

"There's been some trouble, my lord. Your priest is dead."

"Dog's blood! What happened?"

I told him the story. "So you see, my lord, I don't think a crime has been committed, but the right of high justice is yours."

"Ordinarily, I'd agree with you, and I don't think that I could bring myself to hang so lovely a woman even if she were guilty. But you're missing the point here. A *priest* was killed, and a priest's wife killed him. Well, maybe she wasn't a wife as you say, but it's not for us to decide. We don't have jurisdiction. This is a canon-law matter, not civil law. The matter must come before an ecclesiastical court."

Oh no. If the Church was as inept at settling this thing as it was at handling my inquisition, poor Francine might be a long time getting to France. "What should I do, my lord?"

"Well, you're here now, so you might as well spend a day or two looking over the work being done. When you return to Three Walls, you must write up the particulars of the case and send them to the Bishop of Wroclaw. Get Sir Miesko's advice on the proper form. He used to be a clerk.

"Don't bother coming back here until the matter is delivered. The last thing I need is more trouble with the Church! Oh, yes. And while you're here, write up a request from me to the bishop for another priest. Father John used to do that sort of thing for me. No one else but you can do it now."

"Happy to, my lord. But, for after I'm gone, isn't one of Lady Richeza's schoolteachers here at Okoitz?"

"Yes, but I'd forgotten about her. One doesn't think of using a woman for that sort of thing, but I suppose she'll do in a pinch. Not that I'd *want* to pinch that old hag.

"So Lady Francine is one of your waitresses now! That might be worth a trip to Three Walls to see!"

The next morning, I stopped to see Sir Miesko. He was surprised that the death had occurred. He hadn't even known that Lady Francine had stopped at his manor with the caravan. After some discussion, it was decided that he should return with me to Three Walls to write up the matter himself.

Lady Richeza came with us, and brought her four youngest children. "The oldest boy is twelve now," she said. "It's time he had a try at running the manor himself." In another two years the kid could be married. The history of the Middle Ages is largely the history of children.

Sir Miesko worked three days and made up separate affidavits from each of the witnesses, the innkeeper, the innkeeper's wife, the priest who eventually examined the body, myself and, of course, Lady Francine.

"If you want the matter to move swiftly, it's best to give them all the information possible on as many separate sheets of parchment as possible," Sir Miesko said.

Just like modern times. Flood 'em with paperwork!

It was Lady Richeza's first trip to Three Walls, and she was quite impressed with the plumbing, kitchen, and bathrooms. She was less favorably impressed with the inn, though of course she didn't stay there, but in my noble guest quarters.

Lady Richeza and Lady Francine spent a lot of time together, talking.

When the parchment work was completed, I thought it best to deliver it myself. For one thing, Anna could make it to Wroclaw in a day, where it might take a week to go by caravan, and a month could go by before one was going in the right direction at this time of the year.

For another, we were spending huge amounts of money to keep the brass works supplied with Hungarian copper. In the twentieth century, Poland is one of the world's largest exporters of copper, and I had a pretty good idea of where the mines would be, a halfday west of Wroclaw, near Legnica. I wanted to scout out the area and see who owned the land. Maybe I could buy it on the cheap.

Then, too, I'd never been to medieval Wroclaw, and I was having a minor case of cabin fever. Over everyone's objections, I went alone.

Anna can run like the wind, and leaving at earliest dawn she ran all day almost nonstop until we got to Wroclaw at dusk.

The city had the usual squalid suburbs, but its center was built on an island, Ostrow Tumski, in the middle of the Odra River. This was well fortified with a sturdy brick wall, as much against floodwaters as against any invader. Above it rose the towers of the centuries' old cathedral and the solider bulk of Piast Castle.

The guard at the bridge snapped to and saluted as I rode up. He had probably never seen plate armor before, but he recognized the wolf skin cloak I wore, since I'd given identical ones to Duke Henryk the Bearded and his son Prince Henryk the Pious. Wroclaw was the center of Henryk's power, and had been the family seat for centuries.

In a rather thick German accent, the guard gave me directions to the bishop's residence. The duke had many Germans on his staff, in part because the German laws of primogeniture left a lot of German younger sons landless and thus available for foreign service, and because the duke's wife, mother, and paternal grandmother had all been German. The German princes had as many princesses to dispose of as they did younger sons, and with the concentration of wealth that primogeniture always results in, they could afford whopping big dowries. It was a strange sort of invasion, but an invasion nonetheless.

The porter at the door of the bishop's residence let me in and called forth the chamberlain. This worthy heard that it was a legal matter and delivered me to the bishop's clerk. "Ah, the illustrious Sir Conrad Stargard! Please be welcome. The bishop is indisposed, but I can doubtless arrange an audience in a week or two."

I had the distinct feeling that an honorarium paid to the clerk could get me in to the bishop immediately, but fortunately I didn't want to see the old blowhard at all. "That's unfortunate, as I was looking forward to paying my respects to his excellency. Kindly give him this package. It concerns the death of one of his priests."

"It what?"

"It was a bloody death by violence, done by a member of the man's own family. But perhaps I shouldn't talk about it, for fear of causing embarrassment to the Church."

The man was looking at the seals on the package of documents. Sir Miesko had insisted on sealing it with his own seal, the personal seal ring that I'd had made for myself and my seal as Master of the Hunt, which I'd given to him as token of his authority. If a dozen other seals had been available, he would have used them as well, just to make the thing look more important. He also had written the bishop's full name and titles on the outside, along with "personal" and "confidential" in bold letters under it. I'd suggested "For His Excellency's Eyes Only," and Sir Miesko had written that too, liking the phrase.

All this meant that the clerk didn't dare open it, and

he didn't dare delay the matter in the hope of squeezing a little graft out of me.

"But surely you can tell *me*! I hold the bishop's every confidence."

"I'm sure you do. It's all written down in these documents. I believe that his excellency will want to see them without delay."

"Well, perhaps I could arrange some interview."

"No, no. I wouldn't think of disturbing his excellency when he is indisposed. I shall pray for his speedy return to health." I got up to leave.

"But surely—"

"Not another word. I couldn't possibly disturb so great a Churchman as your master. Once he is feeling better, if I can serve his excellency, I shall be at Piast Castle."

And I left, chuckling to myself. Hit me up for a bribe, would he? Now let him die of curiosity until the bishop felt like informing him of the matter. What's more, I was sure that clerk would push the package right through just to satisfy his own curiosity.

Chapter Five

DINNER WAS being served at the castle when I arrived. I was ushered to a seat at one of the lower tables, but the duke noticed me and invited me up next to him at the high table, which was quite literally a half yard higher than the others. About the height of a standup bar.

He had to bump down a baron to do it, who bumped a knight at a lower table, who bumped someone's squire farther down. Furthermore, each of these worthies took his wife or lady friend down with him, but nobody seemed to mind. Apparently, it happened all the time.

"Well, boy. What brings you to Wroclaw in this weather?"

"Two matters, your grace. There was a priest killed on my land, and the bishop had to be informed."

The duke wanted to hear more, so I gave him a brief synopsis of the death of Father John.

"Ha! That'll set the bishop down a peg. Now tell me the whole story the long way, and tell it loud enough for everyone to hear!"

One didn't argue with the duke. Direct orders are direct orders, and Lady Francine was going back to France soon, so she wouldn't be embarrassed by the publicity.

The crowd was suddenly quiet, so I said in a loud voice, "You know, your grace, that Lady Francine was the granddaughter of a bishop in France. She was brought up in a proper household and had every expectation of making a good marriage, being one of the most stunningly beautiful women I've ever seen. But when the

55

Church's Gregorian reforms were put into effect there, forbidding the marriage of the clergy, the barbarous laws of that foreign land decreed that she was suddenly illegitimate! The best that she could do was to marry a poor young priest from Poland, where the Gregorian reforms have not been approved. If there was a dowry, I've never heard of it.

"That is to say, they went through the legal and holy ceremonies of marriage, but whether it was truly a marriage or not remains to be seen. Lady Francine and Father John came to Poland and lived for several years as man and wife as far as anyone could see, but there was a problem.

"To put it as simply as possible, Father John was not physically capable of making proper love to a woman. He, ah, couldn't get it up.

"They lived with this horrible situation for years, but eventually they quarreled. She knew that she wasn't really married, for a marriage must be consummated to exist. She left him and came to work at my inn at Three Walls to earn passage money back to France. Many of you know that a woman must be a true intact virgin to work there as a waitress. I operate inns, not houses of prostitution. The innkeeper's wife physically checks for the presence of a hymen. Lady Francine qualified.

"Father John found her, tried to drag her back to Okoitz, and pulled a knife when she refused. She hit him with a stool in defense, for the uniform she wore was nearly nothing at all and she carried no weapon with which to defend herself.

"To the surprise of all, this blow killed him. I came to Wroclaw to deliver proof of all that I've said to the bishop."

The crowd's reaction was mixed. Some, headed by Prince Henryk, were shocked and more were feeling sorry for Lady Francine, but half of them shared the duke's contempt for the clergy and thought the tale hilarious.

"That's rich, boy! So now the priest's wife is tending commoners at an inn, and doing it near naked besides!"

"That was her choice, your grace. Are you familiar with the Pink Dragon Inns?"

"Yeah, stopped at the one in Cracow. Had to pull rank just to get in, it was so crowded! When are you going to build one for us here at Wroclaw?"

"This spring, your grace, with your permission."

"Permission? Boy, you have orders! Just pick a site and I'll see that you get it. What sort of taxes are you paying at Cracow?"

"Between the town council and the Bishop of Cracow, about one-sixth of profits, your grace."

"Well, I run this city, and that's what you'll pay to me. If the bishop's men give you any trouble, you send them to me."

"Yes, your grace."

"You going to send us Lady Francine when you get this inn built?"

"If you wish, your grace, I'll tell her that you requested her presence here. You understand that she's not sworn to me and I can hardly *order* her to come. But until the legal matter is solved, I've forbidden her to leave Three Walls."

"Well, don't worry about that, boy. I'll be responsible for her. The bishop can hardly object if you follow my orders. Was this inn the second matter you wanted to talk to me about?"

"No, your grace. The second matter concerns something far more profitable. But I think it's best talked about in private."

"As you wish, boy. See me tonight after the festivities."

After a seven-course meal that was a little overspiced for my taste, a company of clowns and jugglers entertained us for an hour, but the routines were a bit too coarse for me. The highlight of their act was a two-man "horse" routine which ended with the horse shitting on the polished stone floor in front of the duke's table. He thought it was marvelous, and tipped them well. The man who had to clean up the real horse turds looked less amused.

The clowns were followed by some dancing, mostly waltzes and mazurkas, a craze which I had inadvertently started myself. At least it was better than the half punker-style stuff they were doing before. I was demonstrating a polka, still in my plate armor, when I saw the duke leave. I bowed out shortly after that and was directed to the duke's chamber.

I stayed at the doorway and said, "Your grace, were you serious last time about not wanting formal courtesies in private?"

"What? Of course not! I want you to grovel so that I can act magnanimous and tell you not to. Now bow and get it over with!"

"Yes, your grace." I gave him my deepest bow.

"Smart-aleck kid. What's this you wanted to talk to me about, and sit down, dammit."

"Yes, your grace." I sat and he pushed his gold wine cup toward me. It was the same one that he was drinking out of. In offering it he was doing me a considerable honor, local customs being what they were. I took a long pull from it. To not do so would be an insult to the duke. I just hoped that he hadn't spit in it.

"Now, what's this you wanted to talk about?"

"You know that I come from the future, your grace."

"Of course. I told you that I worked that out of your priest. So?"

"So in the twentieth century, Poland is one of the world's largest copper exporters, whereas right now, what with all the copper my brass works has been buying out of Hungary, we might be one of the world's largest copper importers. A lot of Polish money is going into Hungary, and making King Andrew rich."

"Huh. Andrew has been less than polite to me lately. So where is this ore at?"

"Maybe fifteen miles outside of Legnica. I'll have to find the exact location and find out who owns the land."

"You've already done the second, boy. The lands for forty miles around Legnica have been in my family for centuries. So I own copper. What do you want out of it?"

"Well, if I could lease the land, your grace, what if I paid you a sixth of the profits in taxes?"

"A sixth, hell! I should get only one-sixth of what I already own? I'll give you a third for finding it and getting a smelting operation going."

"But your grace, the cost of setting up an efficient mine, factories, and other buildings will be very large. It will take hundreds of thousands of pence. If I'm to pay that..."

"So who says that you are? We'll do it on *my* lands and they'll be *my* factories and mines. I just want you to run them for me, the way you built those clothmills for Count Lambert. He's making a fortune off them, or he would if his Hungarian wife didn't get half the cash he rakes in."

"Interesting, your grace. I'd often wondered why Count Lambert was always so eager to bargain or bet with cloth, but not with money."

"Well, now you know. Well, do we have a deal?"

"Do I have complete control of the whole operation?"

"Hell, yes. Do you think I'd want to dirty my hands with commerce? You do things your way, and I'll leave you alone, just so you turn in a good profit after the first year."

"The workers would be as well taken care of as those at Three Walls? And they would all be sworn to me?"

"It's a waste of money, but yes to the first question. And you wouldn't get much out of them if they were sworn to somebody else, so yes to the second. Anything else you want to steal from an old man?"

"Tariffs, your grace. There will be a lot of transportation going on. We'll be taking coke from Three Walls, hauling it by mule and barge and mule again to the mine, smelting the copper there, then hauling the copper back to Cieszyn. There are eleven toll booths along that route. Can anything be done about it?"

"Plenty. That'll be *my* coke and *my* copper. You tell that to any petty baron who tries to tax them. If he gives you any trouble after that, bring me his head! You can throw away the rest. I wouldn't want anybody that dumb in my service."

"Thank you, your grace. I believe we have an agreement."

"Done. You write this up and bring it to me tomorrow. I won't be around all that much longer, and I want this binding on both sides. Of course, the way you keep getting into fights, I just might outlive you. That was some of your judo stuff you used to break that Crossman's arm at your trial, wasn't it?"

"Similar to that, your grace. It's called karate. I didn't have any choice. He was really a better fighter than I was. My sword was stuck in his shield and I couldn't get it out. I had nothing but my bare hands to fight with!"

"Haw! Here I thought you were just playing with him! Then why did you throw away your shield?"

"Again, your grace, I had to. That first blow to the head he gave me would have killed me without this new plate armor. As it was, it twisted the helmet around and jammed it. I could only look over my right shoulder. I couldn't use my shield at all. I couldn't even see it! Fortunately, I once learned a style of sword-fighting that doesn't use a shield, but only a sword. It's a sport in my era called fencing, because in the interests of safety, the combatants originally fought on different sides of a fence. I used that on him."

"Hah! And you beat him with new tactics!"

"Not really, your grace. He was still better than me. I beat him mainly because his ten or twelve killing blows didn't hurt me. This armor I'm wearing defeated Sir Adolf."

"Interesting. Could you make similar armor for my men?"

"I intend to, your grace. But this armor cost me eleven thousand pence, a dozen times what chain mail would cost. In a few years, I'll have machines such that I can sell it for five hundred pence, and I'll be making suits by the thousand."

"Good. I'd like a suit of it myself, and one for my son."

"Well, your grace, there's no reason why we can't make a few more suits by hand. I'll have two suits made for you and the prince, as a gift, but please understand that they must be exactly fitted to your body. Plate doesn't stretch the way chain mail does. You'd each have to spend some time at Three Walls while they were being made."

"I wanted to visit you anyway, as much to see what new wonders you'd come up with as to get a good look at Lady Francine's tits! I'll be there in the spring."

"Wonderful, your grace. We'll all be looking forward to your visit. Be sure to bring your armorer along so that we can show him how to maintain it properly."

I left his chambers glowing. If I was right, Lady Francine had a near royal protector, so she needn't worry about any legal problems. The duke *was* the law. If he liked her, she was safe, Church court or no Church court. An old man is the ideal protector for a young woman. He has the wealth and power to keep her well, and lacks the ability to get her pregnant. Not many modern girls realize this, but their ancestors were wiser.

More importantly to me, the duke was going to finance the whole copper works! Oh, I'd have to make sure that he got a fair return on his money, but if things got tight, the duke had no idea what a modern engineer can do with creative accounting. After all, I trained my accountant myself!

I went to the pleasant room assigned to me by the castellan and told the servant they gave me that I wanted a table, four lamps, parchment, ink, and pens. Once that was delivered, I told him that I wanted a pretty young girl for the night and after that he was free to go away.

It seemed that a lady would cost extra, unless I wanted one of the noblewomen who had bribed him to suggest themselves to me. He was completely open about it, and on questioning him I found that he had heard that I was a wizard who knew everything, anyway. He knew he couldn't get away with a lie, so he figured that his best chance of survival was to tell the absolute barefaced truth.

There are certain advantages to having a strange repu-
tation.

There hadn't been anyone at dinner that I found attractive enough to be worth the hassle, and none of the
ladies mentioned was single. The last thing I needed was
an irate husband challenging me to a duel. On inquiring
about other ladies available, I was told that the cost was
a penny or two. I gave him four and told him that I
wanted someone young, pretty, enthusiastic, and obedient. I wanted her in an hour, and if she wasn't up to
snuff, I'd take it out of his hide. I guess I was in sort of a
manic mood. Ordinarily, I wouldn't say things like that,
but when everything is going right, you get sort of wild.

He said that he would do what he could, and what did
I want told to the ladies who had bribed him?

"Just say that I have killed sixteen men in the last
year, and I don't want any jealous husbands on my
soul."

"That should do nicely, my lord." And he left.

I was close to completing the duke's contract when
the servant returned with two young ladies.

"I wasn't sure of your tastes, my lord."

I glanced up and said, "The redhead will do." I gave
the blonde a penny for her trouble and dismissed her
along with the servant. I told the redhead to undress and
get in bed, and went back to writing the contract. Once I
was through, I blew out three of the lamps, undressed
and joined her.

I was beginning to think that Count Lambert was
right. The easiest way to treat subordinates was to give
orders and expect them to be obeyed.

In the morning, the duke read the contract, said it was
what we had agreed on, and gave it to a clerk to have
some fair copies made.

I grabbed a bite in the castle kitchens, packed a lunch
big enough for six and was pleased to see that the servant had Anna ready.

"There was no bridle, my lord, and you aren't wearing spurs!" he said, handing me my hefty new lance and
shield.

"Anna doesn't like bridles and spurs. Tell the duke's servant that I may or may not be back tonight."

I took the south bridge from the island so as to be on the west bank of the Odra River. It was frozen over, but river ice can be treacherous, especially on horseback. Anna can do some amazing things, but I didn't want to risk drowning for no good reason.

An hour's run took us to Legnica. From there we headed northeast until we hit the river, then followed it upstream until it made a wide bend to the east.

I'd toured the mines once, and they were just off the river, I think at this bend. Of course, that was in the twentieth century, when most of the forests were gone, and this was—would be—a built-up industrial area. And rivers change course.

It was dusk when I thought I might be at the right spot. We hadn't seen any sign of human habitation for hours and Anna said that she couldn't smell anybody. Fortunately, I had brought my old backpack along and I had some experience with winter camping.

Anna said that she'd be just fine outside, and there was plenty for her to eat.

Sleeping in plate mail isn't all that bad. It's sort of like laying down in a well-designed contour chair and twigs and stones on the ground don't bother you in the least. The only problem was that I'd closed my visor to keep my face warm, and there was half an inch of condensed frost inside my helmet when I woke up. I had to remove the helmet (no easy job) and scrape it out. Even then I'd missed enough so that when it warmed up the next day, I had water running down my neck.

In the morning, I found that Anna had eaten most of a medium-sized hazel tree!

This surprised me, and we talked about it. It seems that she could eat anything organic. Given her choice, she preferred fresh green grass and, after that, grain, but in a pinch, wood was just fine. Hazel was better than pine, and fruit trees were downright tasty. She didn't like coal because she didn't like the taste of sulfur, but coke was okay.

"Anna, you never fail to astound me. Can you do anything about helping me find where we should put the mine? We're looking for copper ore. It will be copper sulfide, which is a black, heavy stone."

She said that something was stinky around here and went off to look for it.

I finished off my food and had my gear packed by the time she came back. I saddled her up and we went off to look at what she'd found. They were heavy black stones, all right, and Anna said that they smelled like sulfur, not that I could smell anything. We spent the morning gathering up about six dozen pounds of the stuff, Anna pawing at the snow and me swinging my old camp hatchet to free them from the frozen ground. About noon, I loaded them into my backpack and told Anna to head for Wroclaw.

She never has to backtrack. Once she's been somewhere, she always knows the direction between here and there.

We got there in time for me to take a bath before supper, and this time I didn't have to dance in armor. The duke was miffed because I'd forgotten to get permission to leave, but he cheered up when I showed him the ore we'd brought back. We signed and sealed both copies of our contract that night.

"One other thing, boy. I said I'd put up two hundred thousand pence, and you've said that you can't start until late spring. That's the thin time of the year for me. Most of my taxes come in right after the harvest, so I'm going to pay you the money now. You can pick it up from the exchequer when you leave."

"May I have permission to leave in the morning, your grace?"

"Granted. I'll come visit you during spring planting. Everyone else is too busy to talk to me then, anyway."

As ordered, the redhead was waiting in my room.

Chapter Six

EVEN LOADED down with the ore and all that money, Anna still got us to Three Walls by dusk, which was good because the last few miles were through a heavy snowstorm.

The snow didn't let up for three days, and by that time we were completely buried. It was six weeks before anyone could get in or out. Work went on as usual, of course, and we had plenty of supplies to last us, so it wasn't too bad. But there was no way that I could get to Okoitz to make my monthly visit to Count Lambert.

One day, after we'd been snowed in a month, I heard a commotion outside. I ran to the rear balcony to see what it was, and everybody was pointing up and back over my head. I had to run to the front balcony to see it.

Count Lambert was flying his balloon! It had red-and-white vertical stripes and a huge white Piast eagle on a red shield sewn on its side. Only judging from the size of the basket, the balloon was much larger than it should have been.

I waved, and I think he waved back. But there was nothing else I could do.

Eventually, a merchant made it to Three Walls and told us that the snow was really deep for only about the last mile. Shamefaced, I went to see my liege lord. I found him in his chambers with a basketwork cast on his leg.

"Sir Conrad, where have you been?"

"I was snowed in, my lord. What happened to your leg?"

"A likely story. I broke my leg coming down out of the sky! Or rather when I was dragged along just after that. I tell you that I flew halfway to Kiev!"

"What happened, my lord? I thought that you were going to tether the balloon."

"I did, but it broke the tether rope as if it was a piece of thread. That was the second balloon, of course."

"The second balloon, my lord?"

"The first one wasn't quite strong enough to lift me with a decent supply of charcoal. With me alone, and the fire burning high, it couldn't quite get me off the ground. Well, you warned that this might happen, so I made a second balloon to your plans but twice as big."

"Twice as big, my lord? You mean twice the volume?"

"I suppose so. We just took every measurement you showed and doubled it. It took a deuced amount of cloth, but I had plenty."

"Yes, my lord. I expect that it took four times the cloth and had eight times the volume. It probably had a dozen times the lift of the first one."

"I think it might have. It just snapped the rope and up I went like a frightened bird! I think I headed south at first, at least I think that was Three Walls I saw. Things certainly look different from up there!"

"We saw you, my lord."

"How wonderful! You saw my proud Piast family device? Some of my ancestors doubtless bore it with more honor, but none of them ever carried it higher! I think a lot of other people must have seen it as well, because I think the winds shifted and I'm sure I saw Wawel Castle. That was another strange thing. I could see the wind blowing the trees, but I couldn't feel the wind myself! I was in a dead calm the whole way! Yet I was moving! Can you explain this strange thing?"

"Of course, my lord. You were traveling with the wind. You feel the wind only when it is moving at a different speed than you are."

"That doesn't make much sense, but if you're not worried about it then I won't be either. I tried to land at

Wawel, but I couldn't make the balloon go down! I stopped feeding the fire, but the cathedral towers on Wawel Hill were gone before I started to get low. By then, I was over another forest and had to build my fire quickly. I tell you that I was touching the treetops before I started to go up again. And once started up, it continued to a vast height. And so I went, up and down until my charcoal was exhausted. Then I went down and stayed there. I came down hard as you can see." He gestured to his broken leg.

"Why didn't you throw out your sandbags at the last instant, my lord."

"Because I didn't have any. I know you said to carry them, but it seemed to me that I would be better off taking the same weight in charcoal. After all, I could always throw out the charcoal at the end, just as I could have the sand. And the charcoal could be used to take me higher, if that was necessary. But as it was, I could never find a big field to land in. Most of the world is forest. You don't realize that traveling on the roads, but it's true!"

"At least you're alive, my lord, and you've had an adventure that most men only dream of."

"More adventure than you know, Sir Conrad. Once I was down, and lying there helpless and alone, a crowd of damn peasants wanted to burn me for a witch! They were all jabbering in that half understandable Ruthenian tongue. If a nobleman hadn't seen the Piast crest on my beautiful balloon, I think I might be dead now. As it was, he took me home, and three days later a dozen of my men finally caught up with me. But my lovely balloon is no more. The peasants ripped it to shreds. I'll bet that every peasant in Red Ruthenia has a red-and-white raincoat!"

"Small loss, my lord. Surely you wouldn't have used it again."

"And why not? I'll learn the way of it next time."

"Next time you might come down in the middle of the Baltic Sea!"

"Well, what of it? Why should any sane man want to

die of old age? If you want to think of something frightening, think about being wrinkled and crippled and sick all the time! That's old age and I don't want it! The Baltic would be a glorious death, and would give me as much fame as falling in battle."

I tried a different tack. "In eight years, we have one of the biggest wars in history coming up. You don't want to miss out on that, do you?"

"You mean the Mongols? Of course not!"

"Well, you have to be alive, or they won't let you fight in it. It's a rule. What if you could render great service to your lord the duke in that war? What if you could be on high and see exactly where the enemy was, and be able to inform his grace of their every movement? Wouldn't that earn you undying fame?"

"By God it would! I must start on another balloon immediately!"

"Not a balloon, my lord. A balloon would drift away from the battlefield and leave you a laughingstock. Some would even say you ran away."

"We could tether it."

"And what if the battle moved, as they sometimes do? Anyway, you saw what happened to your last tether."

"What are you suggesting then?"

"Let's go the whole route and build aircraft! An airplane can be piloted up or down at will. You can fly them in any direction you want and you can outrace the wind!"

"But you said that aircraft were too complicated for us to build!"

"They will certainly not be easy. It will take us years, but think of the prize to be won. To fly like a bird!"

"If men can do it, Sir Conrad, *we* will! How do we start?"

"I think we will need to build a whole town dedicated to flight. We will need some of the best carpenters and seamstresses in Poland. And for our future pilots and designers, we should start with young boys. We will start with boys ten or twelve years old and have them build small model aircraft at first. We'll have to try a lot of things, and we can save time by building models first. As the boys grow, so will their models, and in a few years they'll be making full-sized aircraft."

"But why boys? Why not adults?"

The truth was that keeping tabs on a hundred boys would keep Count Lambert busy and safe, but I couldn't tell *him* that. "Young people have free minds, my lord. There's more work to be done than you and I can do in our lifetimes. We'll need help. But from where? Can you imagine a bunch of peasants trying to learn how to fly? The merchants? The priests? It's ludicrous! And the nobles are too involved with their own affairs to give it their full energies.

"But boys would, especially if we took them to a new town away from their parents and other distractions. It might be best if we restricted them to the sons of the nobility, because we'll need adults around to do the carpentry and so on, not to mention cooking and cleaning. It would be best if the boys had some authority over the common workers."

"You're right, Sir Conrad! What boy wouldn't jump at the chance to come?"

"I'll worry about designing the facilities. You should pick the land. We'll need about a square mile of it, most of it dead flat, but with one big hill on it. Do you have such a place on your lands?"

"Several. But I'm minded of the old tomb. At least they say it was a tomb, but it could be just a hill for all I know. You know Krak's tomb near Cracow? It's about the same, only it's bigger. It's also covered with trees, but we can make short work of that!"

"Excellent, my lord. Is it far from here?"

"About three miles. Have one of the other knights show it to you. Have your plans ready for just after the spring planting. I can get you a thousand workers then."

"A thousand, my lord?"

"Two thousand, if you can use them. I'll have each of my knights send me a dozen peasants for two months. I can pay them in cloth. That should be enough to get us started, anyway. We'll call the town Eagle Nest!"

"Yes, my lord."

Going back to Three Walls, the more I thought about the project, the more I liked it. Of course we wouldn't get decent aircraft in the foreseeable future, but having a bunch of bright kids in what amounted to an engineering school could be great! Those were my future engineers!

Furthermore, it would give Lambert something to spend all his spare energy on. Keeping up with a few dozen youngsters will wear down any man!

On the other hand, it meant one hell of a busy spring and summer. I had two major installations to put together at the same time, when peasant manpower was available between the planting and the first hay harvest.

When things get hairy, the magic word is KISS: Keep It Simple, Stupid! Do what you've done before. Actually, the structures needed first were housing, just as at Three Walls.

I'd start by ordering the same tools I'd had made last summer, with only minor changes where experience had shown a better way. Only now I'd order two sets, one in Count Lambert's name and one in the duke's. I'd go to the same craftsmen as before and demand the same prices.

The apartment buildings would be the same as at Three Walls, except I'd bend them into hollow squares instead of a straight line as at Three Walls, because they would stand in the open instead of closing off a box canyon. But the hard parts, the kitchen and bathrooms, had all been designed. What's more, my people already had experience making and installing them.

I would put together two teams of experienced carpenters and masons and have them be my leaders during the construction phase, with peasants hired temporarily to do the grunt work.

I was tempted to go straight to Cieszyn and start ordering stuff, but all my drawings and notes were back at Three Walls. My head was bubbling with my new plans and I didn't stay long. At dawn the next day I was

on the road again and in an hour I was talking to the
Krakowski brothers.

A year had made quite a difference in both them and
the brass works. Twelve months earlier they had been
literally starving to death, and each had lost a child during the winter. Now they were solid, prosperous citizens. They and their families were healthy and each had
added a new member, with more already on the way.

Their factory was booming, with over fifty workers
and twelve pouring ovens. They had back orders for the
brass parts for twenty-three windmills as well as a lot of
other things.

I told them that they now had four more windmills on
order, and these took precedence over other work. Also,
I needed all the plumbing we'd used at Three Walls duplicated twice, and had some other things besides.

They got upset at having to delay their other cus-
tomers, but when I told them that half of the stuff was
for Count Lambert and the rest was for Duke Henryk
himself, they quieted down. Nobody was going to object
strongly about being bumped by the duke. It wasn't
healthy!

Finally, I told them about the copper mine I'd discovered. That got their interest! They were all angry about
the prices they'd been paying and the idea of digging and
smelting their own copper apealed to them.

Thom said that when he was a journeyman he worked
at a smelter for a year, so I asked him to supervise the
works the next summer. It meant leaving his wife behind
for a few months until the housing was up, but that
didn't bother anyone. It wasn't as though they were
newlyweds. And I hinted that if the Legnica installation
worked out well, we'd move the brass works from Cieszyn to there to cut down on transportation costs.

We talked a bit about having an entire city devoted to
the mining, smelting, casting, and machining of brass
and copper and I could see the lights going on in their
eyes.

I gave Thom half of the ore I'd brought back, and he
was suddenly depressed. It wasn't any kind of copper

ore he'd ever seen. The ore he was used to was red-colored, and a little heavier. I told him that it had to be roasted over an open fire before it could be smelted, and he said that he would try it. But I could see that he had grave doubts about the project.

I'd make a believer of him. I hoped.

I was lucky in that Tadeusz was back in Cieszyn from successfully starting a Pink Dragon Inn in Cracow. It had already paid for its construction cost and was generating healthy profits.

He was absolutely delighted that the duke himself had requested a Pink Dragon Inn in Wroclaw, and vowed that within the week he would leave for that city no matter what the weather was like. I gave him a letter of introduction to the duke, sealing it with my big seal ring. I also told him about needing another small inn at the copper mine near Legnica by the end of the summer. *No problem!*

Then I spent two days haggling with blacksmiths and carpenters to get the tools I needed. The duke's name impressed everybody, and I got done in two days what had taken me two months last summer.

I also looked up the cloth merchant that I'd contracted with last summer. We made arrangements for delivering the two thousand yards of cloth agreed upon. He wasn't happy about the deal, because the price of cloth had dropped since we had agreed on the price, and he would loose money by honoring the agreement. I wouldn't let him off, though. I never told him to be a capitalist!

Then back to Three Walls where people still weren't too clear about what had happened. It took a full day with my foremen to settle out who would be going where to do what.

And besides all of the above, work was going on at Three Walls, and we had to agree on a schedule to keep things going even though we were losing two-thirds of our best men and having to hire a bunch of rookies. Most of those going to Eagle Nest would be coming back, but the transfers to Copper City would be permanent.

I was having a wonderful time!

I had the new buildings drawn up in four days, largely because of Sir Vladimir's help. He was becoming a good draftsman, and I'd make an engineer out of him yet.

But looking at the amount of wood that had to be sawn in a few months, it would take three of our walking-beam sawmills to do the job at each of the new installations.

The quality of the work turned out by the brass works had been steadily increasing. It was time to try our hands at a steam-powered sawmill.

We were casting pipes. A tubular boiler wouldn't be difficult. We were machining bearings and bushings. Cylinders, pistons, and rods wouldn't be that much harder. We were making high-pressure water valves. Steam valves should be possible.

The only hang-up was how to fasten the end-caps to the cylinders. I didn't see any way to do that except with steel machine screws. The few screws we had made so far had been filed by hand, which was expensive and not nearly accurate enough.

I needed an engine lathe to accurately cut screws and to make good taps and dies. And an engine lathe needs accurate screws to feed the tool along the stock. I had to have a screw to make a screw!

I laid the problem aside, hoping my subconscious would come up with something, and worked on the rest of the engine. We had to cut huge logs, two and three yards thick, so a circular saw would have had to be six yards across. This was beyond our capabilities. We could probably make a big bandsaw blade, but such a blade has to be very flexible, and I doubted the quality of our steel. I sketched up a big enough bandsaw and it was huge, difficult to move, hard to make, and expensive. KISS.

Then I took one of our four-yard ripsaws and sketched a three-yard-long cylinder at each end of it. By alternately pressurizing the rod ends of the cylinders, they would pull the saw blade back and forth. I set the cylinders horizontally, so the machine wouldn't have to be built in a pit. A manually operated screw pulled the log into the blade, and a mechanism for holding the log at the proper angle was straightforward.

A tubular boiler, a pressure gauge, and a safety relief valve came off my board within a day, and finally I put the whole thing on wheels. It might take a dozen mules to move it, but at least we wouldn't have to disassemble it to move it. In five days flat I had a complete set of drawings.

The world's first steam engine!

But I still hadn't figured out how to make a good screw. Finally, I just drew up a simple engine lathe, even though I didn't see how we could possibly build one. By this time, we had pretty much duplicated the machinery from the brass works at Three Walls, complete with pigs in huge hamster cages turning the lathes, so I gave the drawings to Ilya and told him to make me one.

Ilya was a good man at a forge, but he didn't have the machining experience of the Krakowski brothers. I gave this difficult project to him because the Krakowski brothers were reasonable enough to ask questions until they understood something, and I didn't have the answers to match their questions.

Ilya, on the other hand, was never reasonable. His ego was such that he would never admit that there was anything that he didn't quite grasp. He was belligerent, intolerant, and bullheaded, but he wasn't stupid.

The engine lathe would be the most complicated piece of equipment we owned, but I gave the project to him as casually as if I was asking for an axe head. I simply explained what it did and why, and asked to have it done as soon as possible. He stared at the drawings for a few moments and then said that if I wanted the silly thing, he'd build it.

For the next five weeks, it was hard to get anything else out of the blacksmiths, and repair work was done only grudgingly. I finally had to step in and split the section into a forging group and a machining group, just to keep the carpenters and masons in tools.

At one point I was walking through the plant and saw

Ilya carefully wrapping a woman's bright red ribbon around a smooth brass rod, and carefully scribing on the brass where the top of the ribbon came to as he went along. I didn't say a word.

Another time I saw him deliberately pouring fine sand on a set of running gears, while on another machine one of his assistants was running an iron nut back and forth on a long brass screw. The nut was in two halves and clamped back together, and it too was dusted with fine sand. The assistant said that he had been doing this boring work for two weeks, but I didn't want to get involved. If Ilya somehow did the job, great. If he fell on his ass, the humiliating experience might make him easier to live with.

But Ilya did it. The engine lathe worked better than I had expected, and Ilya's ego was so monstrous that he wouldn't even accept praise for it. He pretended that he could do that sort of thing every day. So I put him in charge of making the steam-powered sawmills, and told him not to take so long this time.

Most modern factories are built on flat, level land. My material-handling equipment was limited to men with wheelbarrows, and the coal came out of the mountain several hundred yards above the valley floor. I used the slope of the valley walls to help out.

From the tunnel mouth, loads of coal were dumped in a pile almost at the door. Below that was a cleaning and sorting area and the tops of the coke ovens were lower still. I built the top of the blast furnace lower than the bottom of the coke oven, about level with the entrance to the boys' cave, where the iron ore came out.

It was still wheelbarrow work, but at least we didn't have to push stuff uphill.

Ilya was vastly skeptical about using anything but charcoal to make iron, but I bullied him into it and with our coke and our iron ore, he eventually turned out decent wrought iron. He insisted that charcoal was better than coke, especially for the cementation process of making steel, but that last took very little charcoal.

As soon as the weather broke, the masons were busy

assembling the blast furnace. They had been cutting sandstone blocks for it all winter long, and we had good supplies of coke and iron ore.

After five days of steady burning, we made our first pour, knocking in the clay plug with a long iron rod, and getting out of the way as a long stream of molten iron sprayed out. After that we tapped it four times a day.

Chemical engineers often refer to themselves as "bucket chemists," as opposed to the "test tube chemists" who work in laboratories, because they often do their experiments with large quantities of chemicals. Reaction rates and sometimes even the end products can vary depending on the quantities used, so these people mix things by the bucketful.

I was a bucket chemist of vast proportions. I got the blast furnace going by building a full-size blast furnace and experimenting for months with the quantities of coke, ore, and limestone required. What little iron we turned out in those first months was simply tossed into a pile for later refining, because it wasn't worth much in its present state.

It was simply that there was no way of doing things on a smaller scale, not without some way of measuring temperatures. Brute force had to substitute for finesse.

Did we need more air in the furnace? We didn't know. Build more bellows, put more people to pumping them and see what happens!

At first, all we could do with the pig iron was to cast it in long troughs formed in the sand, but we could always melt it down later by throwing it back into the furnace. I had Mikhail Krakowski come down and set up our casting operation for us. He used the system he knew, pouring into hot clay molds rather than the sandcasting used in modern foundries. But it worked, and I saw no need to change things. If anything, he got a much better surface finish using clay than I had ever seen using sand.

So the stench and dirt of a blast furnace was added to the stink of the coke ovens.

The bloomery we built next to the blast furnace was less experimental. It produced wrought iron the same way Ilya had back at Okoitz, only on a far larger scale. One of the first steam-powered machines built after the steam saws was a steam hammer to beat the wrought iron blooms, taken from the furnace, into iron rods. It worked on waste heat from the furnace itself, a tubular boiler having been built in the chimney.

Ilya was proud of that bloomery, and worked it at a fine peak of efficiency. But he hated the blast furnace. He could see little use for cast iron, which was made at much higher temperatures, had vastly more impurities and was so brittle that it had to be cast into its final shape, because you couldn't bend it without breaking it. What use was a piece of iron if you couldn't beat on it?

I finally had to put another man in charge of the blast furnace, since Ilya considered it a waste of good ore and coke.

But cast iron is a useful material. Before too long, we were producing a line of consumer goods from it, potbellied stoves, pots and pans, and large kitchen ranges that my great grandmother would have been proud of. And cast iron is the best material for making large machine bases. It is rigid, dimensionally stable, and the fibrous crystalline structure absorbs vibrations. If you look at cast iron under a microscope, it looks like a pile of needles—not that we had a microscope.

Furthermore, cast iron is the starting material for making large quantities of steel, and it was going to take large quantities to beat the Mongols.

But try convincing Ilya of that!

Chapter Seven

In the twentieth century, there are many racial stereotypes, and most of them are derogatory. You know the sort I mean—Englishmen are all stiff, formal, and supercilious. Frenchmen are all drunkards and hung up on illicit sex. Germans are all warmongers who spend their off time making ridiculously complicated toys. Blacks are all lazy criminals. Americans are all loud, boorish, and rich. Jews are all sneaky shysters. Poles always do everything backward.

Everybody knows that these statements are mostly nonsense. The people of any group are diversified. Some of them are good and wise, some are bad and stupid, and most are indifferent.

Yet there is a grain of truth in many of the stereotypes. The British *are* more formal than most people. The French per capita consumption of wine *is* frightening, enough so that any person from another country who drank what they *average* would be considered an alcoholic. And historically, the Germans have started an *awful* lot of wars, losing most of them.

While I am not going to admit that Poles do everything backward, I will admit that we are very good at looking at things from a different angle than most other peoples. The typical Pole has no difficulty dealing with a concept like the square root of a negative one, for example, a thing that can make a tightly logical Englishman catatonic.

That particular concept is regularly used in electrical design, and in America, where there has been a tendency for different nationalities to gravitate into specific trades, perhaps half the electrical engineers claim Polish descent. In the same manner, many of the architects and construction workers are Italian, and the Arabs have started to dominate the mercantile trades.

It's not that any of these nationalities forces the others out of their bailiwick. It's that an individual tends to work at what he can do best. What I am trying to lead up to is why I built a mile-high smokestack, sideways.

I suppose that I could claim that structural limitations in the materials available and the absence of certain types of machinery necessitated building the stack against the side of the mountain, but that's not the way it happened.

Besides setting up to produce cast iron, wrought iron, and lime for mortar, I wanted to produce bricks, tiles, and clay pipes. I'd once read about an ancient Chinese invention called a dragon furnace, a long kiln built up the side of a mountain. You filled the kiln with unfired products and started a fire at the bottom. The rest of the kiln functioned as a chimney, and the bricks farther up were at least warmed up and dried out as those on the bottom were being fired.

Then you started another fire farther up in the furnace. Air coming up the furnace was heated by the hot bricks near the bottom, so it took less fuel to bake the bricks farther up. As time went on, you kept starting new fires farther and farther up, letting the old ones die out. It took a week to fire all the bricks in the furnace, at which time you took out all the baked bricks and put in green ones. The system had a lot in common with the modern reverse-flow system.

We soon added a second furnace along side the first so that we could keep working continuously.

One of the coke oven workers was being ragged by his wife because of the stench he spent all day generating. He came to me with a proposal for a set of flues to take the coke oven fumes to the dragon furnaces and so get them out of the valley. He even had a well thought out set of drawings showing how this could be done.

With only minor changes, we tried it and it worked. The stench was reduced and the valley became a good deal more livable.

Furthermore, the fumes contained a fair amount of unburnt gases which were ignited in the hot dragon furnace, and fuel consumption in the dragon furnaces went down. As time went on, we made the dragon furnaces longer and longer until they reached the top of the highest mountain there. Then we built a smokestack at the top, and everything noxious went up it.

I made the man the guest of honor at the next Saturday night dance, publicly gave him three hundred pence as a bonus, and promoted him as soon as possible after that.

This got me the damndest collection of weird suggestions you could ever imagine. I'd wanted to encourage thinking on the part of the workers, but I hadn't expected to be inundated by dumb ideas. I finally had to set up a review system, where suggestions had to filter up through channels, and pay additional bonuses to workers' bosses so that they wouldn't squash everything.

But the system worked. Not only did it result in a lot of useful devices, but it singled out workers who could benefit from further engineering training. As the years went on, I had to do less and less of the design work myself. This was good, because management work was taking up more and more of my time.

Eventually we got notice that the duke would be arriving the next morning, so I had the band ready. They had collected or had made seven brass instruments, mostly trumpets, and I had taught them a few fanfares. That is to say, I whistled the tunes and they figured out how to make them come out of a horn. Their wives had improvised some gaudy band uniforms, and they made a fairly impressive display, along with their drummers, playing the *Star Wars* theme from the balcony as the duke rode in.

Duke Henryk arrived with his son, his armorer, and twenty men. Since I'd promised them two complete suits of plate armor, I put the girls to making each of them a suit of parchment armor, as they had done for me.

A few months before, at my Trial by Combat, my helmet had been bashed around and jammed at a right angle from where it should have been, so I could only look over my right shoulder. It darned nearly was the death of me. Naturally, I had redesigned the helmet. Instead of a clamshell affair that split down the middle and required a helper to put on, the new version looked sort of like a "Darth Vader" helmet with the bottom edge fitting into the ring around my collar. A separate piece, called a beaver, fit into the front half of the ring and covered the bottom of my face. Two easily removed pins fastened the beaver to the rest of the helmet, and a visor could be flipped down to protect the eyes at the price of decent visibility. The big advantage was that you could put it on and take it off by yourself, even if it was bent.

Naturally, his grace and the prince got the new model helmets.

I'd also had the smiths do a lot of preparatory work, making up each of the pieces in advance, but oversized, so that they need only be trimmed down, finished, and assembled. Even this took the whole crew ten days to do, and I didn't let them off for Sunday, for fear of boring our highborn guests.

As it turned out, I needn't have worried, for the duke stayed two days longer than he had to. He was vastly impressed with the plumbing in our bathrooms. He demanded that I duplicate the system at both Piast Castle in Wroclaw and Wawel Castle in Cracow. I told him that it would be expensive, but he didn't seem to care. He wanted it, so he got it. He even paid the bill without complaining.

I showed him my plans for what I'd started calling Copper City, and he seemed pleased. "Just so it works, boy!"

We were lucky in that Ilya had just completed the first steam sawmill, or I don't think I could have gotten him to work on armor, duke and prince or no duke and prince. The walking-beam sawmill was still in use, how-

ever, so I showed that to my guests first. They watched
sixty women walking back and forth and the huge logs
being cut into boards for half an hour. They were suit-
ably impressed. Then we demonstrated the new steam
mill, which cut more than twice as fast as as the walking-beam mill, and required only a single operator. They
were astounded.

"Damn, boy! That thing has the power of two hundred
women!" The name of the unit stuck. At one time I had
been worried that we would use "pig power" the way the
Americans use "horse power," much of our early machinery being powered by pigs in huge hamster cages.
But after the duke's statement, all our steam engines got
rated in woman power, and operators talked about how
many women they tended. I tried to stop it, but I
couldn't. The best I could do was to redefine it so that it
would fit into our system of weights and measures.

I'd had some of the girls trained to act as food
servers, in case the duke demanded it. Fortunately he
thought that eating cafeteria-style was an interesting in-
novation. This was good because after that, if any noble
visiting us commented on our strange ways of eating, we
had only to say that the duke liked it and that ended the
matter. I saw no point in paying for servants.

Actually, the duke took most of his meals at the inn.

I showed them a blast furnace pour at night, when the
splashing white hot iron is most impressive.

The duke ordered twenty clocks, and two of our huge
kitchen stoves, but he spent most of his time at the Pink
Dragon Inn. After the first night, he demanded, and of
course got, the exclusive waitressing of Lady Francine.
The innkeeper was no fool, and if anybody objected to
losing the most beautiful waitress in Poland, he had
sense enough to keep his mouth shut.

The best time of day to take a shower was just after
breakfast, when most of the men were at work and the
water was hot from the breakfast cooking. The place was
nearly empty except for some of the women on the afternoon shift, and they tended to be younger than those
working mornings. I was debating whether to invite

a certain blonde to join my household when Prince Henryk walked in.

"Good morning, my lord." I bowed. It was the first time that I had seen the prince naked and I couldn't help noticing that there was something strange about his left foot. It was a moment before I realized that on that foot, he had six toes.

"Strange looking thing, isn't it, Sir Conrad?" He wiggled his left toes. "Runs in the family. My grandfather had the same thing. You needn't look so awkward. I've had it all my life."

"Yes, my lord. Forgive me for staring." I took some soft, locally made lye soap and smeared it on a luffa.

"Nothing to forgive. These hot showers of yours are marvelous things, but what do they have to do with defeating the Tartars you said were going to invade us?"

"Directly, my lord, almost nothing. Indirectly, quite a bit. These showers and the sewage system and better food and clothing are all part of a program to keep my workers healthy. I don't want to spend years training a man only to have him die of something that could be easily prevented. Then, too, it is going to take a lot of money to train and equip an army big enough to beat the Mongols. By selling plumbing parts and other consumer goods, I can generate that money. I could never sell it without showing people what it does, and where better to demonstrate it than here?"

"Interesting. That armor you're making for my father and me looks to be effective, but it's taking all your smiths weeks just to make the two sets."

"It's worse than that, my lord. They spent a lot of time doing preparatory work. But in a few years, I'll have sheetmetal rolling mills, stamping presses, and dies by the dozens. We'll be able to turn out armor fast and cheap."

"And the copper mines you'll be opening for my father?"

"Copper is needed for more things than windmills and plumbing, my lord. These things earn money for now, but the same lathe that bores out the center of a bushing can bore out a cannon."

"And what might a canon be, aside from the law of the church?"

"It's a device of war, my lord. One smaller than a man can kill a dozen men at a time. I hope to start working on them by next year."

"That sounds dishonorable and horrible. It's hardly the thing to use in civilized combat."

"True, my lord. They *are* horrible and I pray that they will never be used on Christians. But you and the rest of the nobility must learn that the Mongols are neither civilized nor honorable. They lie, they cheat, and they steal. They will do anything at all so long as it brings victory. One of their favorite tactics is to take enemy prisoners, especially women, children, and the aged, and put them in the front lines to shield their own men. Facing that, you must decide between letting them advance without hindrance, or murdering your own subjects. Against an enemy like this, there can be no question of fighting them as if they were an honorable enemy. You must exterminate them in whatever way is possible."

"It is hard to believe that any people could be so vile."

"You must believe it if you want to survive, my lord. They *are* vile. They will eat anything at all, including rats, dogs, and their own prisoners. I know of one occasion when they ran short of supplies, so they ate their own allies. They also never bathe. It is their custom to put on new clothes on the outside and let them rot away from within."

"Yes, Sir Conrad, I'd heard that you can smell them miles away. I suppose that you will have to build these cannons and doubtless other devilish devices. But you can't expect me to like it.

"On the other hand, this new church you've built is wonderful! How did you ever get such huge logs set up like that?"

"It was quite a job, my lord. You see . . ."

*   *   *

Duke Henryk and Lady Francine hit it off very well together, and it was because of her that he stayed two days longer than he absolutely had to.

She left with his party, and rumor had it that he paid her two dozen pence a day for her services, whatever they were. That was six times what my top people were paid, but nobody demanded a raise because of it.

As soon as the duke left, however, I got hit with a major protest meeting from the women at Three Walls. They had all seen the tryouts on the steam sawmill, and they were against it. Last summer, they had objected vigorously to having to saw wood. Now they were even more against losing their jobs. And their husbands were with them.

I listened to them go on and on about how they couldn't possibly make it without the half pay they'd been earning for their half day's work, just to let them get it out of their systems. Then I stood up and cut off the last woman, who had been repeating herself. "All right, ladies. I've listened to what you've had to say. Now you'll listen to me.

"You've said that you can't possibly survive without the half pay you've been making sawing wood. I say that's dog's blood! You and your husbands can survive quite well without any pay at all!

"You were all starving in Cieszyn before I brought you here, and if you left, or if I threw you out, you would go right back to starving there! I could stop paying you all and you would keep on working here. You'd do it because it's the best thing that's ever happened to you!

"Who pays for all the food you eat, that some of you are getting too fat on? I do! Who got the cloth you're wearing? I did! Who puts the roof over your head? I do! Who built the church you go to? I did! I even pay the priest!

"And what do I get for this? Do I get your loyalty? No! All I get is complaints! What would Count Lambert do if his people met like this and complained to him? He'd have half of you flogged, and you know it! What would the duke do? You'd all be hung!

"But you think that because I've been good to you, you can get away with being bad to me. Well, you can't!

"You complain that you will be losing your jobs because of the new steam sawmill. Well, you'll lose your jobs when I tell you to lose them, and not before.

"Is there anyone here who actually *likes* to walk back and forth on that walking mill? Because if you do, you might as well leave now; you're too dumb to make it around here!

"We are building three steam mills. The first will go to Count Lambert's Eagle Nest. The second will go to the duke's new Copper City. And the third will be set up right here at Three Walls. And when it's working, we'll tear down the walking mill and saw it up for lumber.

"I took an oath to take care of you, and I have, even though you have as much as accused me of being an oathbreaker. And seeing your disloyalty, I am half tempted to throw out the lot of you!

"But I won't. I take our oaths seriously, even if you don't. Things are going to go on just as they have been. Women with children will work half a day for half a day's pay. Those without children will go on working a full day for full pay.

"You will work when and where I or my managers tell you to work. You will continue working until I tell you that you have lost your jobs. If you want to change jobs, come to us as individuals and maybe we can work something out. Or maybe not!

"But the next time you organize a protest meeting against me, I'll throw the leaders out and have the rest of you working without pay for a month!"

I stomped out, pretending to be madder than I really was. Had the matter been about food or housing, I would have been easier on them. But I couldn't tolerate protests over every new machine I introduced. Those were going to start coming in fast and furious.

But Count Lambert is right. You can't use reason on a mob. You have to tell them what to do and expect to have it done.

Chapter Eight

I WAS taking a group of seventy-nine men, fifty-six mules, and eight women to Legnica to build Copper City.

Another crew of about the same size was already at Eagle Nest where, their spring planting done, Count Lambert's peasants were starting to arrive. The Krakowski Brass Works and Three Walls were running with skeleton crews leading a bunch of rookies.

Annastashia was due for her child, so I'd assigned Sir Vladimir to take care of Three Walls. He'd have his hands full, since Ilya was the only real foreman left there.

We were taking it in easy stages, averaging about two dozen miles a day, or about a tenth of what Anna could run in the same time. Despite my precautions, we'd had to take the steam saw in two parts, since the roads were worse than I had imagined. Between them, the pieces occupied half our mules.

On noon of the third day, we were near the boundaries of Count Lambert's county when one of his knights, Sir Lestko, his horse lathered with sweat, overtook us.

"Sir Conrad, thank God in Heaven I've found somebody! You must come quickly and bring all your men! Something terrible is happening in Toszek!"

"What do you mean? What's happening?" I said.

"I'm not sure! But there are soldiers there and they are killing people! They are some kind of foreigners, and they are burning people alive at the stake!"

Toszek was about a mile up the road. The village where the trouble was happening was about a quarter-mile from a wooden castle sitting prominently on a hill. I detailed two men and all the women to watch the mules and baggage, and led the rest, mostly armed with axes, picks, and hammers, to the town. I'd tried to leave Piotr with the baggage, since he had too good a brain to lose, and he was too small to be of much use in a fight, anyway. But he wouldn't stand for it. He was still trying to prove something to himself, or maybe to Krystyana, who was with us. There was no time to argue with him.

We surrounded the place, a process that, for lack of training, took a quarter hour. A modern man has at least seen enough war movies to have a vague idea as to what to do; these men had no such background, and I almost had to tell them individually what I expected of them.

Dirty smoke was rising above Toszek, and we could hear screams and shouts. I knew that people were dying while we blundered around. Yet if we went in like a mob, trained soldiers could cut us to rags!

When the men were all in position and understood that they were to advance when called, keeping the men on either side in sight, Sir Lestko, Tadaos the bowman, and I went into the town. I'd brought Tadaos along to help provide meat for the camp, but I had other uses for him now.

A few dozen peasants were standing some distance away, cowed and frightened. In the middle of the square, eight stakes had been set in a line, and tied to them, slumping, were the burnt bodies of eight women. Three dozen soldiers and some priests stood around them.

The clothes and hair are the first things to burn, and I think that some of the thrill these filthy bastards got was watching the clothes burn off the women.

Tadaos rode his mule to the side of a shed, stood up on its back and climbed to the roof, where he could cover the square with his longbow.

Sir Lestko and I were actually in the square before the soldiers noticed us. Soldiers? The assholes didn't even have sentries out! Women had died because I had overestimated the opposition. I made a solemn vow to myself that next time there was trouble, I was going to just charge straight in and let the chips fly any way they would.

"You people are all under arrest!" I shouted. "You are outnumbered five to one and we have you surrounded! Drop your weapons and raise your hands!"

The soldiers and priests looked at each other, confused. They started babbling to one another in something that might have been Spanish, but which I didn't understand.

"Don't any of you bastards speak Polish? Speak up or we'll shoot you down!"

"I speak a little, knight. What is it you want?" An older priest said in very broken Polish.

"Want? I want you to drop your weapons and raise your hands! Tell them that in whatever tongue you speak, or I'll have the lot of you killed right now for resisting arrest!"

He hesitated a bit and then announced something to the crowd. One of the soldiers shouted something and drew his sword. He got one step closer to me before a steel tipped arrow tore through his throat. Tadaos was on the ball.

"That's *one*, you old fart! Anybody else want to play target practice? Tell them to drop their weapons!"

There was some more shouting that I couldn't understand. These murderers acted as though they were doing the most natural thing in the whole world, and that I was a strange person for intruding on them!

"You're taking too long, old man! I said that you are under arrest! You men surrounding the town! Advance slowly with your axes high!"

My men came up between the houses and barns, looking less sure of themselves than I would have wished.

"Last chance, old man! Surrender or die!"

There was still more unintelligible shouting. Then two soldiers dropped their swords, but three more drew theirs and charged me. Two went down quickly with arrows in their throats, but the third arrow missed, to bury itself in the chest of a priest standing behind. I had been so overconfident of Tadaos's shooting that I hadn't even drawn my own sword. The soldier was only a pace from me as my blade cleared its scabbard, but I needn't have worried.

Anna kicked the man in the face with a forehoof. There was a satisfying crunch and he crumbled into the dirt.

I tried to act as though I'd expected that. Pointing with my sword, as if that was the reason I'd drawn it, I said, "Form them into a line along there. Search them carefully for weapons!"

Of course, the enemy had still not surrendered, but I was using what a capitalist salesman calls an "assumed close." Pretend that your opponents will do what you want them to do, and maybe they'll do it.

They didn't.

Another soldier drew his sword, one of the plumbers took a clumsy chop at him with a pickaxe, and missed. A second soldier stabbed the plumber in the arm and was struck by a carpenter's axe.

A general melee broke out. They had swords and armor, but we outnumbered them two to one and were not much more disorganized. We had two men mounted while they were all on foot. And we had Tadaos.

His last dozen arrows streaked into the center of their mass, hollowing it out. I saw Sir Lestko take out three soldiers, and Anna and I hopped around, looking busy.

At one point a group of soldiers threw down their weapons, but my workers didn't have brains enough to accept their surrender. Or maybe they didn't understand what was happening. In any event, two unarmed soldiers were cut down with axes before I could disengage and get over there. The rest of the soldiers naturally picked up their swords again and the fight went on, costing me two of my own men that didn't have to die.

Then suddenly it was over. In front of the eight smoldering bodies lay those of four priests, nineteen soldiers, three masons, two carpenters, and a blacksmith, besides numerous wounded.

Piotr was standing nearby with a strange smile on his face and blood on his axe. He had killed his man, which is the other major rite of passage in this world.

I had the surviving enemy stripped naked for fear of hidden weapons, then had them tied up and put in one of the barns under guard. Other men were assigned to guard the battlefield, because the peasants might loot it before we could properly share out the booty.

I'd had the presence of mind to bring my medical kit with me, and naturally I took care of my own people before I bothered with the Castilians, for that's what they turned out to be.

I had seven people in tourniquets and was sewing up an eighth, the man's leg laying on my lap, when Count Lambert rode up with a dozen knights. Sir Stefan was with them.

"More of your witch's work, Sir Conrad?" Sir Stefan shouted.

I ignored him and addressed Count Lambert. "Good afternoon, my lord. You'll forgive me if I don't stand."

The dead still lay where they had fallen, and the burnt women were still tied to their stakes. Clothes, weapons, and blood lay thick about the village square.

"Sir Conrad, what the hell goes on here?"

"Well, my lord, the short of it was that Sir Lestko came to me and said that a bunch of foreigners were burning people to death. I came here and found it was true. I put them under arrest, but they resisted, with the result you see. The survivors are in that barn."

"Dog's blood! Sir Conrad, you have the damndest talent for finding trouble! What was Baron Mieczyslaw doing while this was going on?"

"Who, my lord?"

"Baron Mieczyslaw. These are his lands. That's his castle over there. Where is he?"

"I'm afraid I've never met the gentleman, my lord. I've only been here an hour myself."

"Sir Lestko! Go with my men to the castle and see

how matters stand there. Come back as soon as you may. I want to talk to the prisoners."

Count Lambert went to the barn and I went back to my doctoring. I was an amateur, but I was the best available.

Tadaos came back from helping secure the prisoners and started retrieving his arrows. "There's a lot of stuff laying around here, my lord," he said, gesturing to the booty scattered about.

"You'll get your share. We'll sort it out once things settle down. That was some pretty good shooting. You probably saved my life."

"I still owe you a few, my lord."

"Except for that fourth shot, of course. Missing a man clean at only a hundred yards. I'm surprised at you." I tried to say it in a humorous way.

Tadaos looked genuinely hurt. "That was an old arrow, my lord. A feather came loose as I let fly. The glue must have gone bad."

"I was only joking. Those things happen. Look, when you finish up with that, count the bodies, get the men together, and dig some graves. But leave things here as they are for a while. Count Lambert might want another look."

I was finishing up with the last of our men when Count Lambert came back. "Sir Conrad, do you realize that some of those prisoners are priests?"

"I know that some of them were wearing priest's robes and have their heads shaved, my lord. I believe they are impostors. Real priests don't fight and real priests don't commit murder."

"That's true enough. Still, you can't be too careful. What do you advise we do?"

"Well, I suppose we ought to hold a trial, my lord. We have to find out what these people were doing here, and why they seemed to think they could get away with committing murder in broad daylight and in public. For all we know, there could be other bands like this around."

"Yes. We'll do it in the morning, once we've all had a

chance to think." He was walking up the line of burnt bodies. "These were all old women."

"Except for the one on the end, my lord. She might have been sixteen, but it's pretty hard to tell."

"Dog's blood. How could anybody do something so ... so ..."

"Evil, my lord?"

"I think that's the word I wanted, but it doesn't seem bad enough. Well. Have your men clean up the mess here, and distribute the spoils as you see fit. I don't want any of it. It seems unclean."

Sir Lestko came up with six knights.

"Count Lambert, the castle was empty save for Baron Mieczyslaw. All of the servants seem to have run off. I left half your men there to secure the place."

"Good. You other knights, go to that barn and relieve the peasants securing the prisoners. Sir Maciej will be in charge. Sir Lestko, what of the baron?"

"My lord, the baron is in a very bad way. He cannot speak. He is bedridden and cannot move half his body. It is very strange. It's as though a line were drawn from head to navel, right down the middle of his face. All that is to the left of that line is cold and insensitive. It's as if he were half dead."

"Dog's blood! That smacks of witchcraft!"

"No, my lord, that smacks of a stroke," I said. "It's a common enough malady among the very aged. Is the baron very old?"

"Very. He served my grandfather," Count Lambert said.

"That explains it, then. You probably don't see much of it around here because you all die so young of other things first. It's all too common where I come from."

"I see. Can anything be done for him?"

"Not really, my lord. In time, he may regain some of his faculties, but until then he must be tended like a baby. There are a few women back with my baggage. I'll send two of them up to the castle to tend him until someone permanent can be found. But beyond that, there isn't much that I can do."

I had the baggage train brought up and sent two mature women to tend the baron. Taking care of a stroke victim is hardly a job to dump on a squeamish young girl.

Our field kitchen was set up, and Krystyana got a meal going. Some of the carpenters dismantled a shed to make coffins for our dead and the burnt women. The Castilians were simply thrown naked into a pit, the general consensus being that they didn't deserve any better.

When we tried to find the village priest to hold the funeral services, we discovered that his was among the dead bodies in the pit. Somehow, he had gone over to the enemy. We had to send a man to the next village to get someone to do the burial services.

Sir Lestko said that he didn't want any part of the booty either, so I told my people that those who had killed an enemy would get first pick of souvenirs.

"Just weapons, now. Any money and jewels will be divided up evenly later. Tadaos, you did yeoman service today. You get first pick. Piotr, I saw your axe bloody. You go next. The rest of you, well, you know who you are. Get in line. The others will keep you honest."

Piotr took a handsome sword with silver mountings and a matching dagger, while Tadaos found a pair of weapons that had plain steel mountings but very good quality blades. The differences in their characters, I suppose.

I saw Piotr looking proudly at Krystyana, but she just looked away.

After they were through, I had the others, including those who had stayed with the baggage take their choice, and had to be reminded about the women tending the baron. Their husbands chose for them.

As for the rest, I kept the armor for myself, not being as proud as certain others, and we added their horses and mules to our own. They had a surprising amount of money with them, surprising until you realize that there were no banks or travelers' checks in this world. If you were traveling, you had to carry all your money with you in cash, which made for a highwayman's heaven.

Every one of my people got almost three month's pay.

But the real surprise was the church vestments and altar furnishings in their luggage. I began to worry that maybe these really were priests. But even if they were, they were still murderers, so I earmarked the religious things for our church at Three Walls.

Who knows? Maybe they looted a church.

By dusk, there was some semblance of order in the village and the villagers were starting to filter back in. Some of them had been in the woods for days.

Krystyana, Natalia, Natasha, and I were invited to the castle for supper, only to discover that they were down to field rations up there. Dried meat and dry bread and not much of that. When the servants had run off, they stripped the larder.

There was plenty of extra food down at our field kitchen, many of the men not being hungry after their first experience with combat. I sent down for some, and none of the nobility complained about eating the leftovers of the commoners. None, that is, except for Sir Stefan. But after insulting the food, he ate his share. I got to ignoring him as just a bad noise.

Count Lambert was unusually taciturn that evening, and that put something of a damper on things. Questioning him, I found that he'd been notified by a boy from the village. A twelve-year-old kid had run from Toszek to Okoitz, a distance of four dozen miles, in a single afternoon and night, getting to Count Lambert at dawn. He had come immediately.

"In my land, that kid would get a medal," I said.

"And what might that be?" Sir Bodan said.

"It's sort of like a very large coin that is hung from a ribbon pinned to the tunic over the heart, or hung around the neck. It's given as an honor to those that have done some exceptional deed for the good of the community or state. They are of bronze or silver or even of gold, depending on the degree of the honor. Each branch of our military has several of these, ranging from mere participation in a campaign to one for outstanding valor."

"Interesting. So in your land a man may not dress as he chooses?" Sir Lestko said.

"Not at all. A person's clothing is up to him, except that certain professions and the military wear uniform clothing when on duty. It's just that someone wearing a medal that he had not earned would be a laughingstock when he was found out."

"You said, 'each branch of the service,'" Count Lambert said. "You have more than one kind of fighting man?"

"There are three, my lord. An army for fighting on land, a navy for fighting on the seas, and an air force."

"So you fight in the skies as well! Which was your branch?"

"I am an officer in the air force, my lord."

"Then you fought in the skies!"

"No, my lord. My duty was to oversee the maintenance of certain equipment, and during my four years of active duty, we were not at war. Not one man in a hundred was actually on flying duty."

"That must have been frustrating."

"The job had to be done. 'They also serve who only stand and wait.'"

"Well. There is the question of Baron Mieczyslaw. Sir Conrad says that it will be long before he can again perform his duties, if ever.

"My grandfather raised the baron to his rank for valor, but the fact was that his lands were not enough to support any subordinate knights. And while outstanding in combat, the baron drank and gambled to such an excess that it was never felt wise to enlarge his lands. He would only have wasted them.

"Further, he never took a wife, and has neither child nor near relative. His lands therefore escheat to me, yet I would not have him deposed, for as I said, he served my grandfather well. Therefore, someone must act as caretaker here, to be lord in all but in name.

"Sir Lestko, you have been in my county for four years, yet you have not actually sworn to me or mine, but have merely attached yourself to Baron Casimir."

"Ah, my lord. In truth, I am more attached to Baron Casimir's daughter," Sir Lestko said.

"So I had heard. Being lord of a barony might improve your suit. If you would swear to me, I would put you in charge of the lands and castle here. Baron Mieczyslaw will be lord in name until his death. Should he die, you will be invested with his lands, but will not be made baron. That title was in a way only honorary here, and dies with the man.

"Should the baron live and again be able to do his duties, I will see to it that you are rewarded with greater lands elsewhere. What say you?"

"I will do it gladly, my lord."

"Good. We'll swear you in tomorrow as soon as the sun is high. Do not be kind to the villagers here, for they have allowed harm to be done to their lord and to their fellows. The castle servants have robbed and abandoned their lord in time of his dire need. The least of them deserves a severe whipping, and you have my permission to hang those you see fit.

"Sir Conrad, you once talked of the manner of your people concerning trials. I would see how it is done. You will be in charge of tomorrow's trial. I shall be judge and these noblemen shall be jury. The other offices you shall appoint yourself. Have it ready by midmorning.

"For now, I am tired, and I wish you all good night. Sir Bodan will set up the guard schedule."

Later, I saw Natasha going to Count Lambert's room. The girls seemed to think that it would be most improper—and a waste—for him to have to sleep alone.

The next morning, after Sir Lestko was sworn in, I explained the duties of prosecutor and defender, and appointed Sir Bodan to be the defending attorney, since he was articulate and seemed to be the most sympathetic toward the prisoners. I removed Sir Lestko from the jury, since he was a witness, and found bailiffs among my own people. Natalia acted as court recorder.

I took the role of prosecutor myself, and Sir Bodan and I spent the morning interviewing witnesses, until Count Lambert sent down and told us to get on with it. In the Middle Ages, trials were often over in minutes, and justice suffered.

We held it in the church, that being the only building big enough to seat everybody.

I arranged the seating like that of the usual modern courtroom, and we were under way by noon. I started by explaining what we were doing, and that each witness could only say what he had actually seen with his own eyes. Hearsay was not admissible, which surprised people. They felt that they should say what "everybody knew."

One by one, the accused were interviewed through an interpreter, and the witnesses were heard. I could see Count Lambert getting increasingly bored and fidgety, but I kept on with it. It was almost dark when the last had been heard, and some of the witnesses had to be excused to get supper going.

The story that came out was this. The prisoners said that they had been charged by the Inquisition to go and to root out witchcraft wherever it was found. They had performed this office through Spain, through France, and then through Germany over the last year, burning, by their own admission, over a hundred people. They had no written authorization from the church, and they did not feel that it was necessary to consult with local temporal or ecclesiastical authorities.

On coming to Toszek they found the baron stricken in a manner that was certain proof of witchcraft. On questioning the villagers, they found that seven old women lived in a cluster of huts apart from the others, proof that they were up to no good. One young woman had taken on the duty of supplying them with food, and so was obviously of their number. Performing their duty, they had cleansed the world of them.

Then they had been murderously attacked without provocation by Sir Lestko, myself, and my people. They demanded justice.

The villagers said that a year ago, there had been an argument between some old widowed women and their families. To smooth things out, Baron Mieczyslaw had ordered that some huts for them be built apart from the others, and had appointed one girl, the granddaughter of two of the women, to collect food and to take it to them. Some measure of peace had resulted from this arrangement.

Sir Lestko's story told what I have said above, and each of my workers confirmed it.

We met again after supper, and Sir Bodan and I made our closing statements. He said that the prisoners were only doing their duty as they saw it, and they should be released with all their property returned.

I think I showed that the women burned were innocent of any wrong doing, and that the girl's only faults were obeying her lord and simple Christian charity.

I said that the accused had no proof that they were working at the behest of the church, and even if they did once have such proof, they had no right to take any such action without the permission of the local authorities. The Bishop of Wroclaw was never consulted, nor was Duke Henryk. Only Count Lambert had the right of high justice here, and to kill, other than in self-defense, without his permission was murder.

I demanded that they all be hanged. I then suggested that the jury members discuss the matter among themselves, and tell us their decision in the morning. Count Lambert, bored to tears, heartily agreed.

That evening, he said, "Damn but this goes slow! Did you have to bring forth every peasant to tell the story that the one before him had told?"

"Yes, my lord, I did. What if one had said that all the others were liars? What if the truth was something different from what we had been told? The lives of twenty-three men are at stake, as well as who knows how many so-called 'witches,' if they are allowed to leave unmolested."

"It would have been simpler to kill them all out of hand."

"True, my lord. But would it have been more just?"

In the morning, Count Lambert's instructions to the jury were, "Are any of you fool enough to think these bastards had the right to usurp my justice?"

Sir Stefan started to say something, but Count Lambert glared at him and he shut up.

The foreman stood and said, "No, my lord. Hang them."

Not quite proper procedure, but an improvement over the usual way of doing things. At least the accused were allowed to have their say in court.

One of the peasants in the town had been a hangman in Wroclaw, so he was given the job.

The prisoners were permitted to say confession to their own priests while ropes were slung over the branches of a huge old oak tree. Most of the condemned swore at us, and the priest who spoke Polish swore that he'd see me in hell.

"Damn foreigners," the hangman muttered. "You hang them with a new rope and still they complain!"

The sight of the Castilians being hung wasn't pretty. They weren't dropped, so as to break their necks, but were hauled up so as to strangle. Criminals were hung naked, their clothes going to the hangman as his fee.

It was an ugly sight. Most of the murderers urinated and defecated, and over half had an ejaculation, which I thought curious. Some actually died with a smile on their lips. Perhaps hanging really is a merciful way to kill somebody.

It was brutal, yet it was necessary. People cannot be allowed to take the law into their own hands. Anyway, burning eight women wasn't pretty either.

We left them hanging as we rode out about our duties. I suppose that somebody buried them.

I expected to get a lot of flak from the Church over the thing, but there wasn't a word. And in later years, when the insanity of witch-hunts was all the rage in western Europe, there were none in Poland.

The buck stopped here.

Chapter Nine

ΛΛΛΛΛΛΛΛΛΛΛΛΛΛΛ

ANNA FOUND the mine site without difficulty, and we went to work. We had temporary shelters up in a few days, and then the carpenters started felling trees, the masons collecting stones, the miners digging for ore.

The mules were sent back to Three Walls to get lime for mortar, the sawmill was set up, and word was sent to the surrounding towns and villages that we were hiring workers temporarily for the summer. If they did well, they might be sworn in permanently.

There was no lack of applicants, since word had spread quickly about how well my people lived. The winter before, I'd made up some blocks and puzzles of the sort that modern psychologists use, and tried to get some idea of the men's intelligence. I tried to hire the bright ones, because there was no hiring all the applicants. Thousands came and there was only room in the budget for three gross on a permanent basis and a thousand more temporarily. I hated to send so many of them away, but what could I do?

The ore was right on the surface, so tunneling wasn't necessary. We could dig it out of an open pit, which was much safer and cheaper.

The duke had sent six knights to take care of security, so that was one headache I didn't have to worry about.

In a week, things were progressing well enough for me to leave for Eagle Nest. I left Yashoo, my carpentry foreman, in general charge, and only nominally subordinate to the duke's knight, Sir Stanislaw. I took Natasha along, since she was handy to have around, and Anna hardly noticed her weight. By evening, Anna had us at Eagle Nest.

Vitold, Count Lambert's carpenter, was in charge there and things were going well. There were probably more men available than could be efficiently administered, but they were mostly logging and digging, which doesn't take much supervision.

Count Lambert had left the day before, and the setup was his idea, so I didn't change anything. We left for Okoitz that afternoon and got there in time for supper.

One of my miners was getting the coal mine dug without problems, and the cloth factory, with its two hundred attractive and available young ladies, was going full blast.

Count Lambert rather proudly offered me a cold beer. "You were right again, Sir Conrad. A cold beer is a wonderful thing on a hot day! I'm glad you talked me into finishing the icehouse below the grain mill."

The next morning, I was at Three Walls and found that Sir Vladimir and Annastashia were the proud parents of a healthy boy.

Trivial matters delayed me a few days, and then I headed to Copper City again, this time with Yawalda riding Anna's rump.

The whole summer went that way, with me constantly racing from Three Walls to Copper City to Eagle Nest to Okoitz and back to Three Walls, the whole circuit taking us a week to run. Since many of my workers were separated from their families, and since they could read and write now, I was playing postman as well as roving supervisor. It was fun and exciting at first, but it got *very* old after a while.

By fall, things were settled down to the point that Copper City only needed to be visited once a month, and I tried to keep my traveling down to two weeks a month, staying at Three Walls as much as possible.

We had another good harvest in 1233, the third in a row. Everyone gorged on sweet corn and watermelon, honeydews and zucchini, pumpkins and muskmelon. The beehives were a great success, and the price of honey and beeswax dropped by a factor of twelve on the open market.

The grains, potatoes, and legumes I'd brought with me had done well, and I computed that in two years we would be eating them rather than keeping it all for seed as we had been. And glory be to God, we had sugar beet seeds, over a hundred pounds of them! Next fall, I'd have to worry about refining sugar.

The new plants were almost untouched by insects, which cut heavily into most crops since insecticides weren't available. Most insects are very specialized in their eating habits, and the local ones couldn't cope with the crops that I'd brought in. They'd catch up with us eventually, but for the time being we were getting a free ride.

In fact, the only sour point was the squashes. I hadn't realized that they could interbreed, and they had been planted too close to each other. The bees, or whatever pollinated them, had made a mess of things. We got veggies that were half butternut and half spaghetti squash, and every other combination possible. Lambert and I set up a breeding program at six widely separated manors to try to breed back to the original forms, but that would take time. I moved six varieties of beans to those same six manors just to be on the safe side.

Most of Lambert's knights and barons were quickly taking up his new crops and other improvements, running only a year behind him. And everyone was using wheelbarrows now, and the entire harvest was gotten in early, almost without loss.

Piotr was doing a lot more traveling than I was. He had to make a monthly visit to the inns at Cracow, Cieszyn, and Wroclaw, besides the installations at Three Walls, Copper City, Eagle Nest, where we were taking care of the bookkeeping, paying all expenses and charging Count Lambert in cloth for it, and Okoitz, where we had built a small Pink Dragon Inn at Count Lambert's request. If the duke had one at Wroclaw, Count Lambert had to have one at Okoitz.

That summer, I'd formalized the mail service, setting

up a post office at every one of our inns. Besides serving our own people, we carried the mail of anybody who asked, and charged for it. It became a profitable sideline.

We never carried money or valuables, since Piotr had to travel alone and I didn't want to make him a target for thieves, but I did set up a system of postal money orders.

By spring, volume had grown to the point that I had to put on a full-time letter carrier, who made the round on about a weekly basis on a fast horse. As more inns were added, the number of letters sent increased as a cube function. In a few years, letters left each inn daily, and a letter could get to any major city in Poland in a week, for a price.

And like a modern post office, we were absolutely scrupulous about respecting people's privacy and about getting the mail through.

By late fall, the smelters at Copper City were in full production and the other facilities were just about complete. I sold the Krakowski Bros. Brass Works at a very healthy profit to Count Lambert's brother, Count Herman. I did this with the clear written understanding that I was taking the best of my workers with me to Legnica, and that we would be producing products there much like those that were made in Cieszyn.

I don't think the guy understood that people are as important as things when it comes to getting something done. It takes both the tools and the man who knows how to use them to accomplish anything, but many would-be industrialists don't realize that. He got all the buildings, machinery, and facilities, as well as two years worth of back orders and my blessings. But deep inside, I didn't think he'd be successful.

Most of the people from the brass works were moved to Copper City and formally sworn to me. They hadn't been up to that time, except for the Krakowski brothers themselves and their wives, and I wanted all the workers to be treated the same. I also swore in those workers hired that spring that had received the approval of the foremen, most of them, actually.

Thom Krakowski was put in charge of the smelting and mining operations, and being the eldest was also overseer of the whole city. His brothers had charge of the casting and machining sections. In fact they were used to working as a committee, and that's the way I set it up. Oh, they were always arguing like a bunch of kids over a game, and sometimes it got pretty loud. But somehow inside they were a smooth team. It takes all kinds.

My ladies had each spent months at the city and at Eagle Nest duplicating their own bailiwicks there. Krystyana got the kitchens going well; Yawalda had the barns running efficiently. The stores and offices were set up, and all the girls had chosen to come back to Three Walls. I was flattered, but they explained that if they stayed out in "the woods," as they described it, they might be stuck there. But things were always happening when I was around, even if I wouldn't marry them.

Tadeusz had put his youngest son in charge of running the inn at Copper City. He was worried. He was now out of sons. How could we expand further? So we worked out a training program for innkeepers, with each of his sons training a man, and with promotions to larger inns if a man did well. There was also a bonus system for the trainer.

Piotr had junior accountants at each of our installations by then so that he only had to check their work rather than doing it all himself. There just wasn't time.

The priest from Italy finally arrived, and I nearly fell off my chair when he announced his name. It was Thomas of Aquinas!

Saint Thomas Aquinas was the greatest theologian and logician of the Middle Ages, perhaps of all time! And here he was, a young man of twenty-two, running my church and school system. I tried to treat him the same as any other priest, but secretly I was in awe of him. I told him what I wanted to accomplish, but generally I let him do as he felt best, offering advice only when asked.

Interlude Two

I HIT the STOP button.

"He really had Thomas Aquinas working for him?"

"Yes and no. The man's name was Thomas and he really was from the Italian town of Aquinas. But *the* Thomas Aquinas you're both thinking of was seven years old at the time, and no relation to Conrad's schoolteacher. Conrad's history was about as accurate as yours.

"*Summa Theologica* still got written in Conrad's branch."

He hit the START button.

Chapter Ten

WE HAD just finished installing our first rotary steam engine, our first double expansion device. It turned an overhead shaft that had leather belts driving the lathes, grinders, and other machines we had lined up below it. Wicker baskets covered the belts, a safety feature.

I was getting ready to go to Eagle Nest to greet the first batch of four dozen boys when there was a commotion at the gate of Three Walls.

In front of the drawbridge was a ragged mob of some sort of foreigners, and Sir Vladimir was not about to let them in without my permission. There were over a hundred of them.

They had darker complexions than we did. Their hair was black and their eyes brown, sometimes green. They were of medium stature and had the thin, wiry bodies one associates with Armenians, or even Arabs. Yet they weren't quite exactly like either of those peoples.

Their leader, who was about as ragged as the rest, spoke only a smattering of Polish, and the others spoke none at all. It took me several hours to find out what they wanted, and I would have given up on them if I hadn't caught the words "Novacek" and "alchemist."

A year before, I had asked a merchant friend, Boris Novacek, to send me a chemist, if he ever ran across one, since I was weak in practical chemistry. Apparently, this man was the thirteenth-century equivalent of a chemist. He had with him three pottery jars of what smelled like acids, and intimated with gestures that he had made them.

Well, I badly needed a chemist. We were throwing away all sorts of things that could be useful if treated properly. Coal tar, for example, is a sticky guck that is a mixture of thousands of chemicals, some of which can be very useful. I knew that it contained aspirin and dyes and wood preservatives, to name but a few. But I hadn't the foggiest idea of how to go about purifying the stuff. But I needed one chemist, or maybe a few. I didn't need a hundred!

I tried to get this idea across, but it was slow going.

The lunch bell rang, and I was getting hungry. Looking at the crowd of refugees, for that's what they turned out to be, I realized that they hadn't eaten in days, and had had damn little in the months before. We had plenty of food, and there was no reason to be uncharitable. I invited them in for lunch, trying to communicate with gestures that this was a temporary invitation only, and that I was not permanently hiring them.

Problems started almost at once. Where I come from, when you're a guest, you eat what's put in front of you, and at least pretend that you're enjoying it. But they wouldn't touch our beer, insisting on drinking only water. Many Poles feel that you can't trust a man who won't drink with you, and to refuse a man's generosity is an insult.

The leader questioned me at length about the kind of meat we were serving, and I finally had to draw him a picture of a pig to get the idea across to him. He acted like I was trying to feed him human flesh, and on finding out it was pork he said something to his followers such that they contented themselves with bread and kasha. At least they were cheap to feed, even though they ate three times what my own people did.

In the course of the afternoon, either his Polish improved or I got better at gesticulating. It seems that his name was Zoltan Varanian, although I wasn't sure whether "zoltan" was a name or a title. In any event, I got the idea across that he and his people were welcome to stay for two weeks, but after that they would have to leave.

I also insisted that they take a bath before we put them up for the night, which caused other problems. My people didn't have a nudity tabu, and his did. Men and women didn't bathe together.

This caused all sorts of screaming every time one of my workers of the wrong sex walked into the shower room at the wrong time. Their men even screamed when a pretty girl went in to join them. Culture shock all over the floor.

Their clothes were in shreds and we had cloth coming out of our ears. Lambert had been paying for all the work at Eagle Nest in cloth, and I hadn't gotten around to disposing of it profitably yet. I had Janina issue them enough cloth to make a set of clothes for each of them.

Supper that night featured lamb, and that they'd eat. We put them up in the lowest two floors of the noble guest quarters, since there wasn't room for them anywhere else. They were stacked in like firewood, but even so, if the duke paid an unexpected visit, I didn't know what we'd do. Put them up in the barns, maybe.

The next morning, I really had to get to Eagle Nest, being a day late already. I assigned Natasha to Zoltan, with the understanding that she was supposed to do what she could about teaching him some Polish. I said that I didn't expect her to sleep with him. There are limits to hospitality.

Natasha took the job with the same cheerful acceptance that she did everything else. I never decided whether she was odd for being so compliant, or all the rest of the women in the world were strange for not being exactly like her. Any man who wouldn't marry the girl was a damn fool, including myself. Of course, I got her without having to get married.

Four dozen boys were waiting for me at Eagle Nest, bright young kids about ten or twelve years old, the scions of the local nobility.

Most of them had a servant or two along, and these people expected to have the cushy job of waiting on one small person. I put a stop to that, assigning most of the servants to housekeeping, cooking, and cleaning, which freed up many of my own people for more productive work elsewhere.

The boys were assigned six to the room, and one responsible servant was put in with them, mostly to keep the kids in line. There was room for eight times the number of people we had, and each of the boys could have had a room to himself, but boys of that age are tribal in their outlook. I wanted to get them to form long-lasting friendships and a sense of teamwork. For the first few days, I let them switch roommates as they liked, but after that room assignments became fairly permanent.

Count Lambert had picked the headmaster, and I liked the man. He would be teaching two classes of two dozen each, one in the morning and one in the afternoon. He was to teach the standard subjects, reading, writing, and arithmetic. When not in school, the boys were under the supervision of one of my carpenters, a man who was good with kids.

This system gave us a morning team and an afternoon team, which was intended to create friendly rivalry. A good amount of time was spent on team sports, and competitions were set between the shifts on weekends.

I started the boys out with kites, and had them build their own. And not just ordinary kites, but controllable kites with two and three strings. By the end of the week, I told them about gluing sand to the strings, so that you could cut another kite's strings.

Competition got fierce! And hopefully the boys learned something.

Returning to Three Walls, I got to thinking that a uniform might help with the feeling of solidarity I was trying to build among the boys. Count Lambert's factory turned out quite a nice red wool cloth, and Copper City could turn out brass buttons and military doodads by the ton.

I decided on white trousers and a white turtleneck sweater, with a red open-collar jacket. The trousers and jacket would have pockets in the modern fashion, since carrying everything in belt pouches is a nuisance. Black leather boots, belt, and gloves. Brass buttons, buckles, insignia, and epaulets. And either a red or a white peaked hat, depending on which shift they were on.

At the end of the year, I'd let the boys design a class dagger, and none but them would carry one of that design. Each class would have its own, just as many schools have a class ring.

Instructors would wear a similar outfit, except they would have a black hat. Other workers would have the same, but with much less braid on their outfits.

I debated with myself on whether or not the kids should be required to sew their own uniforms, since skill at sewing was needed to make canvas-covered aircraft. I decided against it because boys of that age grow quickly. If the kid had made it himself, he wouldn't feel right about handing it down once he'd outgrown it, and the obvious economy of hand-me-downs was standard in this century, even among the highest nobility.

Natasha and Zoltan made a remarkable amount of progress in the week I was gone. It was actually possible to communicate with the man. Some of this was Natasha's patience, but mostly it was because Zoltan was a very accomplished linguist with eleven other languages. Oh, he still had the vocabulary of a five-year-old, and much of our time together was spent discussing the meanings of various words, but he was able to tell his story.

He and his people were originally from thousands of miles east of Three Walls, east of the Caspian Sea. They had been from the city of Urgench, a part of the Khoresmian Empire, which stretched from the Arabian Ocean to north of the Aral Sea, and from beyond the Hindu Kush to the shores of the Caspian. To hear Zoltan talk of it, it was next door to Eden, with skies that were never cloudy and the waters ever abundant in the great Amu River that washed down from the never-failing snowfields of the Himalayas.

Ponds and orchards and fields of grain went on forever, all irrigated by the mighty Amu. Dozens of cities rose white and glorious in the sun, each with populations of more than half a million, for the empire was densely populated. Yet such was the abundance of the land that there was plenty for all.

Then the Mongols had come from out of the mountains to the northeast, and had killed the Shah and taken Samarkand and the capital city of Bokhara. The cities were destroyed, and their entire populations murdered. With their armies completely obliterated, with their Shah dead, or some said hunted beyond the shores of the Caspian Sea, with no hope left at all, the Prince of Urgench submitted to Genghis Khan. In return for a ruinous tribute paid to the conqueror, he bought some measure of peace for a few years.

But the tribute demanded increased yearly, and to it was added the demand that all the healthy men must enlist in the armies of the Khan, to fight in foreign wars. Already the required tribute in grain and gold and slaves meant starvation stalked the land. Without the aid of the healthy men, the tribute could not be met. The women, children, and aged might be able to support themselves, if poorly, but there would be no surplus. Without the tribute, the Khan's armies would return, and there would be none to defend against them.

The Prince of Urgench joined with other princes in rebellion against the Mongols, and Urgench was the last city to be destroyed. The surrounding countryside was desecrated in days, and every town, village, and farmhouse was put to the torch. The orchards and vineyards were chopped down for no other reason than the pleasure of their destruction. Women were raped within sight of the city walls, and then their throats were cut when the rapist was done. Whole families were lined up just beyond bowshot, and slaughtered.

Urgench held out for five months against the Mongol horde, until all the arrows had been exhausted, all the food was gone, and even the rats had all been captured and eaten. Then the Mongols had proposed a truce. They said that if the prince would surrender himself, they would let all others in the city live, for only the prince had rebelled against his masters, the others were but dupes who had followed him. The Mongols swore this to Allah, and to their own pagan gods.

The prince took counsel with his nobles, and then voluntarily surrendered himself. As arranged, the prince went out the city gate, and Mongol soldiers took charge of that gate. They beheaded the prince within sight of his subjects, and marched their army within the walls.

Then they said that all must leave the city, for they had sworn to leave the people with their lives, but the city itself was to be destroyed. The people could take what they could carry, but that was all.

As the citizens went through the gate, they were searched, and all weapons were taken from them. They were then sorted into groups, according to their occupations. Each group was separately guarded.

Military officers were the first to be murdered. They were bound hand and foot in sight of their families and then some were strangled and others slashed to death. Their families were soon butchered as well, except for a few hundred attractive young women, who were stripped, chained, and set aside.

Other groups followed, and the systematic killing went on for days. When the people complained to the Mongols that they were not keeping their oath to their gods, the Khan answered that he had promised not to kill those within the city, but that they were now outside its walls.

When none were left but a hundred of the city's best craftsmen with their families in one group, two thousand young women in another, and eighty thousand healthy men in a third, the killing stopped for a time.

While the butchering had been going on, and all the heads of the murdered stacked in neat pyramids, others of the horde had been systematically looting the city, although in fact most of the portable wealth had been in the baggage of the refugees.

The city was then burned, and the captive men were put to tearing down every wall, every palace, every mosque, and every hovel. When that was done, it still was not enough to satisfy the Khan. The captives were forced to dig a canal and then to dam the mighty Amu so that the river cut a new channel right through where the city had been. This destroyed the irrigation system, and without irrigation, the fields dried up and the very soil was blown away. Nothing was left of once beautiful Urgench that once held half a million people. The eighty thousand workers were then slaughtered and their heads added to the pyramids of skulls.

The Mongols made Hitler look like a piker, and Stalin look like small change.

Zoltan had been master alchemist of the city, and his family had been spared so that the Mongols might have something to threaten him with. This was also the case of the others in his small group.

The young women were taken off separately and never seen again. Zoltan's group was led off in the direction of Karakorum, the Mongol capital, with a guard of twenty men.

The prisoners were forced to cook for the guards, and Zoltan was as knowledgeable of vegetation as he was of minerals. He concocted a poison from the roots of certain desert plants, and slipping it into their food, used it to kill all the guards.

He then led his people west, and for seven years they had wandered in search of a home, constantly thrown out of Christian lands because they were Moslems, thrown out of Moslem lands because they were considered heretics and deathly afraid of going near the lands of the Khan.

Once there had been over five hundred of them, but four out of five had been lost along the way. A hundred were all that were left from a city of half a million.

It was a pitiful story, and I felt sorry for these people. But darn it, I had problems of my own! I had to make sure that what happened to Urgench didn't happen to Cracow! To do that, I needed the continued support of the Church, of the state, and of my own people. Having this crowd of refugees around wasn't going to help.

They were Moslems, of a sort, but as best as I could tell, they were all members of some heretical sect. Or at

least Zoltan said that all the other Moslems were heretics, so I guess it amounted to the same thing. That was
the last thing that I needed. Members of small religious
sects tend to be fanatics eagerly searching for converts.
The Church was already conducting an inquisition concerning me, and if they found out that I was harboring
and encouraging Moslems, and heretical Moslems at
that, it could go bad for me. And if the refugees started
making converts out of good Christians—well, I didn't
want to think about it.

I got very firm on the point that his people were not to
try to talk my people into joining his Church, or whatever one does to become a heretical Moslem.

He said that this was not a problem, and went into a
long theological argument which I could not follow but
that apparently proved to his satisfaction that we could
never qualify to join his sect, and therefore no attempt
would be made to save us.

This ticked me off even more! Where the hell did he
get off telling me that I wasn't good enough to join his
damned sect? I was good enough to join anything, not
that I'd wanted to. By that point, it was pretty late, and I
felt it best to call it a night. Much longer and I would
have decked the bastard, and that's not how you're supposed to treat a guest.

I spent the next morning catching up on things. Come
spring, I planned to build a second housing unit (or defensive wall, depending on how you wanted to look at
it), a dozen yards outside our first one. The new one
would be made of brick, with a tile roof. Also, I planned
a sawmill and cabinetry shop to be built outside the town
proper, down where a small stream would make it easier
to transport logs. Our valley was as logged over as it was
going to be, the trees left being kept for decoration.
Hauling huge logs uphill to our existing sawmill was silly.

And there were the hundreds of trivial things that
have to be done when you play manager.

It was midafternoon before I could get back to Zoltan,
but I was resolved to throw him and his people out at the

end of the week. I felt sorry for them, but there was too big a cultural difference between us for it to ever work out. We absorbed a group of Pruthenians last year without much difficulty, but those were children whose families had been murdered by the Knights of the Cross. They'd needed new families pretty badly, and were fairly malleable. These Moslems, or whatever they were, were a tightly knit community. Such a group can maintain its culture indefinitely. They had to go.

I know that sounds cruel, but they were cruel times. There was a limit to what I could do, and if I took responsibility for this band of a hundred foreigners, it meant that there were a hundred Poles somewhere who could otherwise have been helped, but weren't. My own people were dying every winter, and I owed more to them than I did to someone from a country I'd never heard of before.

But while they were around, and I was footing the bill, I wanted to pick Zoltan's brain for everything I could concerning practical chemistry. This proved difficult. Part of the problem was the lack of a mutual vocabulary. Zoltan learned the Polish word for "door" when Natasha pointed at the door and said "door." A bit of discussion might be needed to make sure she wasn't talking about the door knob or the door frame, but it didn't take much time. But how the hell do you get across the concept of potassium nitrate? I couldn't say that it was the major constituent of gunpowder. He didn't know what gunpowder was. It's a white crystal? So are table salt, sand, and a million other things!

I tried to start with the simplest atom, hydrogen. After an hour talking about atoms, Zoltan allowed that he had read an old Greek text about atoms, but was sure that the concept was silly. It didn't fit into his system of moist substances as opposed to dry substances, hot versus cold, and the whole earth, air, water, and fire cosmos that he not only believed in, but that he unshakably *knew* was true. A thousand times he had used the theories he had been taught by his master and had gotten good results. How could anyone doubt it?

It was late when we finally called it a day with little progress made. The next four days were about as bad, although Zoltan's Polish was improving astoundingly.

The truth was that I had a good background in theoretical chemistry, with little practical knowledge. Oh, I'd had the usual college lab courses, but they all involved taking prepackaged chemicals and mixing them according to a formula. For all the practical knowledge I gained, I might as well have been in a home economics class. It was worse than cookbooking. I hadn't the faintest idea of how most chemicals appeared in nature. A housewife at least knows what a chicken looks like!

And Zoltan knew quite a bit about practical chemistry. He had jars of hydrochloric, sulfuric, and nitric acid with him. He proved it by dissolving a bit of gold. He was also convinced that he could transmute lead into gold, once he got good enough at it. He just hadn't found the right procedure yet.

We had no common ground between us.

And my people didn't get along with his. There had already been two knockdown fistfights, and another incident where knives had been drawn before the men involved were pulled apart. And it wasn't all a matter of the rich settlers molesting the poor refugees. That damn raghead had no business grabbing a married woman, even if she did walk into the shower room naked at the wrong time of the day!

If this went on, somebody was going to get killed.

On the morning before their scheduled departure, Zoltan approached me with the idea of his people feasting some of mine. His Moslems would cook the food and provide the entertainment for, say, forty of my best men. It seems that among his people, a proper feast was for the men only. Women and children ate later from the table scraps.

Well, okay. It was my food they would be serving, but I could see where it was intended to be a goodwill gesture.

If there was to be entertainment, fine. Aside from rare bands of minstrels and clowns, in the Middle Ages, entertainment was what you did on your own. Variety would be welcome.

I said we would hold it that evening in the living room of my apartment.

Chapter Eleven

^^^^^^^^^^^^^^^^^^^^^^^^^^^^^^

FROM THE DIARY OF PIOTR KULCZYNSKI

When I returned to Three Walls, I found strange things there. A band of foreigners had been invited temporarily within, and a notice had been posted restricting the baths to them during certain hours of the day.

I discussed this with Yawalda, whose friendship I had been cultivating in part because of her friendship with my love Krystyana. Also, she is in charge of the stables, and takes very good care of my horse. It seemed that the men all wrapped their heads in towels, and were embarrassed if any saw them without such strange garb. The women always kept their faces covered, even around other women. They had been invited in because Sir Conrad had taken pity on them, but they would soon be forced to leave.

But Yawalda had another far more interesting piece of news, and she swore me to secrecy before she would talk of it. They weren't sure yet, but it looked as if Krystyana was with child!

Sir Conrad's ladies had long been using a method of preventing this taught them by Lady Richeza and known as the rhythm method. Yet it appears that not all of God's children have this rhythm, for Krystyana had missed her time. This excited me, for now she would have to be married or be called strumpet! If Sir Conrad would not have her, and he had often said that he would not, then perhaps at last my suit would be considered! I might yet win out and marry my love!

I was thus in a wild mood when word came to me that I was invited to Sir Conrad's apartment in an hour's time for an evening's entertainment! But my first hopes were soon shattered, as it was to be given by the foreigners and was to be a men-only affair.

I came dressed in my best, which was quite good now that I could afford such things, and of course I wore the beautiful sword and dagger I had won in combating the Castilians.

I soon found myself sitting uncomfortably on a cushion, with Sir Conrad to my right and Ilya to my left in Sir Conrad's great hall, or living room, as he insists on calling it. This large room takes up the entire top floor of the place, is fully eighteen yards to the side and is above any other room in the whole building, the floor being higher than the adjacent rooftops.

The ceiling is more than twice that which is usual at Three Walls, which is tall in itself. There are no velvets or tapestries hanging, yet the room has a certain rude splendor to it. I know for a fact that Sir Conrad had originally planned something far more modest, for I was there when Sir Vladimir insisted that it was occasionally necessary to impress a noble guest and Sir Conrad went along with him.

The west wall is done in rude limestone blocks, and those of the north and south are in rough timber, the slabs of wood each a yard wide. The ceiling is supported by other huge logs and the east wall is the raw natural face of a limestone cliff. Into this solid rock is cut a fireplace big enough for twenty men to stand, had the fire been out. Now it was roaring high. Yet for all its roughness, the hall had a certain vibrant strength about it that suited Sir Conrad's character.

Three foreigners were playing musical instruments that I recognized as coming from our own band, but their manner of playing was extremely odd. They were far out of tune, and the music had a strange sliding quality that I disliked at first, but eventually started to enjoy.

The leader of the foreigners, their zoltan, introduced each of his men to Sir Conrad and the rest of us. Their

names were all so strange to me that I could not remember a single one of them, but he gave their titles in
Polish as well. This one was a master tanner and that
was a master goldsmith. There were swordsmiths, pot-
tery-makers, armorers, jewelers, leatherworkers, astrol-
ogers, bootmakers, glassblowers, and dozens of other
trades mentioned, as well as some that had no word for
them in Polish. And all of these men claimed to be masters of their crafts, which I took with a bit of mustard, as
the saying goes. If I was in a strange land, I might claim
to be a master as well, for who could catch me at it?

Sir Conrad followed suit, introducing all of his men
present. Since I was by his side, he introduced me first,
and the zoltan translated this into whatever language
they spoke. I felt obliged to stand, as one would at a
Christian banquet, but in so doing I nearly fell over.
After sitting in such an unnatural position, all sensation
had left my legs!

Sir Conrad said that the rest should remain seated,
and continued around to Sir Vladimir, who should by
rights have been first, being the only other nobleman
present, but Sir Conrad often puts the last first and vice
versa. Myself, I think it part of his philosophy.

Food was served after the introductions were finished, with men doing the serving rather than women,
and while I knew that all of it had come from our larders
here at Three Walls, much about it was strange. There
were noodles that were as tiny as grains of wheat, and a
sauce on the mutton that was like nothing I had ever
tasted before. I thought that it might have been some
foreign spicing, yet Yawalda had said that these people
had come to us with absolutely nothing but the rags on
their bodies. It remains a mystery to me.

We ate with brass spoons and the forks that Sir
Conrad had shown us the use of, but the foreigners,
being of course uncivilized, ate with their hands, and
only with their right hands, I noticed. I heard later that
this was because they wiped their privy parts with their
left hands, not having learned the use of hay balls, or
apparently, wash stands.

The zoltan stood and made a speech in his barely understandable Polish. He said that he was thankful for our generosity to his people, and thanked Sir Conrad publicly for the food and clothing he had given so freely. Our lord would be remembered in their prayers, even if we did call God by a different name than they did.

Sir Conrad made a speech in return, but I thought he wasn't very sincere about it. He said that he regretted the necessity of their departure, but that each might take with him as much food as he could carry, and there would be a parting gift of a hundred sheep, which he asked that they not slaughter until they had left Count Lambert's lands, because of that lord's laws regarding ewes.

The zoltan then announced that as part of the entertainment, his daughter would dance for us.

The music was stately at first, or as stately as that slippery foreign stuff ever gets.

A woman came up the steps wearing one of the huge garments favored by these people. Word was they dressed that way to cheat Sir Conrad out of more cloth, for I'm sure that clothing them took six times what he had expected. She was covered from head to foot, and even her face was heavily veiled.

After a time, the music became quicker, and she threw off her face veil, revealing a lovely face and huge green eyes. She tossed the veil at Sir Conrad's feet, for he like the rest of us had stretched out to relieve the cramps in his legs.

At my side, Ilya said, "I know that girl! Been talking with her for two weeks. Met her in the dining room."

"Why does she bother with you?" I asked.

"Because she's very discriminating! Also because I'm mature enough to talk without pawing her body every chance I get like a young buck would."

"How were you talking then? I thought that none of these people could speak Polish."

"That's mostly what we've been doing. Teaching her how to talk. I think there's a fellow from the night shift that's been helping her during the day."

"So the relationship has been purely platonic?"

"Naw, we didn't talk no philosophy. Just what words mean."

The tempo of the music increased again, and the speed of the dance with it. The girl took off her outer garment, revealing a more form-fitting one underneath. Her long black hair was flowing free.

"Not a bad body," Ilya said. "If I'd have known what was under that tent two weeks ago, maybe I *would* have done some pawing."

I nodded, but was too interested in the dance to speak.

Again the tempo quickened and again the dance became faster. Her blouse was thrown to Sir Conrad's feet, revealing a thing of straps that covered her breasts. She was a remarkable beauty, far more attractive than any that I have ever seen in my life, and I tour the Pink Dragon Inns monthly as part of my job. Those inns are reputed to have the most beautiful waitresses in the world!

Again it became faster, and she was stripped to the belly, wearing only a long thin skirt that had many slashes from hem to belt. Not an eye in the room was on anything else but this incredible apparition. At least I can't imagine that anyone was looking anyplace else, though I didn't waste the time to check! She was moving her hips in an incredibly rapid fashion that sent ripples down her skirt. I wouldn't have thought it possible for a woman to move so, yet there it was.

And again the music became impossibly faster, and somehow the dance quickened with it. She was totally nude now, and there was not a hair on her body below the neck. Her privy parts were as smooth as a baby's.

"See how smooth she's shaven!" Ilya said. "These people must make some damn fine steel!"

I didn't bother even to nod, so entranced was I with her dance. Then suddenly the music stopped, and the girl was lying at Sir Conrad's feet, the sweat glistening on her body.

The room was silent for a moment, for we were all

dumbstruck. Then the room erupted with applause that vibrated the walls and must have been heard halfway to Sir Miesko's. But the girl never moved.

The cheering went on for a long while, but finally the zoltan stood with his arms up and his palms out, and it became quiet.

"You like, yes?" he said.

Again there was great applause until it was stopped.

"And you, noble Sir Conrad. You like it also?"

"I liked it very much, Zoltan."

"This girl she is name Cilicia. She is my only daughter. She is my only family that is alive. But so great are your gifts to us, that we must give in return. I give her to you. She is your slave. Take her!"

Sir Conrad rocked unsteadily on his cushion. He paused before he said, "Zoltan, I thank you for this incredible intended generosity, but I can't accept a slave. Slavery is illegal in Poland. Last year I fought a battle to make it so!"

"Nonetheless, noble Sir Conrad, it is so. This is a most obedient woman, and always she has done what I say. Now I tell her obey only you, and she will obey me in that, though it be my last word to her."

"I'm sorry, but I may not break the law. I cannot accept a slave."

The zoltan came close to Sir Conrad, bent over and spoke privately. Since I was sitting at my lord's side, I think that I was the only other man to hear what was said.

"Please, Sir Conrad. We are now in the far north and winter is soon. We have no place to live and soon we will all be dead. I do not blame you for this. You have done us much good and you have no obligation to support a band of homeless wanderers. But you were our absolute last hope, and now we must die. But please, as a father I beg you. Let my little girl live."

Sir Conrad paused a while. "Put that way, yes. I'll take care of her."

"Thank you, my lord."

The zoltan stood and announced to the crowd, "The noble lord accepts my gift!"

The crowd cheered, but myself, I think that the zoltan didn't want his followers to know the real reason for his generosity.

As the festivities broke up, I saw Sir Conrad return to his chamber, or bedroom he called it, with the girl under his arm. She was still naked.

The next morning at breakfast, the extra meal Sir Conrad insisted on serving, the talk was about nothing but the dance Cilicia had done the night before, and those of us who had been there were the center of attraction. The ladies were all envious, and Yawalda said she'd trade next year's pay to have people talk about her as they did the foreigner.

"Cilicia will be staying with us," I said. "Get her to give you dancing lessons."

"I tell you in front of God that I will ask her!" she said.

"Good. I'd like to see all you women doing it. Myself, I think it was some kind of fertility dance, to induce a man to marriage. It's certain that no woman pregnant could do it, or if she was, she wouldn't be for long. Maybe that's the idea behind it, to show that a man's getting unsullied goods."

"Unsullied!" Natalia shrieked in mock anger, and Yawalda threw a piece of bread at me.

I picked up the bread and kissed it, as is only proper, but also to reprove Yawalda for throwing it, for bread is in a way sacred. Then I put it back on the table and she, of course, ate it.

"Well, the nobles seem to want that sort of thing. A commoner must be content with what he can get."

I might have gotten more playful abuse, but Sir Conrad came in and signaled that he meant to speak to us all, so the room fell silent.

"A year ago I asked my merchant friend Boris Novacek to send me an alchemist, for we have need of a man with such skills here at Three Walls."

"Two weeks ago, Zoltan's people arrived on that invitation. My thought at the time was that while we needed an alchemist, we did not need a hundred of them. Therefore I told them that they were welcome to stay for a while to rest from their journey, but after that they would have to leave.

"I did not then realize that all of the other men with him were masters at one craft or another. Many of them have skills that we do not. There is a glassblower in the group. If we can get him the proper tools and supplies, we could all soon be drinking our beer out of real glass vessels! We could have real glass in our windows and the church could have stained glass walls!

"They have a papermaker. You probably don't know what paper is. It is used as a sort of parchment, but it is a thousand times cheaper to make!

"They have a porcelain-maker. Porcelain is like pottery, but much finer, and with many more colors than we now have.

"There are many other skills besides. I have talked with their leader Zoltan, and he has agreed to stay here with his people. Each of his masters will be taking on at least one young Polish apprentice. A list of the positions available will be posted in a few days, and young men interested in possibly rapid promotion and pay are encouraged to make application through Natalia.

"Applicants must be approved by myself, Zoltan, and the master involved, but there will be at least three dozen of them now, and perhaps more later.

"These people are from a different culture than ours, and they have a different religion. They worship the same God we do, but they do it in a different way. While I pray that someday they will come to Christ's pure light, I have little hope of that happening soon. Until such time that it does, the discussion of religion with them is absolutely forbidden. If you want to be outlawed, all you have to do is get into a theological argument with one of Zoltan's people. I hope I don't have to prove to you how serious I am about this. Converting them is a matter for the clergy, *not for you*!

"Still, both Zoltan and I recognize the differences and

frictions existing between our peoples. Because of this, we will be moving them out of Three Walls as soon as possible. Some of you know of the small valley just a half hour's walk east of ours. It has a small stream, and should be suitable for a group of the size of Zoltan's.

"If the weather holds, we will be able to build them suitable housing there before the ground freezes, and we will be transferring a few hundred sheep to them.

"Until that time, I shall be very rough on anyone who breaks the peace with them! With luck, we should have them out of here by Christmas. Cilicia will be staying with my household, to see if it is possible to convert one of them to Christianity."

Ilya choked down a laugh at the mention of Cilicia. Sir Conrad pointed a finger at him. "That snigger just cost you a weeks' pay, Ilya! Natalia, make a note of it.

"That's about it. Carpentry and masonry managers, from foremen up, will report to my office at zero six to discuss scheduling changes. Thank you."

Chapter Twelve

▲▲▲▲▲▲▲▲▲▲▲▲▲▲▲▲▲▲▲▲

FROM THE DIARY OF CONRAD SCHWARTZ

Cilicia was the most beautiful woman I'd ever seen in my life, movie stars and the National Ballet included. In the twentieth century, a woman who could dance that way would be in Hollywood if the Bolshoi didn't kidnap her first.

Understand that the Polish girls around were mostly pretty, but then those that were available were all about fourteen years old, and at that age, they're *all* pretty. It's nature's way of getting them married off. But the two truly outstanding women I'd met here were both foreigners, and I have a theory about that.

In a civilized country, people pick their mates for fairly impractical reasons. Is he witty? Do her hobbies and interests agree with mine? Does he dance well? And most important, is she pretty? Will my friends envy me because he's so tall and handsome?

In all cultures, some people never marry, and often those who don't meet the local standards of desirability are the ones who stay single. Over many centuries, this results in a selective breeding pressure toward people who are attractive and socially adept, but not necessarily intelligent, resourceful, or tough.

In a primitive culture, people have to be more practical in their choice of lifetime partners. Can he provide me and my children with enough food for us to survive? Can she cook and sew and butcher an animal properly? Is he a good enough fighter to save us from our enemies?

Is she tough enough to defend our hut when I'm gone?

These aren't matters of personal preference or social prestige, this is survival. If you pick wrong, it could hasten your death. It's so important that in many cultures, the people directly involved aren't allowed to choose for themselves. Older and supposedly wiser heads do that for them, and marriages are arranged by the parents.

This results in a selective-breeding pressure quite different from that of more civilized peoples. People might be more tough and self-reliant, but they are not more attractive. In fact, I suspect that you could take a good guess at how cultured a person's ancestors were simply by seeing if he or she is attractive.

In the thirteenth century, Poland was only two centuries away from a primitive, tribal culture. It would take many more centuries to transform them into a more attractive if less tough people.

But France and the Middle East had been civilized much longer, and that's precisely where Lady Francine and Cilicia came from.

I'm not saying that this is Ultimate Truth, but I'd argue it over a beer.

Cilicia's talents in bed were as outstanding as her abilities on the dance floor, and I'm glad that I didn't have to take her as a slave because I certainly wanted to take her.

She was bright, too. In two short weeks, she'd picked up enough Polish to communicate, and her accent wasn't as thick as her father's. I admit that she talked me into letting her people stay, despite all the problems that we both knew would occur.

Her technique was to examine things and tell me the name of the man in her group who could show us how to do it better. She examined the blade of the fancy dagger that Sir Vladimir and his brothers had given me last Christmas and pronounced the steel to be inferior. My sword met with her admiration, and when she asked if we could do such work, I had to admit that we couldn't. But one of her people could.

She talked about pottery and cloth and glass, but I

think that it was the papermaker that finally convinced me. To really spread knowledge, you have to have plentiful books. There simply was no possibility of producing enough parchment to do that, even if I could automate the process of producing it. It takes the skin of a whole sheep to make a single large sheet of parchment, and there is a limit to how many sheep you can grow. But if we had paper, I knew I could build a printing press.

So that night, between bouts of Mil. Spec. lovemaking, we planned how our peoples could work together without killing each other. Essentially, the program was to keep them as separated as possible, with contacts only for professional purposes. I would give them some land and keep my people out of it, except for apprentices, who wouldn't be allowed to spend the night. Except for Zoltan, her people would leave their land only with my permission.

My people would build hers some minimal housing, enough to get them through the winter, and we would provide food for the first year, after which they would be on their own. One half their man-hours would be spent teaching my apprentices and in R&D work. We shook on it, a novel custom for her, and in the morning her father was delighted with the deal.

Cilicia, of course would be staying with me. My father didn't raise anybody *that* dumb!

So my carpenters and masons stopped what they were doing and started putting up a housing unit. No indoor plumbing, no defensive features, and the kitchens would be detached. It wouldn't be as nice as Three Walls, because we were up against a time limit.

Not only was winter closing in, but I wanted them out of Three Walls before the Great Hunt. I didn't want fifty noble guests, a few of whom had fought Moslems in the Crusades, rubbing shoulders with guests who weren't even Christians! That was asking for trouble.

But after two weeks at Three Walls, I had to make my rounds of the other installations again. I was getting ready to leave when Kotcha, my mount's rubdown girl, all fifty pounds of excited nine-year-old, ran breathless into my bedroom.

"Anna's had puppies!" she shouted.

This announcement left me momentarily stunned. "Kotcha, horses don't have puppies. They have foals. And Anna's not expecting. You can tell on a horse. The body gets bigger and the breasts fill with milk. This is the wrong time of the year for that, anyway."

Children in the Middle Ages didn't have to be told about the birds and the bees. It was normal for the entire family, parents, children, and various relatives, to live and sleep in a single room. Sex was something normal that had happened around them all their lives. And if that wasn't enough, they were mostly farmers, and watched animals doing it as farm children have always done. Making sex a secret is a modern perversion.

"Anna's not a horse! And they look like puppies!"

"The first part is true enough."

"Maybe you'd better come and look. My lord."

"Maybe I'd better."

A crowd had gathered around Anna's stall, and I pushed my way through it.

What I saw turned my stomach. If ever there was a bunch of prematurely born foals, this was it. They really did look like oversized puppies, with tiny spindly legs they could barely crawl on. Born in November, for God's sake, and there were four of them. No wonder they had aborted. It was incredible that they were still alive. There was only one decent thing to do. Put the poor things out of their misery. I got out my good Buck jackknife.

"You people get the hell out of here!" I shouted at the crowd, which evaporated.

"Kotcha, you'd better go, too. You don't want to see this."

"What are you going to do?"

I crouched down to her level. "I know that this will be hard for you to understand, Kotcha, but sometimes things aren't born right. Sometimes, well, something goes wrong, and when it does, the only nice thing to do is to make them not hurt anymore."

"But what are you going to do?"

"These foals, these 'puppies,' won't be able to grow up right. Look, Anna's breasts haven't even started to swell yet. She won't be able to feed them. They'll starve."

"They eat hay, just like Anna does."

"They're too young to eat hay. Small mammals have to have milk, and Anna doesn't have any."

"I *saw* them eating hay!"

"Kotcha, I've tried to explain, but I'm just out of explanations. It's something that has to be done. Now please go away."

"You're going to kill them!"

"Yes, Kotcha. I have to."

"NO!" She ran to the back of the stall, grabbed a pitchfork, and stood in front of the colts pointing it at me. Fifty pounds of sheer courage and no brains at all.

"Damn. Anna, would you talk to her. You know that this is necessary, don't you?"

Anna shook her head No, and stood beside Kotcha.

If I had to, I could always disarm Kotcha and lock her in her room. But if Anna was against me, it wasn't so straightforward. She could whip me easily in a fight.

"Anna . . . damn. There's nothing in our sign language that covers this. Let's go over to the letterboard and talk this over. Kotcha, you can stay right here and watch the babies."

I'd made up the letterboard more than a year ago when I learned that Anna was intelligent. She couldn't talk but she could spell things out by pointing at the letters. If you could call it spelling.

She went over to it and spelled out KEDS OK.

"Kids okay? You're telling me that those are normal?"

She nodded yes.

"They always look like that?"

Yes.

I sat down on the ground. "Oh my God! I nearly mur-

dered them! But what are they going to eat? You don't
have any milk."

ET HAY ET GRAN ET ENEDING

"They can eat anything, the same as you do?"

Yes.

"Your species always has them four at a time?"

Yes.

"Who . . . who was the father?"

NO FADER

"No father? Then how . . . Anna, some fishes and liz-
ards reproduce asexually, parthenogenetically. Do your
people do that?"

Yes.

"Huh. But this isn't a sensible time of the year for a
herbivore to reproduce. Anna, what triggers it? Why did
you have them now and not some other time?"

SHE ASK

"She? You mean Kotcha?"

Yes.

"And all she had to do was ask? You reproduce voluntarily?"

Yes and yes.

"I'll be damned. How long does it take them to grow
up?"

She tapped her hoof four times.

"Four years, huh? Anna, do you like having children?"

Yes and yes.

"Well, having more people like you around would
sure be helpful. You keep on having them until further
notice. Is that sufficient?"

Yes.

"Good. I hope you accept my apology for the stupid
scene I just made. I guess I'd better talk to Kotcha now.
How long before you're ready to travel?"

She gave me the "ready" signal.

"The morning after childbirth? Well, if you say so.
We leave in an hour. I'm through trying to second-guess
you. From now on I'm going to ask."

Yes.

I apologized to Kotcha, but she stayed mad at me, the way a kid will. It was months before we were friends again.

Actually, I was pretty disgusted with myself. I had reacted emotionally and had almost made a horrible mistake because I hadn't stopped to think. I'd known for years that Anna was a member of a different species than a horse. Just because the adults of her species looked like horses was no reason to think that the juveniles would. And since when do you do mercy killing on people? Because Anna *was* people, and I had gotten into the bad habit of forgetting it.

I'd had the saddler make a sort of second saddle that attached to the back of Anna's regular saddle. This let a passenger ride sidesaddle behind me and have someplace to brace her feet. I took Cilicia along to show her some more of the country, to give her a chance to show off some of her new western-style outfits, and for sex, of course. There was no point in messing around with strange ladies when I had perfection at home.

It took us two days to get to Copper City. Anna could make it in one during the summer, but winter was closing in and the days were much shorter. The lack of a decent artificial light cut into travel time as much as it did into industrial production.

My experiments in trying to distill a decent lamp fuel from coal tar had met with a pretty dismal failure. The stuff had so much sulfur and ammonia in it that it cleared the room of people when I lit the lamp. It smoked badly, too.

I was toying with the idea of trying to drill for oil so that we could have kerosene lamps, but the only oil fields nearby were at Przemysl, a city that was originally Polish, and would be again, but had been in the hands of the Ukrainian Duchy of Halicz Ruthenia for fifty years. Getting permission to set up an installation there would probably take a major diplomatic effort.

I was stumped.

When I got to Copper City, the duke was just arriving.

He had Lady Francine with him, and two dozen armed men.

"Damn, boy! Do you always run a horse like that? You'll kill her!"

"Not Anna, your grace. She likes a good run."

"People say that whenever they see you on the road, you're always at a dead gallop and never seem to have time to talk."

"It's just that between your projects, Count Lambert's, and my own, there isn't much time, your grace. I hope I haven't been rude."

"No, but it keeps them talking about you."

"I suppose it does keep me in the limelight, your grace," I said as I got out of the saddle and helped Cilicia down. She was short and slender but surprisingly heavy for her build. A dancer's body is all smooth, hidden muscle, and remarkably dense.

She bowed to the duke, who nodded back, but she stayed out of the conversation until invited in, as a good woman should. In the twentieth century, the ladies would have monopolized the conversation for hours, talking about nothing. The thirteenth was less decadent.

"What the hell is a limelight?"

"It's ..." Daylight dawned in the swamp. "It's what I've been trying to think of for two years, your grace. It's a very bright artificial light made by burning a gas under lime, and it's what will double the production in our factories."

"Double the production? I don't follow you, boy."

"It might even triple it. As things are, we can only work during the daytime, your grace, and then only during good weather in the wintertime. Our expensive machinery is idle almost two-thirds of the time. With a good artificial light, we can shutter up the windows and run things day and night!"

"How're you going to get that much work out of the peasants? Three days of it and they'd fall over dead!"

"Well, you don't work the same men continuously, your grace. You work them in two shifts, one working days and one working nights. We're already doing that with the smelters and the blast furnaces, where we can't stop at night, but the animal fat lamps we use are expensive to operate and don't give off much light. The accident rate at night is three times that of the day shift, and a lot of that is caused by poor lighting. But limelights are as bright as day!"

"But you'd still have to double up on the housing, and that's what most of the buildings around here are, unless you figure to run their beds on two shifts too."

"That would cause more trouble than it would be worth, your grace. Every family needs its own apartment. But the expensive things are not the sleeping rooms. What costs is the bathrooms and the kitchens, and there is no reason why both shifts can't use those same facilities."

"Sounds good, boy. You get it working and I'll want some for Piast Castle."

"I'm not sure that we'd want to put any of them inside a dwelling place, your grace. The gas I'll have to use will contain carbon monoxide, a poison until it's burned. But it should be safe enough in a factory where there's always somebody around to make sure that a lamp doesn't go out."

"Whatever you say, boy. You'll be staying with me at the inn, won't you? I always rent the top floor when I'm here."

"If you wish, your grace, although I have a bed set up in my office."

"No, you come with me. There's plenty of room. I take the whole floor so I don't have to have any strangers around. I have enemies and there's always the chance of a hired assassin. You and your lady join me and Lady Francine for dinner after you've had a chance to clean up."

One didn't argue with the duke. "Thank you, your grace. We are honored."

Cilicia and I got to the dining room before the duke and Lady Francine. I was in a beautifully embroidered outfit that I'd been given last Christmas, and Cilicia wore a lovely woolen gown.

The duke and Lady Francine arrived in a few minutes. She was wearing a sort of miniskirt, mesh stockings and high heels, and that was all. She was topless, as were the waitresses, and she was actually wearing slightly more than they were, but it was unusual and unexpected for a customer to compete with the help.

Introductions were made and the duke noticed me trying not to stare.

"I like it that way," was his only comment.

"A very attractive style, your grace. Count Lambert once told me that when a vassal is on his lord's lands, he should punctiliously conform to his lord's customs. Since you are my lord's lord, it would seem that this obligation is on me doubly. Cilicia, would you please remove your dress to conform with Lady Francine's style?"

Cilicia stared at me for a moment. I suppose that I was being a little rough on her, since she'd grown up among people with a nudity taboo, and while she somehow felt that it was all right to dance naked, she was not used to walking around that way. But having only one of the ladies at the table bare-breasted would have been awkward for all concerned, especially for Lady Francine. Anyway, Cilicia had to learn our customs.

"Yes, master," she said as she stood and unlaced both sides of her dress.

"Master?" the duke said. "After the battle you fought last year to clear Poland of slavery, you own a slave?"

"No, your grace. It's just that she comes from a land east of the Caspian Sea, where slavery is common. Her father 'gave' her to me, mostly to keep her safe. She keeps on calling me 'master,' and I can't seem to break her of it.

"Cilicia, you are not my slave. Please stop calling me 'master.'"

"Yes, master." She pulled the dress over her head, folded it and set it on a stool.

"Dammit! Stop calling me that!"

"You say I am free, yes?"

"Yes!"

"Then I may do as I wish, yes?"

"That's what I've been saying, dammit!"

"Then I wish to call you 'master,' yes?"

Frustrating! How the hell do you answer that one? "You see, your grace? What's a man to do?"

"Nothing, boy. When a woman gets an idea into her head, a man just has to live with it. Or he does if he wants to live with *her*, and this one looks like a keeper."

Cilicia removed her blouse and tucked up her slip so that it was as short as Lady Francine's. Seeing the duke's frankly admiring gaze, she struck a dancer's pose and waited until he'd filled his eyeballs.

Everyone else in the room was trying to act as though it was perfectly normal for a beautiful woman to undress at the table of an inn, for to anger the duke was not wise.

"Boy, you do seem to collect the beauties! You've near outdone me this time, but not quite!" He gave Lady Francine's hand a squeeze.

Lady Francine, who understood why I had done what I had done, quietly said, "Thank you, Sir Conrad. Thank you for everything."

"Yes, it's a style I like," the duke said. "I may not be the rutty buck I once was, but I can still admire good girl flesh. I've half a mind to dress all the serving wenches at Piast Castle this way, just to improve the scenery. In fact, seeing these two ladies side by side, I've got all of a mind to do it!"

"It looks nice on truly beautiful women such as our ladies here, your grace, but it's not a style that would suit every woman."

"So what? If any of my wenches are ugly or too droopy, I'll just replace them with girls who aren't!"

"Then, too, your grace, they keep the inn here warm because of the waitresses' costumes, or rather their lack of them. Your castle is pretty drafty. Wouldn't it be better to wait until spring?"

"Wait? Boy, I just turned seventy. I don't have time to wait! In fact, I'll do it right now. Sir Frederick! Attend me!"

A knight in full armor set down his bowl of soup and came briskly over. "Your grace?"

"Ladies, stand up. Take a good look at these women, Sir Frederick, then go back to Piast Castle and tell the castellan that I want all the serving wenches at the castle looking the same way when I get back."

"Yes, your grace. I shall leave immediately. But . . . these two ladies are the most beautiful that I have ever seen in my life! Where below heaven is the castellan going to find *two hundred* like them?"

"There aren't two hundred like them in the world! I didn't mean that they had to be this pretty, you ninny! I meant that they should dress this way! I want to see their tits!

"And don't leave now. It's dark out there. Go back to your supper and leave first thing in the morning."

I thought that Count Lambert got away with a lot, but the duke could do anything that didn't offend the majority of his major supporters. If the servants didn't like the change in outfits, tough. Their vote wasn't taken.

"Yes, your grace." The knight beat a speedy retreat.

"Sit down, girls," the duke said. "You see what I have to work with, Sir Conrad?"

"He seemed a most courteous and obedient vassal to me, your grace." This was as close as I dared come to criticizing the duke.

"Yeah, but he's stupid. Men like you are rare."

"Your grace, I think that any difference between Sir Frederick and me has more to do with education than with basic ability."

"That makes it rarer, boy. There aren't any schools here like the ones you went to, but I hear that you're working on it."

"Yes, your grace. We now have nine dozen primary schools operating in Count Lambert's county. There is one in almost every town and village."

"Almost? Why not all?"

"Your grace, you must remember that I am a mere knight. I can only try to persuade a baron to do things my way. If he's against me, what can I do?"

"You're talking about Baron Jaraslav, Sir Stefan's father, aren't you."

"Yes, your grace."

"He's a hard-nosed bastard, but he's served me well on the battlefield."

"I'm not speaking against the man, but in this case he's wrong. Education is important! It's not as though those schools will cost him anything. I'm putting them in at my own expense, with the help of the peasants."

"Boy, I don't see why you're pushing this reading and writing business so hard. What good is that going to do a peasant?"

"As things stand, very little, your grace. But things aren't going to stay as they are for much longer. Right now, most people are spending most of their time simply doing grunt work, generating power with human muscles. But you saw that steam-powered sawmill of mine. You said it had the power of two hundred women. Well, the women who used to walk back and forth on the walking-beam sawmill aren't doing that anymore. They're all doing other work now, more skilled work.

"That's just a start. Tomorrow, I'll show you the steam engines we're installing to turn the machines in the shop here, and the others to knead the clay for the mold shop and pump the bellows of the smelter.

"Every time one of those machines goes in, we need fewer dumb peasants and more skilled men. What's more, the skills needed are changing too quickly for men to get by simply by learning the trades of their fathers. They'll have to learn them in schools and out of books. They have to be able to read."

"I'll grant you're right when it comes to factories, boy, but most commoners are farmers. It has to be that way if we're all going to eat!"

"True, your grace, but only so long as we stay with current farming methods. I've already started to change things. There was another bumper harvest at Okoitz this year, but this time they got the entire harvest in, despite

more rainy days than usual. The difference was as simple
a thing as a wheelbarrow. They have a thresher attach-
ment on their windmill, and they were able to store the
entire harvest in their existing storage bins threshed.
Had it still been in the shucks, as is usual, half of it
would be on the ground. In the next few years I'll be
introducing new plows, reapers, and other harvesting
machines. The era of the dumb peasant is over!"

"Interesting. But how far can this go?"

"Quite a ways, your grace. I once spent four years in
a country called America. That nation was the greatest
seller of agricultural products in the world, and its people
are among the best fed. Yet only one man in fifty was a
farmer! Most of the rest worked at trades that are unknown in this country. There aren't even words for
them."

"Yet somehow all this troubles me, Sir Conrad. I keep
asking myself if it's all really worth it."

"They seemed to think so, your grace. Tell me, would
you like to live in a home that was warm in the coldest
weather, that was as cool as you wanted it on the hottest
day? Would you like to have fresh fruits and vegetables
available at any time, no matter what the season? Would
you like to have an instrument called a telephone that
would let you speak to any of your vassals, though they
were a hundred miles away? To any duke or king in
Christendom? Would you like to have doctors so skilled
that they could keep you healthy for many years to
come? Would you like to be able to walk on board a great
silver ship that could fly you to China in an afternoon,
while a pretty waitress brings you drinks as you look
down on the clouds below? And would you like to have
these things not only for yourself, but for the least of
your subjects?

"Tell me, your grace, are these things worth it?"

"Maybe, boy. Maybe. But your priest has told me of
the terrible wars your people have, of weapons so
mighty that one man, pushing a button, could destroy
whole cities. Of hatreds, and of famines when there was

no need for famines. What do you say to that?"

"I say that I'm an engineer, your grace. I can build machines that can heat your home, harvest your crops, and flush your shit. It's *not fair* to expect me to make you love your fellow man as well. *That's not my job!*"

Chapter Thirteen

^^^^^^^^^^^^^^^^^^^^^^^^^

I SPENT the morning giving the duke and his party a tour of the facilities at Copper City. He seemed most impressed with the eight steam engines we were installing, two of which were already operational. They were all single expansion units, and not very efficient thermally, but I had a use for the waste heat. All the buildings had steam radiators in every room, which condensed the steam back to water to be pumped into the tubular boilers again. Cogeneration. Come spring, we'd be installing a leather tannery to use that excess heat in the summertime.

That evening, we again dined with the duke, and Cilicia told the story of how her native city was destroyed by the Mongols. Everyone in the inn's dining room was listening. She told the same story that her father had told to me, but the way she told it got everyone in the room in the gut. I don't think that there was a dry eye in the place, and even the crusty old duke was in tears.

He promised me his continued support, as did every man in the room. Cilicia became my best propaganda device to generate support for the upcoming war, and she was to tell that story a hundred times over the next few years.

I spent three more days at Copper City after the duke left, mostly handling technical problems since the Krakowski Brothers were good managers and didn't need much help in that direction.

We made the run to Eagle Nest in one day, leaving before dawn and arriving after dusk. The instructors were in uniform, but only about half of the boys' outfits were completed so they were all still in civilian clothing.

It was getting beyond kite-flying weather and the hangar was big enough to fly model airplanes in. When we were building the installation we had so much manpower and timber available that I figured that we might as well build it big enough in the first place. The hangar was six dozen yards wide and twelve dozen long, big enough to accommodate any aircraft I could imagine building out of wood and canvas. It was rather like the church we had built at Three Walls, only two of them set side by side, though not as tall and with a dirt floor. Two huge counterweighted doors faced the eventual runway.

But now we used it for model airplanes.

I spent three days, including Sunday afternoon, talking about aircraft, about lift and drag and the other forces on a plane. The type I got them going on was a high-winged glider, halfway between a sailplane and a piper cub. Sort of an observation plane without an engine.

The steam saw was put to work cutting very thin strips of wood, and I headed for Okoitz.

Count Lambert was enthusiastic about my idea for limelights in his cloth factory, mostly because it would permit his massive harem to stay there all winter. He was less enthusiastic about putting in a second shift. As it was, the girls not currently being used slept on cots in the factory itself. Putting in a second shift involved building housing for all of them, and if I was going to do that, I insisted that we put in plumbing and kitchens of the sort we had at Three Walls.

What finally sold him was the thought that he could sort the workers according to sexual desirability and keep the best ones on the day shift, thus improving the quality of his already beautiful ladies.

If that's what it took to get better sanitation at Okoitz, then so be it. Our infant mortality rate at Three Walls was *one-eighth* of what it was at Okoitz. If saving thirty-five children a year meant hurting the feelings of a hundred girls, then let their feelings be hurt!

And yes, I would accept cloth instead of cash for all

the plumbing fixtures, and yes, I would design and supervise the construction of the new buildings as part of my feudal duty to him.

That settled, Count Lambert wanted to talk about the Great Hunt. Sir Miesko had done a competent job organizing the thing. Everything was ready. The local hunt masters all knew their duties, invitations to all the knights in the duchy had been sent, and the enclosures for the killing grounds had been sent and enclosures for the killing grounds had been built. The only problem was Baron Jaraslav and his son, Sir Stefan. They were adamantly refusing to have anything to do with anything that I was involved with. I was hoping that Count Lambert would talk to them.

"What!" Count Lambert said. "They refuse? Do they know that I want this thing done?"

"They do, my lord. Sir Miesko has been very adamant on that point, and they still won't have anything to do with it. If we bypass them, we've left behind a breeding ground for wolves, bears, and wild boar. They know it but don't care."

"Well, *I'll* settle with Baron Jaraslav! I've had enough out of those two! I'll visit them within the week with fifty knights at my back, and they'll obey their liege lord or pay for it!"

"Yes, my lord. Was there anything else you wanted of me?"

"Dog's blood! There is! You and Sir Vladimir will attend me here in one week. Sir Miesko is on your way, so tell him and any others you meet to come here as well."

"Yes, my lord. You are expecting battle?"

"I'm expecting my vassals to obey me. All of them!"

"Yes, my lord." When he was in this mood, it wasn't smart to argue.

Count Lambert had five knights in attendance, and he gave four of them exacting verbal instructions to ride out in the morning, contact certain specific barons and knights, and have them report to Okoitz. Verbal, because Count Lambert still couldn't read or write.

It was an hour before he calmed down. Then he

started hinting strongly that he'd rather like to try out the
wench I'd brought along.

I wasn't happy about lending out Cilicia, but Count
Lambert's current mood still wasn't anything that I
wanted to trifle with. Anyway, he had always been so
generous with me in this regard that it would have been
niggardly of me to refuse him.

"Of course, my lord. But remember that she is a foreigner, and the customs of her people are different from
ours. I'd best talk to her first."

"Do so." And I was dismissed.

Cilicia was not at all pleased at being lent out "like
horse for rent," as she put it. I said that this was a custom of Okoitz, and one must conform to local customs,
but she wasn't convinced. I finally had to say that she
could obey me or she could go back to her father. She
obeyed, and I picked up one of Count Lambert's ladies
for the night.

Neither Cilicia nor Count Lambert ever mentioned
what went on that night, but he never asked for her services again.

Sir Miesko was appalled that Count Lambert was considering war against Baron Jaraslav. He sent a letter,
carried by his oldest son, to the baron urging him to
make immediate apology to their liege and so forestall
any violence, but he had scant hope that the irascible
baron would do so. "I wish I could understand their
hatred for you, Sir Conrad, but it's there. Now it seems
that blood must flow because of it. A sad thing, and a
waste. Nonetheless, our lord calls and we must go. Wear
your brightest surcoat to this, Sir Conrad. We'll want to
make the best and most intimidating show possible.
There's scant hope, but we may yet forestall a senseless
war."

I went back to Three Walls in a glum mood.

Sir Vladimir was also amazed at being called up.
"Count Lambert is going to fight a battle over so trifling
a matter as a hunt?"

"No, Sir Vladimir. He's going to threaten battle because one of his vassals has repeatedly disobeyed him.

Remember that the baron failed to come when Count
Lambert called him to beat the bounds between his lands
and mine."

"I know, and since then he has been claiming that you
stole lands belonging to him, and he just might be right.
Count Lambert was in a foul mood that day, and it would
have been like him to move the boundary in revenge for
the baron's slight. And of course, Sir Stefan has been
making an ass of himself for years, even before you arrived. But none of that is reason enough for war between
knights of the same lord!"

"I agree," I said, "but we have been called and we will
go."

I spent the week designing the limelight system.

The limelights in the old theaters used a hydrogen
flame under a ball of lime, calcium oxide. The hydrogen
was generated by pouring acid on a metal, okay for a
theater but way too expensive for a factory. A far
cheaper way of making hydrogen was the water/gas
method that was used for generating cooking gas before
natural gas, methane, became commercially available.

This involves getting a deep bed of coal burning in a
closed furnace. Once it's all glowing, the air supply is
shut off and water is forced under the coal. The chimney
is then closed off and the fumes are directed to a holding
tank for eventual distribution. The chemical reaction involves the oxygen in the water combining with the glowing carbon, and the hydrogen leaving as a gas.

The only problem was that for each molecule of hydrogen generated, you also make a molecule of carbon
monoxide, which can kill you dead. The carbon monoxide is also a fuel, and is safe enough once it's burned to
carbon dioxide, but a leaky pipe or a flame that's gone
out is dangerous. The safety problem didn't bother the
Victorians who used the system. They simply weren't
concerned. If someone was dumb enough to kill himself,
that was his problem.

I, however, am not a Victorian. The system I put together was as safe as I could make it. First off, I kept it
out of private areas, where kids could get at it. It was

restricted to workplaces, large public rooms, and out-door lighting. Each installation had a full-time safety inspector, who was also responsible for lighting the lights. Ventilation was carefully checked at each location. And each lamp had a valve that anyone could turn off, but required a key to turn on. This last involved designing a lock, which turned out to be one of our most profitable products.

Oh, I knew that somebody would still find a way to kill himself with it, but I tried.

On the appointed day, Sir Vladimir and I rode out in full armor, in our brightest surcoats and with pennons flying. The bandsmen had wanted to play for us as we left, but that seemed to me to be in poor taste. I felt rotten that things should come to this head. We needed to be preparing to be fighting Mongols, not fellow Christians, even if they were a couple of bastards.

We met Sir Miesko at the proper time, and went on to Okoitz.

"Any response from Baron Jaraslav?" I asked.

"None to my letter," Sir Miesko said. "But he has called his own knights to arms, which is response enough. He has thirty-five, you know, and is Count Lambert's greatest vassal. If vassal he be and not oath-breaker."

"Damn."

More than a hundred knights came to Count Lambert's call, even those not required to do so. We filled the hall, and the squires had to make do in the kitchen. Supper was a major feast, but a somber one. Everyone was in full armor, as tradition required on the night before battle, I suppose so that the lord could check his men's equipment. Not that Count Lambert checked anything. A knight was always supposed to be ready, and if he wasn't, it was his own neck that suffered.

Sir Miesko stood and spoke to Count Lambert. "My liege, you know that I have been your willing vassal since first I was knighted. Always have I obeyed you, and always will I continue to do so. But my duty to you is not only to fight at your side. I am also obligated to give you my best counsel.

"It is true that Baron Jaraslav has repeatedly disobeyed you. But it is also true that he is a very old man and the minds of the aged sometimes grow feeble. I counsel you, I beg you to go slowly in this matter. You will not gain in glory or in honor if you shed Christian blood, Polish blood, because of the aberrant wanderings of a senile mind."

Sir Miesko sat down and Count Lambert said, "It is your duty to speak and my duty to listen, but the reverse is also true. I say that without obedience to our superiors, everything that we are falls apart! If I do not obey the duke, and my vassals do not obey me, then why should the peasants obey us? If we let one major crack form in the structure, the whole thing could shatter! Don't you see that we must be together? Because if we're not, it won't be the Tartars who destroy us, we'll do it ourselves! Then the damn Mazovians or some other petty power will come in and pick up the shredded pieces."

I stood. "My lord, Sir Miesko has spoken my mind as well as his own, though he has been more eloquent than I could be. I have heard that some of the problem is caused by Baron Jaraslav's belief that I was deeded lands that are properly his. Rather than see Pole fight Pole, I would willingly give up whatever lands the baron claims.

"Just now tempers have grown too hot. You mentioned the duke. He knows Baron Jaraslav well. Why not ask him to talk to the baron. Surely no man is more persuasive than Duke Henryk."

"Sir Conrad, your lands are your own, and I'll not have you make any sacrifice because of another's malice. As to the duke, it would be proper to go to him if I had a problem with one of my own station. To bring him a problem with one of my vassals would be to admit my own incompetence. If I did so, he might be inclined to remove me, and properly. I'll handle the matter on my own."

"Then may I echo Sir Miesko and beg you to go slowly?" I said.

"You may beg all you damn well please, Sir Conrad, just so you *obey* when the lances drop to charge! Do the rest of you have counsel for me as well?"

Knight after knight attested to his willingness to obey any lawful order, but begged Count Lambert to refrain from pushing matters too quickly to a head.

Count Lambert's mood got darker and quieter until he abruptly got up and left his hall, his meal unfinished.

We were all silent for a bit.

Baron Jan, Sir Vladimir's father, said, "We can but do our duty and pray that we need not shed the blood of our brothers." Then he led us all in deeply felt prayer.

Count Lambert's new priest held an evening mass. We all went and took Communion since tomorrow some of us could be dead.

It was crowded at Okoitz, and I shared a room with Sir Miesko, Sir Vladimir, and one of his brothers. The girls from the cloth factory were probably as willing as ever, but none of us were in the mood. Judging from the sounds, few of the other knights were either. I don't recall hearing a single feminine squeal all night, a rare thing at Okoitz even when it's half empty.

More than half the knights had squires, almost inevitably a younger relative, since the Polish nobility was very family-oriented. Well over a gross of fighting men lined up outside of Okoitz in the gray dawn, as well as two heralds that Count Lambert must have borrowed from someone. The kitchen help hurriedly handed out packages of field rations, a bag containing a loaf of bread, some cheese, and dried meat. There was little chance of the baron inviting us in for a meal.

I thought that Count Lambert would make a speech to encourage his men, but he didn't. He just rode to the head of the column and shouted, "Advance!"

At a walk, we went to Baron Jaraslav's manor.

The roads were mere trails and we had to go in single file, so there was little chance for light conversation, not that there was much inclination toward it.

"Shouldn't we have some point men and flankers out?" I called to Sir Miesko, riding behind me.

"To what purpose, Sir Conrad? No bandit would attack a party as large as ours, and Baron Jaraslav might disobey his liege, but he is not so wholly dishonorable as to attack without warning. Flankers would only slow us down."

Sir Miesko and Count Lambert were probably right, but my own military training made me feel uncomfortable about it.

The baron's castle was a large and venerable building made mostly of brick, with some of the cornices made of limestone. It had a moat and a drawbridge and was not the sort of place that men without siege equipment could easily take.

Count Lambert made no attempt to surround the thing. He simply lined us up in front out of crossbow range and sent the heralds forward. Sir Vladimir was at my left, as a vassal should be, and Sir Miesko was at my right. The heralds rode up to the gate, played a fanfare on their long trumpets, and announced that Count Lambert wished to speak to his vassal, Baron Jaraslav.

They had to have been waiting for us, for within a few minutes, the drawbridge was lowered and thirty-five armed and armored men rode out. Perhaps another twenty men were on the walls with crossbows, the squires, probably, since a full belted knight wouldn't use one. It made me wish that I'd brought Tadaos along, but I hadn't been asked to and I hadn't wanted to risk any more people than necessary.

The knights lined up facing us, a few hundred yards away. We outnumbered them four to one, but they looked prepared to let us know that we'd been in a fight.

One of the heralds stayed with the baron and the other rode back to Count Lambert. With six of his barons, the count rode to the center of the field, to be met by Baron Jaraslav, Sir Stefan, and five other knights.

I relaxed a bit. At least they were going to talk instead of immediately slugging it out.

I couldn't hear what Count Lambert said, but Baron

Jaraslav was shouting at the top of his lungs, so what came through was half a conversation, or less, since I couldn't hear Sir Stefan either.

"My ancestors were here for hundreds of years before anybody ever heard of a Piast!"

Count Lambert said something I couldn't hear.

"I don't owe fealty to a man whose wits are not his own! Your mind has been addled by that warlock you took in two years ago! Yours and the duke's, too!"

Baron Jaraslav's face got redder as his blood pressure went up. I could feel my own face flushing as well.

"It's bad enough, your swiving every wench in the county, turning them into a herd of whores! Now you want to ruin the hunting like you've ruined the women!

"I was a baron when you were still sucking your mother's tits!"

The baron's face and hands were as dark red as dried blood. I'd never seen such a thing before, but I'd heard about it. Not good in an old man.

"That warlock wants to turn the whole duchy into a stinking, dirty factory! I won't stand for it! Better to die fighting than to fall sickened by his poisons!"

The baron became increasingly incoherent. His hands started shaking, he began gasping and suddenly he toppled from his horse.

I didn't know if this was a heart attack or a stroke, but it looked to me that he was in bad need of CPR.

"I'd better go see what I can do for him," I said as I signaled Anna forward.

"Stay back here you fool!" Sir Miesko shouted, but I ignored him.

Besides basic humanitarian considerations, my thought was that if I could do Baron Jaraslav a real service, like saving his life, maybe he and Sir Stefan might not hate me as much. Okay, so it was a dumb idea.

We sprinted to where the baron had fallen. I pulled my gauntlets off as I leaped to the ground and told Anna to go back to the line. I didn't want her to interpret some movement by the baron as an attack on me.

I tilted the baron's head back, cleared the tongue and

checked his breathing. There wasn't any! I started giving mouth-to-mouth resuscitation as I checked frantically for a pulse. A lot of shouting was going on but I ignored it. I couldn't find a pulse but that didn't mean much, since I couldn't get at most of him what with his armor and all. I started pumping his heart, to be on the safe side, a thing that would have been impossible in my plate armor, but was easy enough with the baron's gold-washed chain mail.

Then I took a blow to the side of the head that might have killed me if it hadn't been for my new helmet. It didn't much hurt me, but the force of it, transmitted through my collar ring to my chest and back plates, was enough to send me sprawling.

"Stay away from my father, you filthy witch!" Sir Stefan shouted, sword in hand.

"You Stupid John!" I swore at him. "He's having a heart attack! Without CPR he's going to die!"

I started to move back to the baron. Sir Stefan swung again, only to have his blade parried by Count Lambert's.

"STOP! Both of you!" Count Lambert shouted. "Dog's blood! You have both dishonored yourselves! Sir Conrad, I told you to stay in the line! Get back there, damn you! Sir Stefan, you have drawn steel during a peace parley, a hanging offense anywhere!"

"My lord," I said, "his heart and breathing have stopped! If I don't—"

"If his heart's stopped, then he's dead! Get back to the line or I'll put this sword in your face!"

I could see that Count Lambert meant it, and the baron was probably really dead by this time anyway. I retrieved my gauntlets.

"Yes, my lord."

As I walked back to the line, Count Lambert gave Sir Stefan a chewing out the likes of which I hadn't heard since boot camp.

Maybe I should have just left things alone, but then Sir Stefan would probably have blamed his father's death on my "witchcraft" in any event. It was worth a try, I

suppose. I certainly shouldn't have called him a Stupid
John. The swear words in one language often don't
translate well into another, but that particular phrase is a
deadly insult and fighting words in Polish.

"You're a damn fool," Sir Miesko said as I got back
and mounted Anna. "If ever a man's foul words stuck in
his throat and killed him, it was Baron Jaraslav's. It
looked like a sure Act of God! But when you ran out
there, you took everybody's mind off of what had just
happened. This sorry mess could have ended right there,
but now it's still bobbing afloat. It could still end with
fifty good men dead!"

"Yeah, I guess I screwed it up," I said.

But the parley went on for another half hour, and we
couldn't hear a thing of what was said. Then something
happened. Count Lambert and Sir Stefan turned and
faced the sun, raised their right arms to it and Sir Stefan
swore fealty to Count Lambert.

Count Lambert and his barons came back to us and
he addressed those of us in the line.

"This matter is ended! Baron Jaraslav is dead! Baron
Stefan has sworn fealty to me and will obey me as all of
you have done this day! I thank you all for coming as
was your duty, but now you may disperse and go home! I
will see many of you in a week at the Great Hunt. For
the rest of you, good hunting!"

And so we left, and soon there was no one left on the
field but the dead baron and Baron Stefan, standing over
his father's body.

It all worked out as best as could be expected. Having
Stefan instead of his father for a neighbor wasn't much
of an improvement, but Count Lambert could hardly
have interfered with the right of inheritance. His own
lofty position was based on that very same right.

Chapter Fourteen

THE KNIGHTS and squires broke up into groups as we headed home in our various directions. By late afternoon there was only myself, Sir Vladimir, and Sir Miesko. As we passed Sir Miesko's manor, Lady Richeza invited us in, but there was still time to get to Three Walls before dusk. When we got to the gates, the band was up on the balcony to welcome us home. I wouldn't have given permission for this waste of man-hours, since they must have been waiting up there for half a day, but I had to admit that it felt good. They were playing the theme from *Raiders of the Lost Ark*.

I announced at supper what had happened, that Baron Stefan was our new neighbor, and that the Great Hunt was on as scheduled.

Sir Miesko had set me up as the "Local Hunt Master," using the valley at Three Walls for our killing ground, just as we had last year. Only this year, it would cover not only my lands, but Sir Miesko's as well as those of Baron Stefan and two other knights.

As Master of the Hunt, I got the wolf skins and any aurochs captured on all of Count Lambert's lands. As Local Hunt Master, I got all the deer skins taken locally. As a landowner, I got a share, about one-fifth, of one-half of the meat taken. My workers would get about one-third of the one-quarter of the meat reserved for the beaters. And since I personally would be participating in the kill, I got a share of the one-quarter of the kill that was divided among the nobility present.

Complicated, but profitable, especially since the fashion of wearing wolf skin cloaks was taking hold. I had already sold the six hundred wolf skins we had taken last year at *very* nice prices, and I was looking forward to taking twenty times that number this year.

But Sir Miesko was in fact handling all of the detail work of a Local Hunt Master for me, except for the feasts, and that was Krystyana's problem.

My main worry was getting the Moslems' housing completed so we could get them out of Three Walls before more savory company started arriving. We almost made it, and I told them that they had to get out anyway. They could live in the nearly finished buildings until the hunt was over, and no, they couldn't act as beaters alongside Christians, although they were responsible for sweeping all the wild game out of their valley, and taking care of my herd of sheep, now three thousand strong, during the hunt.

The morning before the hunt, most of the workers walked out to the manors of the knights on the periphery of the hunting district, leaving behind only a skeleton crew to keep the blast furnace fed and a few pregnant women to take care of the small children. To minimize friction, none of my people were sent to Baron Stefan's lands. My own station was at Sir Miesko's.

The plan was to have a line of peasants and workers backed up by a line of horsemen, mostly knights and squires, to take care of any emergencies, such as an irate bear.

Since Piotr Kulczynski was spending half of his life on horseback, I assumed that he would be one of the riders. Sir Miesko objected. "All the other horsemen will be of the nobility, their ladies or at least squires. Some might object at having a commoner in their number."

"But the east line is already low on horsemen," I said. "Pulling Piotr makes it worse."

"Better a thin line than offended neighbors," Sir Miesko said. "If you really want him on horseback, why not make him your squire? It's a simple formality."

I didn't see any reason why not. I was entitled to a squire or two, and Piotr was the sort who would get a kick out of that sort of thing. Being my squire needn't change his pay or duties.

I asked Piotr about it and he was absolutely delighted. No American kid getting his first car on his eighteenth birthday was ever happier.

The ceremony was a simple swearing in and we did it within the hour. Sir Miesko made Piotr the guest of honor at supper that night. Any reason for a celebration was always welcome.

The Banki brothers, three knights who were the special friends of three of my ladies, arrived at dusk. Had we known that they were coming, Piotr probably wouldn't have gotten his promotion, but there was no point in telling him that.

Natasha was managing a field kitchen at a manor where Sir Vladimir and Annastashia were stationed.

Thus, there were exactly as many men as women at Piotr's feast. Natalia, Yawalda, and Janina naturally paired off with Sir Gregor, Sir Wiktor, and Sir Wojciech Banki, I had Cilicia, and this naturally forced Krystyana on Piotr. He of course made no objection to this, but she took it with poor grace.

Having a partner at a formal feast required a fair amount of interaction. Among other things, you shared the same spoon, cup, and bowl. Krystyana stayed polite, but was formal and cold. And at the dance, later, she refused to do a waltz with him, new squire or no new squire.

Why Piotr was so determined to have this one lady was beyond me. There had to be a masochistic streak in the little fellow.

In the morning, the beaters were fed while it was still dark and were lined up in the dawn around the periphery of the hunting district, paralleling the group from the district to the east and meeting up with the beaters to the north. When all was ready, the signal to advance was given and the day's walk began. People swung sticks at the brush and made as much noise as possible. Wild animals are well fed in the late fall, and aren't particularly aggressive, so there were no real problems throughout the day.

By evening, the beaters were shoulder to shoulder and the valley at Three Walls was packed with animals. I had to station guards with torches around the blast furnace workers to keep the animals from bothering them. I swore that next year, I would build a killing ground outside the valley, perhaps surrounding the plain at the valley mouth with Japanese roses.

There were over five thousand people at Three Walls that night, and for the four days thereafter. Somehow, we got them all fed and bedded down, with wall-to-wall people everywhere, even in the church.

Baron Stefan, in his gold-washed armor and gold-trimmed helmet and sword, was at least trying to stay polite, but he and his knights were somewhat standoffish. He had brought his own servants and had them serve him when everybody else ate cafeteria-style, but I made no objection. It was enough that he was no longer swearing at me on every possible occasion. I gave them my living room to bunk down in and that seemed to satisfy them.

In the morning the slaughter began and it went on for four days. We were better prepared to process the meat this year than last. More smokehouses had been built and we had vast quantities of barrels and salt, enough to sell to anyone who wanted them, which was almost everybody. A dozen sausage machines worked around the clock, and everyone ate liver and kidneys, the most desirable parts of the animal by medieval standards, until they couldn't hold any more.

Piotr and Sir Miesko kept a careful accounting of everything and I heard no objections to the final sharing out.

The one sour point happened when one of the duke's men, Sir Frederick, came over and told me that the duke had liked the wolf skin cloak I'd given him so much that he had decreed that none but a true belted knight might wear one.

Wonderful. That cut my potential market for wolf

skins by a factor of a hundred. My profits were going right down the toilet, but there was nothing I could do about it. One did not argue with the duke.

I probably had twelve thousand wolf skins coming in and nothing to do with them. Maybe I could dye them another color and pass them off as from some other animal.

Much later, it turned out that I needn't have worried. Saying that none but a nobleman might wear a wolf skin cloak was almost the same as saying that a nobleman *must* wear one, at least to the fashion-conscious Polish nobility. The demand for wolf skins went way up and the price of wolf skins tripled by midwinter! And who do you think had the biggest stock of wolf skins in the world? My God, how the money rolled in!

One evening, the Banki brothers came to my office, which adjoined my bedroom.

"We have come to formally request the hands of three of your wards, Natalia, Yawalda, and Janina, in honorable matrimony," Sir Gregor said.

This took me completely by surprise. I'd known for a year that the three couples had a thing going, but matrimony just hadn't occurred to me. "Well. This needs some talking," I said. "Sit down and have some mead. Do the girls know that you are here?"

"It was them that put us up to it," Sir Wiktor said.

"That's usually the way of it," I said. "First off, I want to say that I like you three. I think that you would make fine husbands, but, well, I'm not their father. I suppose that I can speak for Janina, since her parents are dead, but Natalia's father is alive and well at Okoitz, as are both of Yawalda's parents. It is from them that you must ask the hands of those girls, not me."

"True," Sir Gregor said. "Yet our loves would do nothing without your permission, and it is not likely that a peasant would object to his daughter marrying a true belted knight."

"I suppose so," I said. "There is the fact that these three girls all have responsible positions here, and they all earn very good money. I'm really not thrilled about losing them. Then too, I don't know anything about your own financial positions. Can you afford to support them properly?"

"You touch on a delicate point," Sir Gregor said. "Our parents have both been dead for years, and while their lands were ample to support one knight, they don't do the best job at supporting four. You see, there is a fourth brother that you haven't met. Stanislaw is probably the best farmer in Poland—I swear that he could grow wheat on a stone!—but he's very much of a stay-at-home. "We aren't by any means wealthy, but if the dowries were adequate, we could easily support our ladies."

That took me back a bit. "So you think that I should not only give you three lovely ladies, three of my best managers, but that I should also *pay* you to take them from me? Women who aren't even my own daughters? Isn't that a bit much?"

"Well, a bride usually comes with a dowry," Sir Wojciech said, before Sir Gregor hushed him up.

"We have talked these very things over with our ladies, Sir Conrad, and the truth is that while they are eager for marriage with us, they do not want to leave their positions at Three Walls. Your adopted daughter, Annastashia, has stayed here after her marriage with Sir Vladimir. He gets no pay other than his maintenance and the dowry you gave him. Why can't we do the same? Surely the presence of three good fighting men would be useful to you, what with all the caravans you have going in and out of here. Don't they need guards?"

"First off, I can hardly adopt the girls in the same way that I adopted Annastashia. Quite frankly, I've slept often with all three of them, and it would feel like incest if they became my daughters! And the 'dowry' that I gave Sir Vladimir was in fact half the booty that we took together in that fight with the Crossmen last year. The duke awarded it all to me, and making part of it a dowry was just a way of giving Sir Vladimir his share without insulting the duke. Count Lambert never pays more than five hundred pence to marry off one of his ladies-in-waiting, and then only when they're pregnant, generally by him."

"But these girls are hardly peasants anymore, and we would not require anything like the amount that you gave to our cousin Sir Vladimir. Say, three thousand pence each. In return, we will swear fealty to you and serve you daily for four years, asking only our maintenance."

I did some quick mental calculating. Eight pence a day and maintenance was fairly standard pay for a knight and his horse. That came to just less than three thousand pence a year. The brothers were offering me quite a deal, about seventy-five percent off. They must have wanted my ladies pretty bad. Anyway, I hadn't slept with any of them since I'd met Cilicia, and it was a shame to let them go to waste.

"Okay, I think we have a deal, providing that the girls continue on as my managers, and providing that you get their parents' permission, post proper banns at the church, and so on. If you're to swear to me, well, you're sworn through Count Lambert's brother, Count Herman, aren't you? I think we need the permission of both counts before I can swear you in. All that will probably take three or four months, so I suppose we'll have the wedding around Easter."

The brothers were delighted and went off to tell their prospective brides, who were waiting out in the hallway, probably with their ears pressed to the door, if I knew that crew, and I did.

When the slaughter was over, and the female deer, elk and bison were driven out of the valley, along with the young and a sixth of the males, and all the catch was carefully divided according to schedule, we held a last feast and a dance. The morning after, our guests departed happy and heavily laden.

The icehouse and storerooms and smokehouses at Three Walls were filled, we had a gross of deer to provide fresh meat during the winter, and there were huge piles of salted down deer and wolf skins. It was time we set up a tannery.

I couldn't properly announce the engagements to all

the hunters present, since the parents had not yet given their permission, but the day after the crowds left, we threw a party in celebration anyway, just a small one for my household.

Anna had stayed in the barn during the time that Baron Stefan was visiting us, since I didn't want to give him anything to start ranting about. But with him gone, she just naturally came up to join the party. The Banki brothers had heard a lot of stories about Anna, of course, but I don't think that they really believed any of them until she came up to the living room and sat down. I introduced them and explained about her speech difficulty, and they were most surprised to find themselves in a conversation with a being who looked like a horse!

I was a little surprised when Piotr came uninvited to the party, which was for my household only, but Sir Vladimir explained that as my squire, Piotr was most certainly a member of the household. I guess I just hadn't thought it out properly. But there was nothing for it but to invite him out of the bachelors' quarters and give him one of the spare rooms in my apartment.

Piotr was delighted with this move upward, but Krystyana was scowling about it. In fact she had been doing a great deal of scowling lately, and I began to think that having a talk with her was in order. It hurts to be hated.

I thought about her as the evening went on, and some of her troubles were obvious. Since I'd met Cilicia, I hadn't had very many other women. Krystyana had always been willing to share me with the others, but now she was having to give me up all together. Then too, she had left Okoitz in the company of four other girls almost two years ago. Now one was married to Sir Vladimir and the other three were engaged, or nearly so, to the Banki brothers. She had always been the leader of that group, and now she was the one left behind. Only Natasha remained unattached besides her, and Natasha was a relative newcomer.

I was looking at Krystyana when I was thinking this out, and I noticed a slight bulge in her tummy. I wasn't sure, but I thought I might have hit on Krystyana's *big* problem.

As soon as I could, I called Natasha aside and asked her about it.

"Of course, my lord. You didn't know? Krystyana is heavy with your child."

"*My* child? You're sure of that?"

"She has touched no other man but you since first leaving Okoitz, my lord. Whose else can it be?"

Now that's as big a fist in the stomach as a man can get! I dismissed Natasha and sat back to ponder it all. I was going to be a father! Cute, bouncing little Krystyana was going to be a mother! It was only when I asked myself if the kid's father and mother were going to be married that I suddenly got cold chills.

In the first place, I'm just not the marrying kind. Maybe it was because my parents' marriage hadn't been all that happy, or maybe it was something in my genes, but that's just the way I am.

In the second place, Krystyana and I didn't have anything in common but a certain sexual attraction, the sort of thing any normal man feels for a healthy fourteen year old, and even that was already fading, at least my half of it.

And in the third place, the whole idea of marriage *scares me shitless*!

I procrastinated for a few days, hoping that some solution would come to me. The only obvious one, a marriage between Piotr and Krystyana, was shot down because of her obvious hatred for the boy. *He* was willing to take her in any shape or condition.

I finally decided that my procrastination was sheer cowardice, and called Krystyana into my office. I simply laid it on the line to her. I said that I liked her like a sister, but I wasn't going to marry her. If she wanted to stay single, that was okay by me. I would always see to it that she and her child were well taken care of and I hoped that whatever happened, she would want to stay on as the kitchen manager, since she was doing such a good job there. But I strongly recommended that she marry, if not Piotr, who loved her, then someone else. I would be happy to provide a suitable dowry.

She didn't answer. She just left, crying.

Some days you just can't win.

Chapter Fifteen

THE DUKE was impressed by the stories he heard about Count Lambert's Great Hunt, and decided that we should do it on all of the lands subject to him, about half the land that would one day make up modern Poland. I was appointed his Master of the Hunt, and delegated all the work to Sir Miesko. He was delighted to do it, since the hunt on Lambert's lands alone had made him a wealthy man. He spent almost six months on the road getting the thing organized, and I didn't much get involved. That suited me just fine, since I wanted to work on the limelights.

Getting the limelights going was another job of bucket chemistry. I had some iron grids cast that would fit in the bottom of one of our beehive coke ovens, to raise the coal off the bottom so we could run water underneath. While that was being done, work was started on the gas tower, a circular water tank in which floated a vast close-fitting, copper-lined, straight-sided barrel. Not that a straight-sided barrel was unusual. They were the only kind in use until I introduced the potbellied variety and proved that they leaked less.

Pipes went under the tank and up to just above the waterline. When gas was produced, the barrel rose, to settle again as the gas was consumed.

How big a gas tower did we need? How much gas was needed to keep a limelight going? Was one coke oven enough? Too much? I hadn't the slightest idea. I just made things big and hoped for the best.

Then, too, I'd never even seen a limelight, I'd only

heard about them. As I understood it, it was a hydrogen flame under a lump of lime. I didn't know what sort of a burner was used, so I used a bunsen burner.

Six weeks and eighteen thousand man-hours later, seventy-five tons of coal was loaded into the converted beehive coke oven and lit on fire. It was necessary to have the grid completely covered with coal so that the steam would be forced through the coals rather than around them.

The system worked to the extent of generating a flammable gas, and filling the gas tower, but the faint blue flame produced was hot enough to heat the lime only to a dull red. Not a very efficient light, which was the purpose of the exercise.

I could think of only two ways to get a hotter flame. One was to use pure oxygen instead of air, since the nitrogen in the air cools a fire considerably. The trouble with that was that I didn't have a good source of oxygen, and we weren't quite up to building an air liquefaction plant.

Oh, I could have heated mercury, a remarkably cheap substance in the Middle Ages. It was an industrial waste product from the manufacture of sulfur. At moderate temperatures, mercury absorbs oxygen and at higher temperatures, gives it off. But having that much mercury vapor around was scary. At least with carbon monoxide you know when you're being poisoned. I'd save the mercury scheme for a last resort, if then.

The other way was to preheat the air and gas before they were burned. I spent a few frustrating weeks getting a burner of this sort going. The trick turned out to be to mix clay with slaked lime and mold the heat exchangers into the lamp itself, then run it through the brick kiln to harden it. A few months later it was discovered that a fire clay lamp painted with slaked lime was stronger and brighter. One problem with this scheme was that it required pressurized air, and thus a second set of pipes running to each lamp. But at least it didn't need a second fancy locked valve at each installation.

But by the time the new lamps were ready, the

Leo Frankowski

weather had closed in and the water under the gas tower froze. In normal operation, this wouldn't happen because the gases themselves would be hot enough to keep the water liquid in the worst weather, but we had shut the system down while I worked on the lamp. We drained the water, covered the tower with straw and circulated hot coke oven gas through it until the crust of ice was melted. Then we started over.

This time the lamp got to a fairly bright orange after an hour or so, and I declared that to be good enough.

Other things were going on while I was playing with lights. Zoltan's people started doing us some good. Their pottery man came up with five colors of glazes made from local materials, and we went into production making tableware, at first for ourselves, but then for sale as well.

Their papermaker was in limited production turning our old linens into very nice rag paper.

And their sword-maker was screaming at the top of his lungs at Ilya, who was naturally screaming back at him, both men being of the opinion that sufficient volume could make up for their lack of a mutual vocabulary. The workers had a betting pool going on which one would kill the other first, and at what time of the day this happy event would take place.

The two smiths went on screaming for over a month with nothing accomplished, so I had to step in and demand that the sword-maker demonstrate to us his methods. They surprised me, being nothing like the Japanese method I'd told Ilya about two years before.

He collected up a pile of wrought iron and beat and cut it into small pieces, about the size of a ten zloty piece, or an American quarter. He put a measured amount of this iron into each of a dozen round bottom clay flasks and packed them full with raw wool. Then he sealed the flasks and took them up into the hills where it was quiet. He built a fire around the flasks and after a day of burning he started gently shaking the flasks and listening carefully. When the metal inside "sounded wet," he let the fire go out. On breaking open the flasks, there was a fused blob of steel inside he called "wootz." This he worked at relatively low temperatures—never red hot—until it was shaped like a sword or knife. Then he hardened and tempered it in the usual manner. The result was watered steel that looked just like the steel in my sword, and kept a fine edge.

It wasn't quite as good as my sword, however. I pared the edge off one of his knives with my blade, which had the swordsmith staring goggle-eyed. None the less, it was better than anything Ilya had done using the method I'd told him about, so we went into production using the *wootz* method.

The glassmaker started to make glass out of sand, lime, and wood ashes. After having him make a very fancy drinking glass as a Christmas present for Count Lambert, I had him make a chimney for the gas lamp, to conduct the fumes away. The chimney made a great improvement in light output, and it took me a while to figure out that the glass was transparent to visible light, but opaque to infrared, which was reflected back to the lime, making it hotter.

All of which shows that it isn't necessary to know what you're doing in order to be able to accomplish something. It's only necessary to be sufficiently persistent. Sort of like the infinite number of monkeys at an infinite number of word processors who wrote everything in existence.

Anyway, we now had good light source, and I gave orders to plumb the factories and furnace areas, and had two gross of the lamps made. By spring, we had light as long as we wanted it, by which time there were eighteen hours a day of sunlight, and we didn't much need the lights.

But *next* winter...

The shops weren't idle either. We made a rolling mill to make sheet brass, and some small punch presses to use the sheetmetal. I designed some simple door locks and padlocks, and they looked to be a profitable line.

Our reinvestment rate was over ninety percent. That

is to say, most of the things we made were for use in our factory system. But we still needed to buy a fair amount of stuff from the outside, and additional cash was always welcome.

Transportation costs were very high in the Middle Ages, especially for land transport. The best mules can only carry a quarter of a ton, can only go thirty miles a day, and must be loaded and unloaded by hand twice a day. Expensive.

This meant that the most profitable products would be small, light, and valuable. Locks, glassware, pottery, cast-iron kitchen products, plumbing parts, and clocks were all being made by spring, as well as our older brass works' lines of church bells, windmill parts, hinges, and other hardware. I wanted to add paper, printed books, and cigarette lighters in the near future.

We expanded the paperworks from a two-man outfit to one where a dozen men worked, and added power machinery to cut and mash the linen rags to pulp. Within the year we added a papermaking machine, which was a major undertaking but not a major headache. I'd at least *seen* a papermaking machine.

For a printing press, I decided to bypass the evolutionary step of the flatbed press and go directly to a simple rotary press, and to cast the type in a solid line, rather than bothering with movable type. I drew up what I thought were some very simple designs, but they took a team of our best machinists along with the Moslem goldsmith over a year to make them work.

And the cigarette lighter took the longest damn time. We actually spent three times as many man-hours developing it than we did on our first steam engine. It had seemed so easy in the beginning.

We had flint, steel, and white lightning for fuel. I drew up a simple Zippo-type lighter, except that I made it cylindrical instead of flat to simplify the machining, and with a pull-off cap because we didn't have a decent steel spring to hold the usual flip-top in place. It was bulkier than the modern equivalent, but these people used pouches instead of pockets, so that wasn't a problem.

The problem was in generating a spark. Flint was harder than any steel we could make. The spark wheel wore away before the flint was touched, and all without a spark. I even sacrificed the disposable butane lighter I'd had with me from the twentieth century. We took it apart but didn't learn much, since the flint was about gone.

But flint gouged up the modern spark wheel as well, which told us that the flint in a lighter wasn't like the flint we were using. This got us to collecting flint from every source we could find, but all of it seemed to be the same.

I finally dropped back and punted. Some of the more expensive modern lighters used a quartz crystal that was struck by a tiny hammer to generate a spark electrically.

I found some quartz crystals in a shop in Wroclaw, and had our jeweler cut several pieces at different angles of the crystal. Within a week, we had a working lighter! After that, it was just a matter of tooling up for a very profitable line.

It can take a half hour to start a fire with flint and steel, but it only took moments with one of our lighters. You just took off the cap, raised the little weight on its slider, let it drop and presto! Fire! We sold them by the thousands! It also gave us a nice market for lighter fluid, which was wood alcohol, after a while.

By then, spring was on us and it was time to get back into the construction business. Transporting coke by pack mule from Three Walls to the boat landing on the Odra River was extremely expensive. After that, transport costs by riverboat weren't nearly so bad, about one-twelfth the cost per ton mile.

Many of Count Lambert's knights had followed his lead in digging coal mines for fuel, now that potbellied stoves were available. Questioning them and going down most of the shafts, I was able to map out the coalfield fairly well.

All indications were that I could dig for coal right on the riverbank. All through the winter, I'd had six men digging a pilot shaft there on some of Count Lambert's land, and they'd struck coal five dozen yards down.

It made all kinds of sense to build a mining-and-coking operation there, so I made a deal with Count Lambert for half a square mile of land and as soon as the weather broke, I got ready to head there with a construction crew.

FROM THE DIARY OF PIOTR KULCZYNSKI

It was early morning, and we were mounted up in caravan fashion to go to the new lands sold to Sir Conrad by Count Lambert near the River Odra. There we would open mines for coal and build coke ovens of a new design.

Sir Conrad rode up the line of loaded mules and three gross men, seeing that all was ready. I was stationed near the front, next to Sir Vladimir. The three Banki brothers were away making final arrangements for their upcoming weddings, which we were all looking forward to.

There was a great commotion at the gate, and I looked to see the merchant Boris Novacek, a friend of my lord Sir Conrad, crawling through the wood gate on his knees and elbows, for he had no hands!

Sir Vladimir shouted for Sir Conrad, and we both rode to Novacek's aid. Yet Sir Conrad passed us and was there first.

"Boris! What happened?" Sir Conrad shouted as he dug out his medical kit.

"What happened?" Boris said, half dazed. "Why, they cut my hands off."

"Who did this?"

"I don't know. We were never properly introduced." Novacek tried to laugh, but tears came out. "Do you have any water?"

Sir Conrad threw his canteen to Sir Vladimir, who sat Novacek up and held that strange metal bottle to his lips.

"You!" Sir Conrad shouted, looking at a young man in the crowd that was gathering, "Run and get Krystyana!"

"You! Run and get a stretcher! You! Have the men stand down. We leave at three!" Sir Conrad ordered while he opened his kit and examined Novacek's stumps.

"What happened to your guard, Sir Kazimierz?" Sir Vladimir asked.

"Sir Kazimierz? He's dead, poor lad. The good Sir Kazimierz is dead. He took an arrow in the eye and I think he did not see it fly at him."

"You were ambushed?" Sir Conrad said.

"Yes, my friend. My lord. Cut down on the road. There's nothing to buy now in Hungary. I sell your cloth and metalwork there, but they have nothing to give for it but silver. Even all the wine they can spare has already been brought here. I carried nothing but silver and gold, all my silver and gold. We had no caravan to protect us, you see, so they chopped my hands off." Novacek spoke as one falling pleasantly to sleep after hard work and many beers.

"He's lost a lot of blood," Sir Conrad said to my love Krystyana, who had just arrived, walking as fast as she could, for she was heavy with child. Of course she would not look on me. He tied off the arteries in the left stump, and left it for Krystyana to sew up, going around the merchant to tend the right one.

"Boris, who put on these tourniquets for you?" Sir Conrad asked.

"The tourniquets? Why, I put on the right one myself, after the fight. The highwaymen put on the other."

"But how could you have tied it without any hands?"

"I still had my left hand then. It was hard, but one can do things when motivated sufficiently." Novacek seemed not to notice the trimming and sewing they were doing to the stumps of his wrists, and I think the tourniquets must have had them completely numb.

"Then how did you loose the left one?"

"They cut off my right hand in the battle, and my sword with it. They cut off my left one that night, in sport. At least *they* thought it great sport. *I* wasn't asked." Boris giggled.

I could see a terrible fury building up on Sir Conrad's face.

"So this happened yesterday?"

"Could it have been only yesterday? It seems much longer. But it must have been yesterday afternoon, for I planned to make Three Walls by sunset."

"And where did it happen, Boris? Can you remember where?"

"It was on the trail from Sir Miesko's. A ways down the trail. About half a night's crawl." He giggled again.

"Anna, can you smell out Boris's path back to the outlaws?" Sir Conrad asked his mount, as he finished tying off and cleaning up the right stump. Annastashia was there, washing her hands with white lightning, ready to sew it up.

Anna nodded Yes, a thing I had gotten used to.

Sir Vladimir was standing between Sir Conrad and me, but I was sure that Sir Conrad was looking directly at me.

"Then mount up! There's work to be done!" The look in Sir Conrad's eyes left no room for argument, or even comment. I mounted my horse, checked my sword, bow and arrows, and followed Sir Conrad and Sir Vladimir out the gate at a gallop.

I heard Novacek yell, "Stop! There are sixteen of them!"

Sir Vladimir turned and said, "What of it? We have God on our side!"

But I don't think Sir Conrad heard him.

Anna had her head to the ground as she ran, sniffing like a hound, which slowed her down some. We would never have stayed with her otherwise, and even so Sir Vladimir and I were hard-pressed to meet her pace.

Sir Conrad never turned around to see that we were following. Sir Vladimir turned once, saw me following and smiled. Then he turned again to the trail ahead, for our pace was wild.

I unsheathed my bow and strung it at a full gallop, as I'd often practiced before. Tadaos the bowman had taught me much of shooting, and there is none better than he at a standing-shot. But Tadaos will not shoot from a horse. In fact, I think that it is not possible to pull his mighty bow from any but a standing position. Myself, I can scarcely bend it even then! But I had taught myself horse archery, riding past the butts and letting fly for many a Sunday afternoon. A good thing to do when your love will not look at you.

Thus I had an arrow nocked and ready in my left hand when Anna suddenly left the trail and charged through the brush.

Sir Conrad was in his plate armor and seemed not to notice the branches whipping by, and Sir Vladimir, in chain mail, would hold it dishonorable not to be able to follow where his liege lord led. Myself, I was in but ordinary clothes and while they had broken off the larger branches in my path, I was still sore pressed to stay with them, and must needs protect my face with my arms and clutch tightly to my bow lest I lose it.

Nonetheless, I got first blood in the fight, for as we went through a meadow at break-neck speed, I saw a sentry in a tree stare at us and nock an arrow.

I let fly and saw that my shot was true. He dropped his bow half pulled, clutched his chest and fell.

Sir Vladimir saw this and lowered his lance.

"For God and Poland!" he shouted.

Sir Conrad's sword had been out since we had left the trail.

The bandit camp was in a clearing, and I think that they must have had such confidence in their numbers that they had not moved it after committing yesterday's crime, even though their prisoner had escaped. Immediately and without hesitation, Sir Conrad charged into their midst, covering himself completely with glory. I saw heads and arms fly as he cleared a swath through them. Sir Vladimir was right behind, and I saw two men fall to his lance on his first pass.

Being unarmored, I dared not follow, but stopped at the edge of the clearing. The brigands were slow to act, stunned by the fury of the attack. I let fly at those at the edges and killed three while they stood there. Then suddenly all were in motion, and I killed but one more with my last eight arrows, though I wounded two besides.

The surviving bandits put all their efforts at Sir Conrad and Sir Vladimir, and I think that they scarce noticed me if they saw me at all. I prayed thanks to God in heaven for this favor, but when my arrows were exhausted, I felt obligated to sheath my bow, draw my sword, and join the others.

I had no chance to bloody it, for it was suddenly over. Bodies and pieces of bodies were scattered about the meadow, many sporting the bright red feathers for which I had paid extra to fletch my arrows.

Not a man among them was left alive. Sir Conrad was looking at them.

"I think we got carried away, Sir Vladimir. We should have taken a few of them alive."

"To what purpose, Sir Conrad? To hang them later? What good would that do? To show people that they shouldn't be brigands? They already know that!"

"We haven't even proven that these were the men who attacked Boris. We have only Anna's word for it."

"Well, there's proof for you. Look there. That's Sir Kazimierz's stallion. I'd recognize it anywhere. And I'll wager we'll find his armor when we sort the booty."

"What of the sentry?" I said. "He might still be alive."

"Sentry?" Sir Conrad said. "Piotr, what are you doing here?"

I was astounded. "Why, I am your squire and you told me to come, my lord!"

"*I* told you? I certainly did not!"

"Wait, Sir Conrad," Sir Vladimir said. "He was standing just behind me when you ordered me to follow you. I, too, thought you meant him to come with us."

"Well, I didn't."

"A bit late to say that now, my lord. Look about you. Those arrows are his. He killed at least as many of the enemy as did you or I. If this were my grandfather's time, and any knight could knight another, I'd dub him right now, for he saved my liege lord—you! You didn't even see the sentry he skewered from a treetop. That man was aiming at you when he did it."

All this was not precisely true. That sentry hadn't had

time to aim at anybody. But I blessed Sir Vladimir for saying it.

"Oh," Sir Conrad said. "Piotr, I guess I owe you an apology, as well as my thanks. Let's see if that sentry is still alive."

He wasn't. Not only had my arrow pierced his heart, but he had broken his neck in the fall.

"It looks like you wasted an arrow, Piotr!" Sir Vladimir laughed. "The fall alone was fatal!"

It was an old joke, but we all laughed at it. These noble knights were treating me as an equal!

We looked through the camp. There were horses and mules belonging to Novacek, and armor belonging to him and to Sir Kazimierz was found and identified. There was also a third suit of chain mail, doubtless the property of some earlier victim. It was small and made for a person of slender stature.

"There's really not much here in the way of booty," Sir Vladimir said. "Novacek's property must be returned to him, and Sir Kazimierz had a younger brother who would appreciate having his horse and armor. They aren't wealthy, and I would feel best if they were given to him."

"Agreed," Sir Conrad said. "I'll see that it gets to the kid."

"That leaves this last set of mail. It's of Piotr's size and I'm minded that he should have it. Traveling as much as he does, he needs it, and he truly earned it this day."

Sir Conrad looked at me and smiled. "Agreed. Piotr, you are now the proud possessor of a set of armor, with helmet and gambezon. Wear it in good health!

"The rest of these tools and weapons are mostly junk. We'll give anything that looks decent to Count Lambert as his share, throw the rest into Ilya's scrap bin, and that settles the problem of the distribution of the spoils, except for one major item.

"Boris was half delirious, but he distinctly said that he had all his wealth with him when he was attacked. As well as he's been doing these past few years, that was probably several hundred thousand pence. Where is it?"

We spent much of the morning looking for the treasure, but without luck. Finally, we loaded the animals for the trip back to Three Walls, and I took a few moments to try on my new armor. It was a remarkably good fit, and even the open-faced helmet sat well, so I made a brave appearance reentering the city.

Naturally, we were the center of attention, and everyone was looking at us. I caught Krystyana's eye, but she quickly glanced away.

Sir Conrad announced that the journey to the Odra River would be delayed a few days, and said that in the afternoon, right after lunch, every available person in Three Walls would go to the bandits' campsite to search for Novacek's treasure.

At dinner, bold in my new armor, I came and sat by my love's side in the dining room. I tried to make polite conversation, but she stopped and stared directly at me.

"It takes more than armor to make a knight, *Squire* Piotr!"

Then she left, her food uneaten.

That afternoon and the whole of the following day, almost a thousand people searched for the treasure. Sir Conrad had Anna try to smell out where they hid it, but all she found was their latrine. There was shit there, and Novacek's left hand, but no treasure. We threw the bandits' bodies on top of their own filth and piled dirt over them.

Sir Conrad lined the people up fingertip to fingertip and marched them for miles from north to south and then from east to west. Every square yard of land for miles around was searched again and again. We found Sir Kazimierz's body, and Novacek's other hand, but no treasure.

One yeoman's cottage was taken apart and the ground under it dug up, for no other reason than he lived a mile from the camp. Then a crew rebuilt it for him.

Countless trees were climbed and no few hollow ones were chopped down, but to no avail.

Novacek affirmed that he had lost just under four hundred thousand pence, and not a penny of it was ever found. The reward on the treasure was never claimed.

Eventually, it became a normal pastime, a thing to do on one's day off, to head into the woods with a shovel, and many young couples claimed that this was what they were doing in the woods as well. It became a standing joke to ask how you dug a hole with a blanket.

Yet it was a game my love would not play.

Interlude Three

I HIT the STOP button.

"So what happened to the treasure?" I asked.

"It was right where Anna said it was. The outlaws hid it under their latrine, or rather they used the hole as a latrine after they buried the treasure, figuring that nobody would look through somebody else's shit. They were right, and the effect was doubled once there were sixteen dead bodies over it."

"Oh," I said. "Another thing, why didn't flint work in Conrad's lighter?"

"Lighter 'flints' aren't flint, kid. They're made of misch metal, an alloy of rare earth elements. Anything else troubling you?"

He hit the START button.

Chapter Sixteen

IT WAS another summer spent running around on Anna, usually with Cilicia riding behind me. I had originally intended to put her on the payroll like everybody else, but at first I didn't get around to it. Then she started teaching dancing to the women at Three Walls, charging a penny for six lessons a week. All winter long she had more than sixty women in two classes, and was making more than twice what anyone else at Three Walls was making, so there was no point in paying her on top of that.

I was even considering charging her rent on my living room, where the classes were held, but then found out that she was giving most of the money to her father. My deal with Zoltan hadn't included giving him any cash. I could see where land, clothes, and food weren't quite enough, so I let it ride. It was years later that I discovered that she was charging him fifty percent a year on his loans.

Had a Polish girl done that, I would have spanked her ass, but these were a different people, with different morals.

Different strokes for different folks.

Cilicia wasn't really eager to spend half her time traveling with me, but she wasn't happy about letting me out of her sight, either. She came, despite the money she was losing by not teaching school. But she made up for it by dancing for the men at each of my installations, and then teaching dancing to the women when she was there. After six months, she had enough girls well trained to act as instructors, and she built an organization that paralleled my own, teaching dancing for all the traffic would bear. About the same time, dancers became standard fare at the Pink Dragon Inns. Oh God, how the money rolled in.

Cilicia's people were survivors. They had to be, after all they'd been through.

Zoltan worked out a sideline of his own, making and selling perfumes and cosmetics. I wasn't all that happy with it, since it seemed a waste of resources, and a girl who can blush doesn't need makeup. But he found a ready market for his products, and there was nothing I could do about it anyway, so I didn't try.

Visiting the duke's castle at Wroclaw, we found that not only were the serving girls topless, but most of the other women were doing it, too. The serving wenches were dutifully clad in miniskirts and mesh stockings, and were clumping around inexpertly in high heels. The noblewomen were wearing clothes reminiscent of something worn by snake goddesses in ancient Crete. But not all of them.

There were two factions. The largest felt that if the duke wanted it, he should get it. But a substantial minority noticed that the duke's son, Prince Henryk, was a lot more straight-laced than his father, and that the prince's wife wasn't going along with the new fad. Figuring that the prince was the wave of the future, these ladies were dressing like Queen Victoria.

The first thing we built at Coaltown, the installation on the Odra, was a brickworks. It was cheaper to manufacture bricks on-site than to haul them in on mules from Three Walls, and we needed an awful lot of bricks.

The previous fall, I'd put Zoltan to work seeing what he could do with coal tar. He'd come up with ammonia and a wood preservative. Further, he knew of a process of combining salt, ammonia, and carbon dioxide to make sodium bicarbonate and ammonium chloride. We tried the ammonium chloride out as a fertilizer. Sodium bicarbonate has lots of uses, but the big one is to melt it down with sand and lime, both of which are plentiful, to make a good quality glass. I wanted plentiful glass more than I wanted steady sex!

Of course, I might not have said that a few years ago.

A beehive coke oven isn't very efficient at producing by-products, so the ovens at Coaltown had to be of the complicated modern design, with brick heat regenerators, chemical separators, and tall brick chimneys.

Okoitz started to get a major face-lifting that summer. During the winter, Count Lambert had repeatedly enlarged my plans for the workers' dormitories until they were bigger than the rest of the town! He not only had room for three gross of young ladies, but moved his own quarters there as well. There were six dozen guest rooms, a huge dining hall, a big new church, and an indoor swimming pool. And plumbing, sewage disposal, limelights in the public rooms, and steam heat.

As an afterthought, he let me add a wing for the peasants as well.

I made the place look like a proper castle, with machinations, crenelated walls, and dunce caps on the towers. There was even a drawbridge over a moat that doubled as a swimming pool in warm weather.

His old castle became an addition to the cloth factory and the peasants' housing was turned into stables.

To build it, he contracted with me to take all the surplus bricks and mortar we could produce for three years, and gave us all the surplus cloth his factory could make for the next five. Essentially, we became his sales force.

I'd long felt sorry about the poor living conditions at Okoitz, even though they were no different than these throughout most of Europe in the Middle Ages. It was just that when I first came to medieval Poland, these people took me in and made me feel at home. This was the first chance that I had to do something really nice for them, and I spent a lot of time on the designs of that building. It was going to be nice!

As to the financial arrangements, well, as long as I

could meet my payroll and keep food on the tables, I really didn't much care who owned what. I was doing my job, I was having fun, and I wasn't missing any meals. Why should any rational man want anything else?

I'd appointed Natasha to take care of Boris Novacek, since without hands he wasn't capable of doing anything for himself, and she had the patience to wait on him literally hand and foot. They hit it off pretty well together and he recovered fairly quickly under her care.

Yet even after he'd reconciled himself to the loss of his hands, he was still in the dumps. His fortune was gone and he saw no way of supporting himself.

So I offered him a job, salary plus commission, as my sales manager. We had not only the products of my factories to unload, but the duke's copper works and Count Lambert's cloth works as well.

At first, he seemed to lack confidence in himself, but within a month he was in the full swing of it and enjoying himself. He was a past master at dealing with other merchants, and I think he used his disfigurement to his own advantage. Gesticulating at his opponents with his handless arms seemed to intimidate them. In half a year, we were not only selling everything that we wanted to sell, we were getting thirty percent more for it.

The money was important because it permitted us to expand faster. I no longer had to worry about whether I could feed a man's family when I hired him. If he looked to be the sort we wanted, I swore him in and found a place for him later.

But I think that Boris's greatest triumph was when he invented the Tupperware party. You see, one of my major expenses was maintaining over a hundred schools in Lambert's county. Our kitchenware line wasn't selling very well, largely because women didn't know how to use them. We made very good cast-iron frying pans, for example, but frying was an unusual way to prepare food in the Middle Ages, probably due to the lack of a decent frying pan!

So that summer, Boris invited two dozen of the

schoolteachers to Three Walls for a week, and saw to it
that they learned how to use every utensil we made. I
even found myself showing them how to make pancakes!

Then he set up a system whereby the schools bought
things from Three Walls at below wholesale prices, and
the teachers demonstrated and sold the utensils to the
other women in their towns at normal retail prices.
Everybody knew that half the money spent went to the
local school, and that the teachers were making a commission on the sales in addition to their salaries. By fall,
we were in danger of making a profit on the schools,
which was a bit much. So we used the surplus money to
put up school buildings.

Up till then, school had been taught in the church,
somebody's house, or even in a barn. Now there were
schoolhouses, and each one of them had a store attached. We expanded the product line available to the
schools to include everything we made, and the smallest
town now had a general store. If they didn't stock it,
they could get it.

Every school had a post office, too. This was usually
just a drawer in the store, but you could send and re-
ceive mail.

Most of the towns were small farming communities,
with only a few dozen families, so most of the schools
had to be small, one- or two-room affairs. But they all
had hot running water, in part to demonstrate our plumbing products.

If most of our teachers only had a year or two of
schooling themselves, well, it was the best we could do
and the quality of teacher education went up in time.

I refused to allow any money to be made off the
schools, so there was nothing to do but expand the system. In three years, we covered the entire duchy, and in
six, all of Poland.

Just in time for the Mongols.

By late fall, Boris knew that he had found a new niche
in life, and he and Natasha came to me during one of my
regular biweekly court sessions. They wanted to be married, and had already gotten her parents' written permis-

sion to do so. I gave them my blessings, and told him that he was a very lucky man, which he was. A fine lady!

Construction never stopped at Three Walls. That summer we added a second housing unit, made of brick, outside of our existing building. It tripled the living space available to the workers. Yet because everyone was on different shifts, our existing kitchen, dining room, recreation facilities and church were still adequate, not to mention the factories. A considerable savings.

We also finished the sawmill and carpentry shop that had been stopped last fall in order to build housing for the Moslems. Besides cutting logs into rough lumber, there was a drying kiln, and power-operated planers, joiners, and routers.

Surprisingly, medieval carpenters didn't know much about cabinet-making. Despite the lack of inexpensive fasteners, they had never heard of a dado or a rabbet or a dovetail joint. Their methods of fastening were limited to butting two boards against each other and doweling them together. If more strength was needed, they had iron straps made up. I had to teach myself cabinet-making just so I could teach it to my own carpenters.

Then there was the whole problem of getting mass production going. They were used to making things one at a time. If somebody needed a chair, a carpenter made one. If somebody wanted three, he made one and one and one. This was an emotionally satisfying way to work, but it wasn't very productive. Equipping one of our dining rooms took a thousand chairs, and mass production was in order.

We needed barrels, chests, and other shipping containers by the tens of thousands. Standardization was necessary, unless we wanted to haggle over the price of every barrel of lime shipped. It took a lot of work and a few temper tantrums, but I made believers out of them.

By midsummer, I had over two thousand men sworn to me and on my payroll, and that's not counting their families.

The place was crawling with kids! Almost every woman continued having a baby a year, but now, with better nutrition, sanitation, and housing, they weren't dying off as fast as they were born. Our infant mortality rate was fast approaching modern levels.

Modern doctors and other medical-types like to take all the credit for the vast improvements in public health, but the fact is that it is the lowly sewer inspector and the despised customs inspector and the humble sanitation engineer who *really* keep people healthy!

So we had a population explosion on our hands, but it didn't bother me. At least these kids were going to grow up clean, well fed, and well educated! We could afford to feed all the extra mouths, and the population of the country wasn't a twelfth of that of modern Poland, which isn't all that crowded.

In the long run? Well, historically, a high standard of living inevitably results in a lowered birth rate. And if that wasn't good enough, there was a whole empty world out there to repopulate.

Everywhere the Mongols had gone.

I was spending more time than I was actually required to at Eagle Nest, mostly because I liked working with the kids. They were the most eager, enthusiastic, friendly, and *earnest* bunch of people I'd ever met. They were so absolutely convinced that they were going to conquer the skies that they damn near had me believing it.

In the course of the winter, they'd each built several model gliders, and many of them were as good as those done by modern boys, despite their lack of balsa wood, silk paper, and quick-setting glues. In the spring, they were back at kites again, and getting innovative about it. The winner of one combat contest was really a section of aircraft wing, with three strings controlling it.

But toward summer, I could see that they were getting a little bored, so I told them about hang gliders, and they built a dozen of them.

A hang glider is controlled by the pilot's moving his

body to shift the center of gravity of the craft, rather than by the more conventional use of control surfaces. What can make them deadly is that in a downdraft, the plane and pilot can experience zero G. At this point, the pilot has absolutely no control over his plane. Shifting the center of gravity has no effect when there *is* no gravity! Coming out of the downdraft, the glider can be in any orientation, even upside down or backward, and a fatal crash is likely.

Downdrafts can't happen close to the ground, and for this reason I forbade them to go more than a dozen yards in the air, under penalty of being grounded for a month. By late fall, most of the boys had been grounded at least once. I even caught Count Lambert flying too high, but I couldn't do much except admonish him for it. The joy of flying was too much for him.

We had our first fatality that year. One of the boys broke a dozen regulations by taking a glider to the top of the big conical hill alone during a windstorm. A shepherd tried to stop him, but the kid was airborne by the time the old fellow got there. They say he was high out of sight before he got into trouble.

His body was sent back to his parents and three other boys were pulled from the school.

But two weeks after that, the new class arrived, twice as large as the first one, and things went on, twelve-dozen boys strong.

Krystyana had a fine healthy boy that summer, and pretended that she didn't notice what anybody said about her lack of a husband. I got to sleeping with her occasionally, mostly because I felt sorry for her, and by Christmas she was pregnant again.

The harvest was again good that year, and the new crops were starting to be plentiful enough to make a serious contribution to the food supply. I had new grain towers built at all our installations, each with a windmill to circulate the grain and keep it in good shape. If grain is just left to sit there, it soon becomes infested with insects, fungi, and rats. But if you regularly pump it to the top with an Archimedes' screw on dry days, any bugs and rats are killed and the grain stays dry enough to retard fungus. This is still the method used in the twentieth century.

We had tons and tons of sugar beets at Okoitz, and I had to figure out how to convert them into sugar. Sugar is a major industry in modern Poland, and entire sugar refineries are regularly sold to other countries. But the more important an industry is, the more specialized it becomes. There are engineers who spend their entire lives working on nothing but sugar refineries, with the result that a generalist like myself simply didn't get involved. I didn't even know the basic process!

Zoltan came to my rescue. He'd never heard of a sugar beet, but he had heard about the process for refining sugar cane, which grew on the eastern shores of the Mediterranean Sea. This was wonderful, because by myself, I don't think that I ever would have thought of adding lime, the caustic stuff that mortar is made out of, to the beet juice to make it crystallize. But between Zoltan's chemistry and my machinery, we got a working plant installed at Okoitz before Christmas. It made a nice "winter industry" for the peasants, something to keep them busy between the harvest and spring planting.

Free popcorn became a regular feature of the Pink Dragon Inns. We had twenty-two of them now.

Every few months, I visited Father Ignacy at the Franciscan monastery in Cracow. He was my confessor, my confidant, the one person in this world that I could be honest and comfortable with.

This time, I found that the old abbot had died, and that Father Ignacy had been elected to take his place.

"Congratulations on your promotion, Abbot Ignacy," I said.

"Thank you, my son, although it was probably more your doing than my own."

"Mine? What do you mean?"

"It was mostly those looms and spinning wheels of

your design that did it. I encouraged my brothers that we should do our own weaving, and the project has been a huge success. Somehow, I received most of the credit for it."

"But I thought that Friar Roman did most of the work there."

"He did, but there is very little justice in the world. However, I'm sure that you would rather talk about the inquisition that the Church is conducting on you. At least you always ask about it," Abbot Ignacy said.

"I take it that there is news?"

The Church was holding that inquisition to determine whether I was an instrument of God, to be eventually sainted, I suppose, or if I was an instrument of the devil, to be burned at the stake. *Yes*, I was *most interested* in what they decided!

"There is. You will recall that I wrote up my report promptly within months of your arrival in this century. My abbot acted briskly, and within a few months sent the report, with annotations, to the bishop here in Cracow, but his excellency felt that perhaps this sort of report should go through the regular branch of the Church, rather than the secular one. That is to say, through the home monastery rather than through his office, so that summer the report was sent to the home monastery in Italy. But the home monastery felt that no, this was a proper matter for the secular branch to handle, and sent it back here.

"The report was therefore sent, with further annotations, to the Bishop of Cracow again. However, by this time you had established yourself in the Diocese of Wroclaw, so the Bishop of Cracow found a traveler going to Wroclaw and sent the report to the bishop there."

"Wait a minute, father. I was there when that report came in. It was at my Trial by Combat, and both bishops were in attendance. So were you, for that matter. Why didn't the Bishop of Cracow just hand your report to the Bishop of Wroclaw?"

"How should I know that, my son? Perhaps he hadn't had the opportunity to annotate it properly.

"In any event, the report was sent to the Archbishop of Gniezno, in northern Poland, who in turn sent it on to Rome.

"The report has now returned, through the proper channels, with a request that the Abbot of the Franciscan monastery at Cracow investigate the matter thoroughly, and report back. It happens that I am now that personage, so I have written a complete report and am currently looking for someone who is going to Wroclaw. Actually, writing it was an easy matter for me, since I had all the facts at my fingertips, having written the original report myself.

"So, you can see that the matter is proceeding smoothly, and as fast as can be expected."

All I could see was that after *three years* all that had happened was that Father Ignacy had written a letter in reply to his own letter! I became convinced that the bureaucracy of the medieval Church was as screwed up as that of the stupid Russians!

"Father, we now have a postal service that covers every major city in Poland. Why don't you just *mail* the report to the archbishop?"

"And bypass his excellency the Bishop of Wroclaw? Heaven forbid! You wouldn't happen to be going to Wroclaw, would you?"

"Not directly. Just mail it to him. It only costs a penny, and it will be there in less than a week."

"An interesting suggestion, Conrad. I'll have to mention it to my superiors."

"Through channels, of course."

"Of course!"

The Great Hunt went off very well, and our new killing ground was ready in time for it, so we didn't have thousands of wild animals running through what had become a substantial city. There were many fewer wild boars and wolves than before, at least locally, and many more deer, elk, and bison. But since I was now getting a rake-off from all the lands owing allegiance to the duke, the total number of wolf skins delivered to me was huge.

I had a problem storing and curing all of them. But the price stayed up and it was vastly profitable. My aurochs herd was up to eight dozen animals, and we started culling some of the bulls for eating.

The wilderness was being pushed back, the land converted to farming and pasture, and large stockpiles of lumber were building up. On Lambert's lands, the rule was that any tree that gave an edible fruit or nut should be left standing, and except for certain areas preserved as forests—about thirty percent of the total—all else should be cut for more pasture area.

And so 1234 wound around.

Chapter Seventeen

THE NEXT year saw our first printed books, our first poured concrete, and our first mass production of glass. It also saw our first cannon.

There are some big advantages to doing something the first time. You can set your own standards.

When it came to printing, there were a lot of simplifications I could introduce, for no other reason than because no one had ever seen anything different. All the characters were the same width, as on an old-style typewriter. The use of lowercase letters was not common in the Middle Ages, so we didn't have any.

The width of a column was standardized at twenty-four characters, and our rule was that any word could be hyphenated anyplace, so all lines were the same width and no space was wasted. All books were printed on paper that was a third of a yard high and a quarter yard wide, since that was the width that our papermaking machine made. And there were three columns on each page. Always.

Once you were used to it, it was easy enough to read, and almost everybody was used to it because all the schoolbooks were printed that way. It was the way you learned in the first place. For those who learned by reading handwritten manuscripts, there was no difficulty in learning something new. Up until then, *every* book had been in a different format.

This made for great simplifications in our type-casting machine. It was a carefully machined iron trough with two dozen long iron sticks in it, set up so the sticks could be slid back and forth. The top of the sticks were square cut to look like a castle wall, and on top of each merlon was stamped a letter, number or punctuation mark.

The operator slid these sticks until the line he wanted was under the casting apparatus. A second operator slid a mold on top of the line of sticks and poured a molten lead alloy into the mold and over the row of stamped letters.

A third operator trimmed the wedge-shaped bars of type and fit them into a drum that went to the printer, once the drum had been turned on a lathe to make sure that all the characters were of exactly the same height.

The printing press was also a simple affair. There was a cast-iron pressure roll on the bottom, then the type roll, and finally some leather-covered inking rolls on the top. There was no paper feed required since we worked only from large continuous rolls of paper, and always the same kind of paper.

Printing the other side of the paper required a good deal of skill on the part of the printer, keeping the paper tension proper, so that the back of the sheet matched up with the front. Paper stretches with moisture, and sometimes print runs were delayed because it was necessary to print the second side on a day with the same relative humidity as when the first side was printed. But it couldn't be the same day because our ink took a day to dry.

But despite the above, a twelve-man crew could print and bind six thousand copies of a fair-sized book in less than a week, whereas hand-copying a single book could take a month, or six months in the case of a bible.

What took a year of development time were all the details. Getting the ink right and finding the right lead alloy that would cast properly and always shrink in exactly the same way, and so on.

The leather ink rollers were a problem because the crack where the leather was sewn together showed up on the printed page, no matter how carefully it was made. They solved this one by using a tubular piece of leather, made from the covering of a bull's penis! Privately, they called the rollers "Lamberts," but I don't think he ever heard about it.

Making concrete required far less finesse and a lot more brute force. Mortar is made from calcium hydroxide. It hardens by absorbing carbon dioxide out of the air and turning itself back into calcium carbonate, the limestone it was made of. Concrete is made of a mixture of things, but mostly calcium silicates. It hardens by polymerization. With concrete, you have real chemical bonds holding things together, which is what makes it so strong.

To make it, you heat a finely ground mixture of coal, limestone, clay, sand, and blast furnace slag in a rotary kiln until it melts together into clinkers. Then you grind it up again. The machinery to accomplish these small tasks took over fourteen thousand tons of cast iron, because we were only making a small one.

The limestone went through a pair of crushing wheels as wide as a man is tall, and three times that diameter. Then the chips went through three sets of progressively finer ball mills. If you can imagine a huge cement mixer filled with cannon balls and limestone, you understand a ball mill.

The rotary kiln was a cast-iron tube two yards across and three dozen yards long, lined with sandstone bricks and turning once a minute.

I loved it, but then engineers love to make big things. It gives you a godlike feeling of power! Mere money doesn't come close!

Once you have the materials, making plate glass is pretty easy if you know the trick, and I did. You just pour the glass onto a pool of molten tin and slowly draw off window glass. This won't work with glass made of wood ashes and sand because the melting temperature of that mixture is too high—you vaporize the tin, I found out the hard way. But with our soda glass, it worked just fine. Our rig was fairly narrow, since none of our outside windows was more than a quarter yard wide.

Within three months, we made enough glass to glaze every window in every building we'd put up in four years, except for the churches. Learning how to make stained glass took a few months longer, and then only because I was able to hire a French glassmaker to show us how it was done.

He knew two methods of doing it. One involved adding dyes to the molten glass and then piecing bits of this together in a lead frame, but it was the second method that we used, for then we could use standard rectangular cast-iron frames.

This involved little more than painting the colors and designs wanted on the glass, then baking it until the glass softened enough to absorb the colors. Easy enough once you know how to make the paints, and this guy did.

But while he was a good enough craftsman, he wasn't much of an artist. He did one window for the church at Coaltown, and I didn't like it. It was trite, and I wanted something glorious.

So I got the services of an artist friend of mine, Friar Roman, from Abbot Ignacy by giving him a thousand prayer books and offering him his very own printing press. Actually, I'd wanted to give the printing outfit to him anyway, since I didn't want to get into the publishing business.

The deal we made had my people training his, and we sold them paper and ink at cost. They could print anything over my requirements that they wanted, sell it as they saw fit and keep the money, but they had to acknowledge that money as my donation to the Church. My work, mostly schoolbooks, was to be done at the cost of materials.

Actually, much of their other work turned out to be my work as well, since we made it a practice to buy a copy of every single book published for every single one of the schools, to build the libraries. We got those at cost, too.

And there were two other strings attached. The first was that everything printed must be in Polish. I wanted to establish the Polish language and Polish culture as a leader in Europe, and having the only printing presses in existence gave us a big edge. In the twentieth century, a Polish boy has to learn English or Russian if he wants to stay at the forefront of engineering and most sciences and German besides if he wants to keep up with chemistry.

That wasn't going to happen in the world I was building. I'd make everybody else learn our language! That can be done by making yourself culturally and technically ahead of everyone else. What's more, once you're ahead, you tend to stay ahead, because while your kids are studying science, their kids are studying your language.

Not one person in a hundred in America speaks a foreign language. *They don't have to!* But everybody else has to speak English just to keep up with them.

Anyway, the Polish alphabet is slightly different from that used in the rest of western Europe, so it wouldn't have been easy to do foreign stuff in the first place.

The second string was that I wanted him to turn out a monthly magazine, a general purpose family-oriented thing that would have sections on current events, household hints, agriculture, medicine, and construction. There would be a sermon written by Abbot Ignacy and there would be something each month for the children. In addition, we would be accepting commercial announcements, for a price.

The abbot was astounded at the idea of writing a book every month, and even more so at my suggestion that an initial print run of six thousand copies would be appropriate. But once we discussed how each of a dozen people would be writing only a few pages a month each, he came around, although I think that it was the thought that six thousand families would be reading his sermons that made him take on the task.

As it turned out, I had to write half of the first few issues myself, until we got enough regular contributors to fill it out. I had to write a manual of style, to keep things consistent, and I had to talk Abbot Ignacy into assigning four friars to the task of writing a dictionary.

The first three issues had only ads from my own companies, but in time I was able to largely disengage myself from the project, except for the occasional article.

The long-term effect of the magazine was astounding. Up until then, the only source of news anybody had was hearsay and gossip. Now they had a source of information about what the duke said in Wroclaw, and how the Palatine of Cracow answered him.

Within two years, we had correspondents in most of the major cities of Europe, and were the first news service. And the magazine was a great way to tell my story on sanitation, housing, and food supplies.

So it was a profitable trip, but I'd ridden to Cracow to get an artist.

Friar Roman had never made a church window, but that didn't matter. We had craftsmen who could do the actual construction. What I wanted was the artwork.

An engineer is probably not the person to choose as an art critic, but I was also the boss and I had definite ideas about what I wanted. I wanted to make a religious statement, and I didn't dare do it in words.

The Church in the Middle Ages depended far too much on fear to get its message across. When I go to pray, I don't want to be surrounded with representations of tortured human bodies.

To me, Christ's message was a message of love. Love for God and love for one another. I read nothing in the Sermon on the Mount about mutilating people for the glory of God!

For the Church of Christ the Carpenter, our church at Three Walls, I wanted a simple naturalistic scene of a young Christ helping Saint Joseph in his carpentry shop. On another wall, I wanted Christ with the little children. The third was to have Christ with the lilies of the fields and the last was to be Christ with the money-changers in the temple, because Christ wasn't a wimp.

So I put Roman on the payroll and set him up with a nice room at Coaltown, where the glass works was located. It had big windows on the north side, a drawing board, and a big stack of paper. I told him what I wanted and let him alone for a few weeks. Then I told him what I didn't like about what he'd done, and had him try it again.

It was four months before he started doing what I wanted, and I had to teach him about perspective drawing in the process. But eight months after I'd shanghaied him, we had the glass hung at Three Walls. Then I got him going on my other four churches.

It was not only important to save Poland from the Mongols, it was also important that I help make it *worth* saving!

There was a bad harvest in 1235. The fall rains had come much earlier than usual, and much heavier. Yet we barely felt the effects of it.

For years, Count Lambert had been selling the new varieties of grains as seed and *by the pound* at high prices. The result was that most of the farmers in Silesia and Little Poland were growing at least some of it.

The modern grains were shorter and had thicker stems than the older varieties, so they stood up to a heavy rain better. Most towns had at least one McCormick-style reaper, and they were able to get in most of the crop on the few dry days that we had.

Many farmers were able to sell their grains to harder hit areas, and made great profits doing it. At least, the sale of single-family plumbing packages skyrocketed, which is some sort of indicator.

My factories didn't buy any grain at all that year, since we had stockpiled enough the year before.

Anna's children were all healthy, and she had another batch of four every six months. The oldest bunch looked like horses now, but they grew slower than regular horses, and Anna said that they took four years to become adults. We had twenty of them, but it would be a few more years before the first bunch would be ready to join the team.

Anna spent very little time with them, only looking in on them every day or three to see that they didn't need

anything. It wasn't that she was a bad mother, it was just
that she was supremely confident that if they had enough
to eat, they would grow up okay.

They were good little survivors. When they got cold,
they burrowed into the hay, and if that wasn't enough,
they burrowed into the ground below the hay. And they
would eat anything. If they ran out of hay and grain, they
would start eating the stall they were in, so you had to
watch them. In fact, I think half of Anna's looking out
for them was to protect the world from them, and not
vice versa.

Krystyana was productive as well. After the birth of
her second child, I promised myself that enough was
enough. I wasn't doing anybody any good by producing
illegitimate children. I stuck with that vow, except for
once when she was crying and making love seemed the
best thing to do.

Once was enough. By late fall, it was obvious that she
was pregnant again.

The previous fall, I'd put Zoltan on the problem of
making gunpowder, or rather the problem of making
saltpeter—potassium nitrate—since once we had that, I
knew the formula for gunpowder. It's seventy-five percent saltpeter, fifteen percent charcoal, and ten percent
sulfur.

But all I knew about saltpeter was that it was made
out of manure, or sometimes old mortar, and that it was
a white crystal. Oh, I could give you the molecular
weight and even sketch up a molecule of it, but that
wasn't going to help Zoltan any.

He'd gamely gone at it, and had gone through seven
frustrating months smelling like shit, as did his young
Polish apprentices. The boys were all having trouble
with their love lives until I ordered them to bathe *after*
work and had them issued extra clothing to wear when
not on the job.

Then one day Zoltan came in with his clothes in tat-
ters, his hair gone, and his beard burned off. His face

was covered with blisters but through them shown a great happy smile.

"I think we have done it, my lord!"

So I gave him the small brass cannon I'd had made up along with a supply of cannon balls. I told him about wetting the mixture down, drying it, and grinding it to turn serpentine powder, which was what he had, into black powder, which was what I wanted.

I explained how to load and fire a cannon and told him that I wanted him to play with slightly different mixtures to see which one could make the ball go farthest, always using the same small amount of powder.

I also made him, his apprentices and everyone around them swear to keep the process for making the powder a secret. I didn't want anybody to know how to make it but a few of his people and his apprentices. They realized the seriousness of having somebody else shooting cannons at *them*, and the promise was kept until well after the Mongol invasion.

Chapter Eighteen

By CHRISTMAS of 1235 I could see that it was all going to come together. There was an awful lot left to do, but I think the seeds of an industrial base sufficient to supply a reasonably modern army were there and well planted.

Getting the army was another matter. I had four knights sworn to me and that's where I had to start.

Actually, it was sort of strange for one knight to be sworn to another, but there was nothing in the rules against it. I had more knights than some of Count Lambert's barons, but all the lack of a baronage meant was that I sat farther down the table at a formal banquet and I wasn't permitted to knight anybody. But I avoided formal banquets whenever possible and hadn't wanted to knight anybody anyway.

The truth is that I am of a naturally egalitarian disposition. I didn't like this separation of people into hereditary cases, this silly business of noble and commoner. If I had my way, I'd scrap the whole unhappy system! But I didn't have my way and giving up my own knighthood would drastically reduce my own efficiency, as well as wrecking my lovelife. But someday I'd have the power to do something about it.

I called my knights together after dinner one day, along with their wives.

"Gentlemen, we are starting to get it together," I said. "We now have most of the raw materials that we need. We now have the beginning of a factory system that can take those raw materials and turn them into useful products. We now have workmen trained to use those factories and the tools in them.

"We also have the biggest, best trained and best lead army in the world coming at us in five years.

"What we don't have is an army of our own! At present, we have no way to save our country from absolute destruction. You've all heard Cilicia's story about the obliteration of her native city. *That could happen here!*

"It *will* happen here, unless we do something about it!

"Our factories can easily be converted from making civilian products to war production. They were designed with that thought in mind. We can turn out arms and armor at a rate that will astound you. Better armor than the world has ever seen, and weapons of awesome power will be ours when we need them.

"But the weapons are worthless without the men who will use them! I can promise you that we will be better equipped than the Mongols, but if we are to win, we must be better trained and better lead as well. That's not going to be easy!

"The Mongols have been diligently practicing the art of mass murder and total destruction for over fifty years, and so far they have never been defeated!

"But they are going to be beaten here and we are going to train and lead the army that will do it! You four gentlemen are going to do most of it, since I'll have to spend half my time on production.

"It won't be the kind of training that you have been used to, because this won't be the kind of war that you have been used to. You have become accustomed to treat war like a game, where polite, Christian gentlemen settle their disputes according to well-defined rules.

"Well, the only rules the Mongols know are 'obey orders' and 'win the war.' They are not Christian nor are they gentlemen. They are greasy, smelly little bastards who can fight like all the demons of hell! They are hard and tough and cruel. The only way that we are going to beat them is by being harder and tougher and crueler than they are!

"You are used to a kind of warfare where only the nobility fights. That too must come to an end. The Mongols will come to us with every single man of theirs under arms. To meet them, we must do the same. Our factories will be able to equip every adult male in Silesia and Little Poland. We must be able to train that number of men. It will be difficult, but not impossible. I can show you techniques that can turn a farmer into a fighting man in six months. Training leaders will take longer, and training the men to train *them* will take longer yet.

"In the spring, we will be building a training base in the northwest corner of my lands. We have already fenced off a dozen square miles of land there, using Krystyana's roses, so we'll have plenty of privacy. I've asked Count Lambert to send me a gross of volunteers right after the spring planting. Those peanuts will be our first class.

"The training period will be eleven months and we will be working at training not warriors, but trainers of warriors. I'll be happy if three dozen of them survive the education we give them.

"After that, you gentlemen will be administrators, and they will be doing all the grunt work. But for the next year and a half, you will all be going through hell yourselves! That's why I invited your wives to this meeting, to explain to them that you won't be seeing much of them for a while, that you will be working for me and not playing around with Count Lambert's harem at Okoitz.

"I know that you are all in fairly good, strong physical shape. You should be, living the healthy, outdoor lives that you do.

"But you are not 'run twelve miles before breakfast' healthy and you're not 'do two hundred push-ups' strong. We will be working on that this winter, and it won't be fun. All I can promise you is that I will be going through the same pain that you will.

"We start physical training tomorrow morning, and we will also be spending two hours a day here in my office doing skull work. Any questions?"

"Too many to remember them all, my lord," Sir Vladimir said. "But the one that sticks in my mind is 'what is a push-up'?"

"You'll learn, my friend. I promise you, you'll learn."

"This running and other physical training you mentioned," Sir Gregor said. "I don't understand the need for that."

"We will be training an infantry force, and some artillery, which I'll explain later. There is no possibility of getting enough war-horses to equip our army. That many horses don't exist! Also, Poland already has a sizable force of cavalry in the conventional knights. I'd estimate that we have thirty thousand of them, plus we should get some help from France and the Holy Empire when the time comes."

"What of the Russians and the Hungarians?" Sir Gregor said.

"The Russians, or rather the Ukrainians, will be largely wiped out in the next three or four years. I don't think that we will find it possible to give them any significant amount of help in that time. As to the Hungarians, well, they'll be attacked at the same time that we are, and will have their hands full with their own problems. It is more likely that we will be able to aid them than the opposite happening."

"This land that you have set aside for training," Sir Wiktor said. "A dozen square miles seems like a lot. And what is this need for privacy? Much of the reason for having a strong military force is to make an enemy think twice before attacking you. Why try to hide it?"

"The Mongols are coming whether we're ready or not," I said. "They won't believe what infantry can do until we show them on the battlefield. There are two reasons for the seclusion of our training grounds. The first is that I don't want our training techniques on public display. They are one of our major secret weapons.

"The second reason is more important, and more subtle. In the course of training, we will be doing two things to our soldiers. The obvious one is that we will be building up their bodies and teaching them how to use weapons. The other is psychological. We will be tearing their minds apart and then putting them back together in a newer, stronger way. It helps to have them in an isolated, alien environment."

"How does one tear apart the mind of another?" Sir Vladimir asked.

"That too is something that I'm going to have to show you, and you won't like it. I trust that you gentlemen know that I have the highest regard for you as individuals and as my vassals. I won't like being rude to you, especially when it's not deserved. But in order to teach you how to train others, I'm going to have to treat you the way you'll be treating the peasants you'll be training. I won't be polite. In fact, I'm going to be as rude as possible. I don't know why this helps to make men absolutely obedient, but it does.

"If there are no further questions, I'll see you all at the gate tomorrow at dawn. Be in full armor with good shoes. We'll start off with a three mile run and then I'll teach you about marching."

It was snowing, but they were standing out there at dawn, and with them was Piotr Kulczynski.

"Piotr, what the hell are you doing here?" I said.

"My lord? I am your squire and when you called out all your knights, I thought—"

"Well, you thought wrong! I need you as an accountant. I don't need you as a training instructor! Now get the hell out of here!"

Piotr left, almost in tears.

"Aren't you being a little rough on him, my lord?" Sir Vladimir said.

"Shut your face, Vladimir! When I want your opinions, I'll tell them to you!"

That set the tone of our training. Such rudeness wasn't needed with my knights, and certainly not with Piotr, but it would be with the peasants and workers we had to train.

Sir Vladimir had repeatedly followed me into battle and fought like a hellion. I had no doubts about the three Banki brothers, either, and I thought that Piotr would walk through fire if I asked him to.

Which gave me an idea. I had once read an article on fire-walking in *The Skeptical Inquirer*, An American magazine organized for the purpose of debunking strange cult practices that abound in that country. Americans take their right to personal freedom to extremes, and permit all sorts of flying-saucer worshipers, Scientologists, and other crazies to abound.

The magazine explained quite carefully how it was possible to walk on a bed of glowing coals, and under what circumstances it was safe to do so.

If anything could convince an army that they were unbeatable, walking through fire should do it! Perhaps as part of the graduation exercises. Yes . . .

So we ran three miles in full armor, and I made sure that I stayed ahead of them even though my lungs were hurting and I could tell that my legs would be sore for a week. The muscles needed for riding on horseback are quite different from those needed for running! This was followed with an hour of calisthenics in the snow, and then some marching. The dinner bell rang, but I ignored it and kept them marching until they could at least stay in step.

"Your *other* left, Vladimir!"

We ate leftovers for lunch and were silent while doing it. Some of the workers noticed, but were smart enough to say nothing.

After lunch, we met again in my office.

"You may speak freely now, gentlemen," I said. "Part of the reason for these afternoon meetings will be to explain and to hash over what we did in the morning."

"Very well, my lord, since you invite it," Sir Gregor said. "I would like to know why you felt it necessary to speak so rudely to us. Had I not been sworn to you, I swear that I would have challenged you to a duel for some of the things you said."

"Well, I warned you that I was going to do it, but you didn't take me seriously enough. Was it necessary to talk to you in the manner that I did? The answer is no, it wasn't. You four have spent most of your lives training for combat. You are eager for it. Your whole system of self-worth depends on you following your liege lord into battle and fighting there honorably.

"But it will be necessary for you to know how to deal with people whose previous life aim was simply to get enough food to feed their families and to maybe lay a little money aside in case of bad times. That is to say, the great majority of people in this world. You must impress them with the importance of instant obedience to a direct order, even when the order makes absolutely no sense to them. I'm not sure why, but somehow shouting at people seems to accomplish this.

"Tell me, Sir Vladimir, what were your feelings when I shouted at you for defending Piotr this morning?"

Sir Vladimir thought for a moment. "Anger, at first, my lord. Then shame. Shame for myself for offending my liege and shame for you for so debasing yourself."

"Exactly," I said. "Anger and shame. But the anger goes more quickly than the shame. I think it would be very unlikely for you to speak up like that again in the same circumstances. Now you are no longer angry at me, in part because of this discussion and in part because we have known each other for a long time.

"The men you will be training will not have the benefit of your previous acquaintance with your drill instructor, nor will they have the benefit of these meetings. They will learn to hate you, and that is a necessary part of the training. Years after it's over, most of them will look back and see you with a certain amount of respect, but that is a very hollow sort of reward. In fact, being a drill instructor is one of the roughest jobs I know of.

"It might help if you tell yourself that this is a necessary thing to save your country, *because it is*."

They were silent for a bit.

"This funny kind of walking, this marching. Does that have some reason for it?" Sir Wojciech said.

"There are two reasons, one practical and one psychological. Tomorrow, I'll be showing you a weapon called the pike. It's like a lance, but it's six yards long. With one, if it's used properly, foot soldiers can destroy cavalry. But carrying something that long, you must walk in step or your pike gets tangled up with everybody else's pike.

"There are two parts to the psychological side. From the standpoint of the soldier, it gives a strong feeling of group belonging. It gives a feeling of power, a feeling that your unit can't be stopped. And if enough of the men really believe that, they truly *can't* be stopped.

"From the standpoint of the enemy, it results in fear. Seeing a thousand men coming at you, all wearing the same clothes and all walking in exactly the same way, their feet hitting the ground at exactly the same time, makes you think that you are not fighting mere men who can be killed. You think that you are up against an unstoppable machine.

"Once our men and their men both believe that we are unstoppable, the battle is more than half won."

The grueling training went on all winter long. Besides the pike, I introduced the rapier, a footman's sword that has no edge to speak of but only a point.

At first we wore the rapiers in the normal way, but this got in the way of calisthenics. Sir Vladimir was the first one to wear one over his left shoulder. He had the tip of the blade stuck into a long dagger sheath at his belt and the rest of the sword covered with a thin leather tube attached to a strap that went over his left shoulder. He could get it out in a hurry, although getting it back in was a bother. Still, it was a lot more convenient wearing it his way than getting it tangled around your feet. Wearing the sword high became one of our trademarks. That, and our funny haircuts.

You see, I believe that every elite military organization known to man has had a funny haircut. The Normans who conquered England wore one that looked as though they put on a beret, cocked it a bit, and then shaved off everything that wasn't covered. The Cossacks shaved their heads except for a pony tail hanging on the left side. The Mongols shaved a big square on the top of their heads, leaving a curl in the middle of their foreheads, in front of their ears, and a thick fringe around the back.

I don't understand the psychology of this brand of

nonsense, but obviously, we had to have a funny haircut too. For a while there, I was toying with going to a Mohawk, but then I decided that the modern military crew cut was as weird as any of them, and took a lot less maintenance to keep up.

We also spent a lot of time on unarmed combat, for a warrior must stay a warrior even if he's unarmed and naked.

But after two weeks, I had to leave and go the rounds of the other factories. There were always technical problems where a few words from me could save hundreds of man-hours, and managerial problems that only the boss could resolve.

I put Sir Vladimir in charge when I was gone, and I gave him a daily schedule of what was to be done. He followed it as best he could. For my own part, I tried to stay with the physical training program even when I was on the road, but it was hard to do.

I especially didn't want to stint the boys at Eagle Nest. Those kids were so *earnest* that I felt a moral commitment to give them all the help I could. It didn't faze them in the least that one of their members had already died in the air. They fully expected to take further casualties and, in typically Polish fashion, were willing to pay the price. It wasn't the ignorant feeling of 'it can't happen to me.' They knew that it *could* happen to them! They just felt that the prize was worth the price, and they went on. This from twelve- and thirteen-year-old boys! If only NASA had such heroes!

What could I do but love them and help them in every way that I could? For now, I got them into sailplanes, and designed a launching device that would be built on top of the big conical hill near there. There was plenty of coal tar stockpiled at Coaltown, so we scheduled an asphalt runway on the plain below the hill. In time, other runways were added so that they could land no matter which way the wind was blowing, and eventually an entire half square mile was paved over. This not only permitted landing in any wind, but on sunny days it caused a lovely up-draft that went up for miles!

Wing struts proved to be a problem. The most efficient sailplane wings are very long and thin, and we had to support them without the benefit of aircraft aluminum. What we came up with was a sort of synthetic bamboo. I had a huge lathe built that could turn an eight-yard-long spruce log. We bored a conical hole down the middle of it, inserted a long iron cone in the hole and turned the outside of the log so that the thickness of the wall was half that of your little finger. Then the iron cone was removed and wooden discs were glued inside every half yard. This assembly had an astounding strength-to-weight ratio. Two of them fastened together end to end at the fuselage ran down the center of the wings. It held.

Count Lambert was often at Eagle Nest when I was there. He complained that they were making great progress with the aircraft themselves, but that I had once described to him an engine that could power an aircraft, and I was doing nothing about developing one.

The problem was that there were a lot of things higher on my priority list than a glorified lawnmower engine. There was the tooling to mass produce armor, a rapid-fire breach-loading cannon to develop, and we needed to be able to mass produce shells, bullets, gunpowder, sword blades, boots, and all sorts of things. I didn't even have a dependable source of lead and zinc yet, let alone sulfur!

But Count Lambert and the boys teamed up on me and extracted a promise. I would start working on an engine once they could build a two-man glider that could stay up for an hour. Knowing the problems involved, I didn't think that my promise would seriously upset my schedules.

There were two major sour points in early 1236, and they both hit me within the same week. I was being sued, twice. One lawsuit was by Count Lambert's brother Herman. He was no longer pleased with the brass works that I'd sold him. Rather than making him money, it was costing him money, due, I was sure, to his poor management. He felt that it was all my fault, and he was a count whereas I was a mere knight, which proved it to his satisfaction. He wanted his money back.

The other one was from Baron Stefan. He had decided that I was still on the land that Lambert had wrongly given me, land which had been in his family for more than three hundred years, he said. He wanted the land back and for me to pay damages for the trees I'd cut down and the fences I'd put up.

They gave me a few months of needless worry until the duke was passing through one snowy day and threw both cases out of court. Or rather, he dismissed both suits because he *was* the court.

Count Herman's suit was dismissed because I had delivered the property agreed upon and had never promised that it would be profitable. He gave the count a fatherly lecture about trusting to the workingman rather than to the man's tools and nobody mentioned the fact that the duke himself owned the factory that had run the count's factory out of business.

The duke became angry when he found that Baron Stefan had failed to come at Count Lambert's summons to beat the bounds between our properties. He said that if the baron lost land because of that, he deserved it, and a horse whipping besides for disobeying his liege lord.

It helps to have friends in high places.

Also that winter, Anna and I scouted out the Malapolska Hills, north of Cracow, where I knew there were deposits of zinc, lead, iron, and coal. She said that winter was the best time for smelling out this sort of thing, since there were fewer other smells around.

We found deposits of zinc and lead fairly close together, or at least there were two different ores and Anna said that they both stank like sulfur and I knew that both ores here were sulfides. Lead and iron had been smelted here for thousands of years, and some archeologists believe that it was here that iron was first made.

But zinc was unknown as a separate metal. It was used as an alloying element with copper to make brass, but the ores were mixed before smelting to make brass directly, or zinc ore was mixed with copper before casting and copper was actually used to reduce the zinc!

Late that summer, I found out why.

The fact is I wouldn't have gotten zinc at all if I hadn't added some pollution-control equipment to the blast furnace there. There wasn't even a real need to control pollution, since our facilities were tiny by modern standards and didn't seriously effect the environment. But the problem would grow unless we started off doing things right, so I was adding dust collectors where possible.

When we tried to smelt the zinc ore, after roasting it to convert the sulfide to the oxide, all we got was slag. No metal at all came out. It was only when we cleaned out the dust collector that we found drops of zinc there.

The zinc had left the furnace as a gas! Small wonder the ancients never found it. They weren't worried about pollution at all!

By the next winter, we were producing zinc in quantity, but I get ahead of myself.

Work started on the training base as soon as the ground thawed. I'd chosen the land because of the varied terrain, with both mountains and plains on it, and because it was the least populated area of my lands. I only had to pay seven yeomen to move their families off it.

Eventually, the main barracks would be a square castle a mile to the side and six stories tall, but it was modest enough to start out. It had bunk-bed space for sixteen dozen men and a dining hall that doubled as a church, both made of concrete blocks. There was a big concrete parade around and a twelve-mile long obstacle course that was rougher than anything that I'd ever heard of.

On schedule, over a gross of peasants arrived from Count Lambert, or rather one from each of his knights. I had specifically asked for rough, disobedient characters. Peasants who were "too smart for their own good."

They certainly looked the part. If ever there were a bunch of men who looked like they should be hung on general principles, this was the gang. With one exception.

Piotr Kulczynski was with them.

Chapter Nineteen

FROM THE DIARY OF PIOTR KULCZYNSKI

I had spent much of the winter in preparation to attend Sir Conrad's warrior school. I had trained one of my subordinates, Jozef Kulisiewicz, to take over my position for a year, taking him twice on my rounds of Sir Conrad's factories and inns, and saw to it that *his* replacement was well trained.

I had artfully observed all the exercises that Sir Conrad and his knights were doing, and diligently practiced them myself. And I had worked on Count Lambert very carefully, and eventually got him to appoint me to the school. This was not easy, for while my father was one of the count's peasants, I was not, being sworn to Sir Conrad. But I persisted with the count, and came up with many reasons why I should go. At last, I irritated him sufficiently.

"Dog's blood! If you were sworn to me, I'd have you whipped! Piotr, you are too damn smart for your own good!"

"Yes, my lord. But isn't that precisely what Sir Conrad asked for? Men who were too smart?"

"By God it was, and I'm going to send you there just to get you out of my mustache! I know what Sir Conrad has planned at that school, and I think you'll be dead in three days if you go!"

"Thank you, my lord."

"You can thank me after he kills you! Now get out of here and get out of town, too!"

My plan accomplished, I left quickly. For I thought it was absolutely necessary that I attend the warrior school. My position as chief accountant gave me an excellent income, pleasant working conditions, and considerable prestige, but it did not give me what I really wanted. It did not give me Krystyana.

She was intent on marrying a true belted knight, or not marrying at all. Although nothing had been said of it, I was sure that those who survived the warrior school would soon be knighted. What other purpose could the school have?

So thus it was that I was standing in line with a gross of the grossest peasants I'd ever seen. It seemed that they had been picked for ugliness rather than for any other reason. They were all huge and hairy and smelled bad. I began to think that I had made a *big* mistake, a serious error in my career development plan.

"Piotr, what the hell are you doing here?" Sir Conrad shouted.

"Count Lambert sent me here, my lord. He said that I was rude and insubordinate and that if I were sworn to him, he'd have me whipped."

"Count Lambert could have you hung, sworn to him or not! Who is taking over your job?"

"Jozef Kulisiewicz, my lord. He's quite competent."

"I'll bet he is! After this stunt, he just might keep your job! You conniving little runt! You planned this, didn't you? Well, you planned wrong! You wanted to come here? Okay! You'll stay here! You're not my squire any more, Piotr. You're just another grunt in this line!"

I was so shocked that I barely heard the things that he said to the others in the line, though he was loud enough to make a snake listen. My position gone? And I was no longer a squire? What had I done to myself? Surely no one would knight *this* bunch of ruffians! I was ruined!

They gave me little time to bemoan my fate. We were marched off to the showers, for Sir Conrad said that we stank too badly for him to stand before us.

They had us strip naked and throw our clothes into a pile, to be burned, they said. Burning was probably the right thing to do with the rags that the others were wearing, but I had been spending much of my pay on nice clothing! My red hose and purple tunic were thrown into the pile of rags, along with my blue hat, my green cloak, and my beautiful Cracow shoes with the longest pointed toes in Silesia! I could only thank God that I hadn't worn my sword and armor, reasoning that none of the others would have such finery.

We were each given a small bag with our name on it for our valuables. We were told that these would be returned to us if we survived the year out, or sent to our families in the more likely event that we did not.

Four old women were waiting for us with sheep clippers, another of Sir Conrad's inventions.

We were each clipped of all hair, from head to foot and all in between, with the old women laughing at the small sizes of our privy members or occasionally pretending to be astounded at the size of others.

It was a vastly humiliating experience, and followed by the knights shouting at us to wash our bald heads and denuded bodies with the foulest smelling soap I've ever encountered.

We were each inspected for fleas before they let us out to air dry in the cold spring wind.

We were issued clothing from stacks of ready-made garments. There were even some that fit me tolerably well, but it was all of the baggy peasant cut that doesn't have to be well-fitted. The boots were sturdy, and of the cut of Sir Conrad's hiking boots, with blunt toes and no style at all.

The other grunts—for that is what they called us—were surprised at the quality of the clothing, but for myself, I thought it ugly. The cloth was sturdy linen, undyed and without any embroidery. The others liked the food as well, for it was like that normally served at Sir Conrad's installations, but it was no new thing for me.

The barracks were of blocks of artificial stone and we must needs sleep in bunks three decks tall, with four dozen men to the room, but all was remarkably clean and orderly.

We soon found out how it was kept that clean, for much of our time was spent in cleaning and polishing. That is to say, much of our time that was not spent doing other things, for they kept us inordinately busy. We were up every day before dawn, to wash in cold water and stand in neat lines before breakfast, to say mass and recite our oath at sunrise, always followed by a run that started at three miles but was eventually extended to twelve. Nor was this a simple run on flat land. It went up and down hills, over obstacles made of huge logs, over chasms hand over hand on ropes, and up and down cliffs. Many of the grunts were injured and no few killed in the process, for great fatigue and dangerous heights are a deadly combination. Whenever someone was hurt, we always got an impromptu first aid lesson, and all things stopped while we watched the victim being sewn back together again. We were constantly marching or running or jumping up and down and doing other exercises. After a week, we were issued weapons, first a pike, then a sword and dagger, and lastly a halberd. Fully a quarter of our day was spent working with these weapons, or the quarterstaff, or learning to fight without any weapons at all.

Another quarter of our day was spent in the classrooms, for it was decreed that all must learn to do arithmetic, and to be able to read and write. As I had already mastered these subjects, I was put to tutoring some of the others, though most had difficulty learning when they were so tired. In fact, more men were dismissed for mental reasons than for physical ones.

Some of the grunts actually went crazy under the strain of it. One man locked himself in a supply closet and when we finally got him out, he was babbling incoherently. He was naked and smeared with his own shit.

FROM THE DIARY OF CONRAD SCHWARTZ

Getting the army going was the hardest thing I've ever done.

It wasn't the arms or armor although that was a lot of

work. The Bessemer converter to make cast iron into steel took many thousands of man-hours, as did the rolling mill that made sheetmetal and the stamping line that pressed out helmets, breast plates, shoulder cops, and the other twenty-seven pieces it took to cover a man. And every piece had to be made in at least four different sizes, so the total number of dies required was huge.

We were making steel using the *wootz* process, so making good pike heads, halberds, swords, and daggers was straightforward, but still a lot of work.

We had decent black powder and making the swivel guns was not hard, once the production line for it was set up, but we hit a snag when it came to the primers. I wanted a breach-loading, bolt-action, clip-feeding gun with brass cartridges and lead bullets, but after two years of trying to come up with a dependable primer, I had to set the project on a back burner. There just wasn't time, not if we were going to get it into mass production in time to train the men to use them to fight the Mongols.

Yet I dreaded going to something like a flintlock. The rate of fire would be so slow that we would need twelve times the guns to do the same job. The advantages of breach-loading and premade cartridges were obvious. The problem was lighting the gunpowder.

I finally hit on the idea of putting a firecracker wick on the back of each cartridge and an alcohol burner in the base of each gun. A shield on the bolt covered the wick until the bolt was turned home, at which time the flame hit the wick, it sputtered for a few moments and then fired the cartridge. Not the best system in the world, but it worked.

During the Hussite wars in fifteenth-century Bohemia, war carts proved to be decisive in many battles. Our guns were fairly heavy, about six dozen pounds each, and the weight of the ammunition alone was more than a man could be expected to carry, not to mention the other arms and armor.

I came up with a big, four-wheeled cart, six yards long and two wide. The wheels were two yards high and mounted on castors such that the cart could be pulled either the long way, for transport, or sideways, for fighting. There was no possibility of getting enough horses to pull the thousand carts that we would need, so thirty-six men armed with pikes and halberds would have to do the job. Six guns and gunners in the cart could be pulled along with the pikers protecting the guns and the guns firing over the heads of the pikers.

One side of each cart had enough armor to stop an arrow, and the top of the cart could be slung six yards out to act as a yard and a half high shield for the men pulling it. It was armored, too.

If the men were well trained, and if we could get the Mongols to attack us, or if we could somehow surround them, they were dog meat. But there wasn't much we could do about their mobility. The typical Mongol had several horses and, in a race, they could easily beat us.

Communications can make up for speed, to a certain extent. No matter how fast your troops are, you must get a message to them before they can move. If we had radios, our effective speed would be doubled. I didn't have a radio yet, and wasn't sure I could do it, our materials' technology being so low, but I set up a crew to learn Morse code over short telegraph lines. If we could make radios, the operators would be ready.

There isn't much to making a telegraph. Electricity goes through a wire and a simple coil of wire makes an electromagnet which clicks or rings a bell. We had wire-drawing equipment and almost any two metals in a jar of vinegar makes a battery. But years ago, I'd tried to string a line between Three Walls and Okoitz and never did get it up. The price of copper was so high that seeing so much of it hanging on the trees was too much for people. Thieves stole the wire faster than we could string it up! We couldn't guard it all, and every time we caught a thief, three more sprung up to take his place. I finally had to give the project up and Sir Vladimir said he'd told me so.

But we could string wire around inside Three Walls, and we did so, mostly to train operators but also for internal communications.

A better line of defense was the Vistula River. We had steam engines running in the factories and paddle-wheel riverboats were well within our capabilities. A fleet of armed and armored riverboats could stop the Mongols dead, especially if the boats had radios.

The rub was that the invasion would happen on March seventh, at which time the river might or might not be frozen over. With the river frozen, the boats would be useless, so we did not dare put all our hopes on them.

But all this was the easy part, for me at least. It just meant nine years of long hours of hard work for me and a few thousand other men and women.

The hard part was training the army itself.

In thirteenth-century Poland, there were no trained, professional fighting men except for the knights, whose concepts of honor and fair play made them fairly useless, except in the polite sort of conflicts that they were used to fighting. By their lights, it was more important to fight nobly than to win, a nice rule for a playing field but not the thing to do when the Mongols were planning to murder every man, woman, child, and household pet in eastern Europe!

I had to train a modern army from absolute scratch. There were no old sergeants left over from the last war. Things had been fairly peaceful for years, despite the fact that the country was rapidly disintegrating because of duchies being divided up among the heirs of the previous duke. Such wars as had been fought were more like sporting events than serious combat. And there wouldn't have been sergeants, anyway. On the rare occasions when the peasants fought, they were given no training at all, and often no weapons except for such agricultural implements as they might own.

Once I knew that we would have the industrial ability to arm an army of fifty to one hundred thousand men, I had my liege lord, Count Lambert, send me a gross of misfits and troublemakers from his other knight's estates, since my experience in the service had been that the best sergeants were misfits at heart. Maybe I was wrong, but it seemed to me that most of them would not have done well in the civilian world. To function well, most of them seemed to need the surrounding structure that the military provides. Anyway, nobody minded giving me their problem children.

We put them through absolute hell. The program was designed to keep them on the very edge of physical exhaustion, near the ragged boundary of insanity. And a lot of them didn't make it.

I deliberately killed two dozen men in that first class, and I don't think that my soul will ever be truly clean again. But I had to have leaders that were absolutely tough and reliable and I didn't have twenty years to nurture and train them. If they weren't good enough, we could loose thousands of men in battle, and maybe the whole country besides.

But it *hurt*. It hurt like hell. And often, after a funeral service, I cried myself to sleep. Me, a supposedly mature man of thirty-six.

FROM THE DIARY OF PIOTR KULCZYNSKI

We were constantly under supervision, with never a moment to ourselves except on Sunday afternoons. Then, one could walk away from the barracks and spend a little time absolutely alone, and it was wonderful.

It was a month before I had the opportunity to speak privately to Sir Vladimir, for I found him sitting alone on a log in the woods.

"How are you doing, Piotr?" he said, as though we were back in Sir Conrad's great hall.

"Very good, sir!" I said, involuntarily bracing.

"Relax. Nobody can see us here."

I tried, but it was difficult to do so. For years, he had treated me like a younger brother, but for the last month he had been as brutal as the others.

"Thank you, Sir Vladimir." I sat down on the log next to him.

"You've surprised us, you know. None of us expected you to last a week, especially Sir Conrad."

"Indeed? But don't you see that I have to? If I fail here, I wouldn't have anywhere else to go. My position is gone and I am no longer a squire."

"Maybe, maybe not. Myself, I think it likely that if you went to Sir Conrad and asked for them back, you would get them. Sir Conrad was annoyed that you circumvented his wishes, but he is not an evil man. I think you need only apologize and admit your failure here."

"The apology is his, had I but a chance to give it. But I have not failed this school. Not yet, anyway."

"Well, if you can take it, you might as well stick with it. Eventually, all of Sir Conrad's men will be attending this school, so you might as well get it over with."

"Then why was Sir Conrad angry with me for wanting to attend it now?"

"Because this is not the regular course! This first class is intended to teach the teachers. The later classes will not be as difficult as this one. We are hoping that one-quarter of you will survive this training. We must have first-rate instructors to train the others. After this, at least half will make it through. Sir Conrad was annoyed at you wasting his time by going through early."

"That's some relief, anyway. When do you think we will be knighted?"

"Knighted? Who told you that? There are no plans to knight anybody! In fact, it is my private thought that Sir Conrad would eliminate knighthood if he thought he could get away with it! I know that the separation of nobility and commoners displeases him, and that it doesn't exist in his native land."

"Then all that I have done has been for nothing, Sir Vladimir. I'd hoped that if I could be knighted, then Krystyana would look differently on me."

"So that's what it was all about! I was curious what it was that made you disobey your lord's wishes. May I speak frankly? Piotr, you and Krystyana are two crazy people! She wouldn't accept you if you were a duke! She wants Sir Conrad, even though she knows that she'll never get him. And you keep chasing after her even though she kicks you in the teeth every chance she gets!

There are plenty of pretty girls out there, and you'd have a good chance with any one of a hundred of them."

"Many girls, but only one Krystyana."

"Piotr, you are digging a hole for yourself, and if you insist that you be buried in it, there's nothing I can do. It's time we were getting back. You go ahead. I don't want the others to think that I have been doing you any special favors, even though I suppose I have, or at least I've tried to."

I often thought of dropping the school, but I could never bring myself to fail or to publicly admit failure. I stuck it out.

FROM THE DIARY OF CONRAD SCHWARTZ

There is more to an army than weapons and training. Even more important than these two is spirit, the elusive *esprit de corps*. The men must believe in themselves and in their organization, and they must believe it in a deeply emotional way, rather than in a coldly logical manner.

You see, war is an absolutely irrational phenomenon. There is not and never was any sane reason to risk your only life attacking someone for some possible material or emotional benefit. Even if one was absolutely immoral, the plain fact is that you have everything to lose and damn little to gain.

It only makes sense to fight when someone else is attacking *you*, and even then there is a large element of the irrational in it.

Any individual man in a battle line can improve his chances of survival by running away. If he runs and everyone else stands and fights, odds are that he will live, while a certain percentage of those that fight will die. Yet if everyone runs, that army will take far higher casualties than if everyone stands and fights. The vast majority of casualties endured by a defeated army happen *after* the battle, during the mop-up operation after the battle line has failed.

So as irrational as it sounds, *on the average* your odds of survival are better if you stand and fight, even though *as an individual* your odds are better if you run away.

It *is* irrational. It's *crazy*! And therefore a winning army must be a special kind of crazy. The people in it must be insane enough to be willing to die so that the army may win. That special kind of insanity is called spirit.

You build spirit in many strange and irrational ways. One is that you stage special ceremonies, and our "Sunrise Service" was our most important one.

I wanted an oath of allegiance that would have emotional impact and be understandable to young and uneducated people. I carefully studied all the oaths that I could remember, but most of them were either too legalistic, like the military swearing-in ceremony, or they really didn't say much, like the American pledge to the flag. By far the best of the lot was the Boy Scout pledge and the Scout law. I modified it slightly to suit our circumstances, but every day of a trooper's life started out with this service.

They woke at dawn to the sound of bugles and were out on the parade grounds before the sun peaked over the horizon. At the first sliver of sunlight, a very short mass was said, less than eight minutes and without a sermon, though it took work to get the priest to do this at first.

I had a small band, some brass and percussion, play Copland's "Fanfare for the Common Man." Then we raised our right arms to the sun and recited:

"On my honor, I will do my best to do my duty to God and to the Army. I will obey the Warrior's code, and I will keep myself physically fit, mentally awake, and morally straight.

"The Warrior's code:

"A Warrior is: Trustworthy, Loyal, and Reverent; Courteous, Kind, and Fatherly; Obedient, Cheerful, and Efficient; Brave, Clean, and Deadly."

This was followed by the orders of the day, where the men were told what they'd be doing for the rest of the day.

The whole ceremony took less than twelve minutes,

but it was done every day of a warrior's life. Forever.

Other things were done to build spirit. You wear the same kind of clothing, so you all look the same and start to think that you all really are the same. You march together, walking in exactly the same way. You sing together, sounding the same way. And you do great and impossible things together. You run difficult obstacle courses and eventually you win battles.

But my army wasn't going to have a chance to win any battles, not until the Mongols arrived. This wouldn't be like a modern war that lasts for five years and gives you a chance to blood your troops before the final conflict. The war with the Mongols would be won in two months if it was going to be won at all.

I needed something else to give the troops that magic feeling of invincibility, and I had two ideas. One was that notion of fire-walking.

Various primitive tribes and the crazy people in California practice fire-walking, or at least walking on a hot bed of coals. If I could show them that they could now walk naked through fire, they would believe that they were unstoppable. And no one will run if he truly believes that he will win.

The other is a curious optical phenomenon, called the glory. If you are on a high place early on a clear morning, and the valley below is very foggy, if everything is right, when you look at your shadow on the fog below, you see around your head beams of light radiating outward. It only shows up around *your* head and no one else's, at least from your perspective. They, of course, see it only around their own heads. I read about this in *Scientific American*, but their explanation for it was unconvincing.

Yet one morning, when I was running the troops through the obstacle course, looking down to my left I saw this very same phenomenon. It was spooky, as though I was wearing some sort of halo!

If I could show the men that they wore halos, that they were individually blessed by God, they would be true believers, absolute fanatics, the kind of crazy people who win wars.

I changed the course of the morning run and made that spot off-limits, saying it was a holy place. Yet I went back there other mornings and three-quarters of the time I could see the same strange effect. I would definitely make it a part of the graduation ceremony!

Chapter Twenty

FROM THE DIARY OF PIOTR KULCZYNSKI

After three months, there were less than half of us left. Eleven men had died, a dozen more were crippled for life, and others simply could not stand the strain of the training, but I was still there.

Lady Richeza started teaching a course on Saturday afternoons. She taught courtesy, and dancing on Saturday nights. Young ladies were brought in to assist her and it was all very carefully supervised. It was astounding to see female human beings again. Three months with none but male company does strange things to a young man's thoughts. Yet when the ladies were introduced, we grunts were all remarkably shy, and had to be ordered to associate with them! I never have understood my own feelings here.

The next three months were equally rough, and we lost almost two dozen more grunts, but after that the drop-out rate fell off, and the only losses we had were due to injuries. It wasn't that the course became any easier. It didn't. But those of us who were left were the sort who could survive anything. Climbing a rope higher than a church steeple didn't bother us in the least. We did it every day before breakfast! Going up or down a cliff twice that high was child's play, and we got to enjoying it. Half a day with double-weight weapons? We could do it!

Soon, we were issued plate armor of the sort that Sir Conrad wore, and we learned to do all our exercises while wearing it, no easy thing at first! We lost a few men on the cliffs when they misjudged their balance or the strength of rocks, but the rest of us learned the necessary reflexes.

Then we got our first guns. Sir Conrad said that guns could be made of any size, but that the larger ones were useful only to attack cities and castles. Our opponents would all be horsemen, and our guns were therefore fairly small. He called them swivel guns, for they were mounted on swivels that enabled them to be easily pointed in any direction. They were as long as I was tall and had a bore that was bigger than my thumb. They could shoot six times farther than a crossbow, and one of the bullets could go through four pigs and four sets of armor. I know, for I did the shooting and helped to eat the pigs afterward.

Six of these guns were mounted on a war cart that carried, besides the guns and ammunition, the weapons and supplies needed by forty-three men. That is to say, six squads of six men each, plus six squad leaders and a cart commander. The carts were large, six yards long, two wide and a yard and a half high, in addition to being a yard and a half off the ground. There were four huge wheels, and these were mounted on casters that could be locked in any of four positions. In transport, the wheels were locked so that they faced forward and back, and then pulled the long way. In combat, the casters were locked sideways, and the cart was pulled sideways so that all six guns could face the enemy.

In combat, the lid of the cart was supported far off to the side on three pike shafts, providing a big shield for the thirty-six men who pulled it. Our armor had a ring in the back, near the waist, for attaching a rope, which was tied with a slip knot. This left the hands of the first rank free to work their halberds, and those of the next five to hold their pikes.

I had been a good shot with a bow, and it evolved that I was one of the best with a swivel gun as well. Part of the joy of being a gunner was being able to ride while the others pulled you along. You were high above them, and

could sneer at them because they had to face forward
and couldn't see you do it.

In truth, my small size also had something to do with
me being a gunner, for the less weight in the cart, the
better. The strongest men were all made first rank axe-
men, and those best at first aid were in the sixth rank,
where they could see any man fall.

The plan was to have thousands of these carts, with
the pikers protecting the guns, and the guns covering the
pikers, shooting the enemy over the footmen's heads.

Except for our eyeslits, our armor was proof against
arrows, and it was difficult to imagine an enemy defeating us. It was hard to imagine anyone fool enough to
fight us!

It was in the ninth month of my military training that
the worst trouble occurred.

My class was down to three dozen men then, from the
gross we had started with, since Josep Karpenski had
died the night before.

It was a cold morning, with a bit of frost on the
ground, so naturally Sir Conrad led us on the twelve mile
run before breakfast completely naked. If the afternoon
was hot, you may be assured that we would be working
out in full winter armor, for he never missed an opportunity to make things as difficult as possible.

We speculated why this was so, over our hurried
meals and in the few brief moments a day that we had to
ourselves. At least I speculated, for the others were convinced that Sir Conrad treated us thus out of pure cruelty. Myself, I was not convinced of that, for I alone had
known the man before this form of hell began, and I
knew that he never caused needless pain.

That there was some method behind this apparent
wastage of time and men was obvious to me, for it was
not the stupid brutality of a dumb peasant whipping a
dumber beast. It had more in common with the raw pain
caused when white lightning was poured on an open
wound to cleanse it, before the ragged edges were
trimmed away and the wound sewn shut.

That is to say, it was a precise, accurate sort of cruelty that was always on the very edge of the intolerable, but could still be survived somehow.

I think this knowledge of my liege lord helped me in some spiritual way, and gave me some advantage over the others to help compensate for my physical shortcomings.

The morning run was an everyday affair, and always done over the same course in one direction or the other.

We were running in step, four abreast and singing one of the songs Sir Conrad wrote for us, as we rounded a curve and found ourselves surrounded by Baron Stefan's men. They were all on horseback and in full armor, and there must have been fifty of them, counting the squires as well as the knights.

Baron Stefan, wearing his golden chain mail, his gold-trimmed helmet and gold-hilted sword, announced that we were on his land, that we were all trespassers and that since Sir Conrad had bewitched the duke as well as Count Lambert, it was time to take the law into his own hands and demonstrate by combat that this land was his.

Sir Conrad said that this was ridiculous. It was against all law for two knights of the same lord to fight. Trial by Combat was not legal under these circumstances, and certainly not when he and his men were naked and the baron's were in full armor.

The baron said that he was not going to fight Sir Conrad, but only make a demonstration by killing one of his peasants, and not even a very valuable one. He would only take the runt of the litter, and he pointed toward me!

Both Sir Conrad and Sir Vladimir, who was also with us that morning, tried to talk and shame him out of it, but the baron was like one out of his mind. He said that I was marked for death!

I thought about running, but on foot it was not likely that I could outrun a rested war-horse. I would be caught when I was exhausted and would have to fight with my strength gone. Further, if I must die, I would rather do it in as honorable a manner as possible. At least I had gone to mass and communion less than an hour before, so my soul was fit for death. I stood at attention and waited, trying to recite to myself a good act of contrition.

Sir Conrad continued trying to reason with the mad baron, but the fact was that the baron's men could kill us all if he ordered it. Sir Conrad ridiculed the baron into vowing that he would fight me alone, and had the baron's men vow that they would stay out of the fight. Then he talked the baron into at least letting me have a stick to defend myself with. A tree was pointed out, and it was agreed that I should have the use of it.

Sir Vladimir talked to one of his cousins who was sworn to the baron, and got me the temporary use of a war axe. Sir Conrad looked at me and softly said, "A pike and a quarterstaff."

The tree was a young pine, tall and straight and as big around as my wrist. I made quick work of it, leaving the bark on to better the grip. Perforce, I returned the axe and went to the center of the meadow. I threw the quarterstaff I'd made to the ground a few yards away and stood with my pike raised and at the parade rest position, with my feet wide apart, my left hand behind my straight back and my pike vertical and at arm's length from me.

I felt a bit silly, standing thus naked, but if anything was going to save my life, it would be the training I'd gotten in the last nine months. This was not the time to forget it! I found myself silently reciting every prayer I knew.

Baron Stefan had his men arrayed to the north and Sir Conrad had his to the south, almost as if this were a legitimate Trial by Combat.

Sir Conrad again made protest at the illegality of the procedure, and vowed vengeance if I was killed. I continued praying, and saluted him when he was done.

The baron went to the edge of the meadow, put on his great helm, lowered his lance and charged. The crowd was silent as that huge black horse thundered toward me. Inside, I was terrified, but I think that I didn't show it, for the habits of the last months had been beaten deep into me. Doctrine was that a knight will seldom fight fairly with a man afoot, and that a Mongol doesn't know what fair means. Therefore, a footman is under no obligation to fight back in a manner that a horseman would call fair. When you were alone and with a pike against a horseman, go for the horse! If you can kill it, you might stand a chance against the knight. But if he's up there and you're down below, the odds are way against you.

You don't always do this if there are more of you than there are horsemen. In that case, only the pikers in the middle go for the horse. Those on the outside go for the rider. If you can mob him, so much the better!

I kept my pike high until the last instant, so as to give the baron as little warning as possible as to my intentions. Then I stepped forward to a crouch with my pike grounded behind me and had the point lowered just in time to skewer his war-horse at the base of the throat.

And it went right in, just like a real pike does into the practice dummies! I threw myself to the side away from his lance, just like I was in a drill. The baron and his horse fell in a woeful heap right where I had been standing! The pike had gone in a full two yards before it had shattered, and the horse moved not at all.

Doctrine was to hit the downed horseman as quickly as possible, but I thought he wouldn't get up and I didn't want the baron's men calling foul on me. I picked up the quarterstaff from where I had tossed it and stood, waiting to see what the baron would do.

He tried to stand, but I could see that his leg had been broken in the fall, just above the knee. I relaxed, foolishly thinking that I had already won.

The baron was struggling to get to his feet, despite his obviously broken leg.

"Sir Conrad!" I shouted. "The baron's leg is broken! What should I do?"

"Ask him if he yields to you! If he does, or if he's dead or unconscious, the fight is over! Otherwise it's still on, so watch yourself!"

I turned to my opponent. "Baron Stefan, do you yield to me?"

"Yield to *you*, you filthy peasant! You've killed my best war-horse and he was worth fifty of you! You're going to die for that!" Then he somehow got up with only one good leg, drew his sword and swung it at me. I was so astounded at his toughness that I almost didn't get out of the way in time. The tip of his sword flashed by just grazing my throat. I actually felt it touch, though it didn't break the skin.

I leaped backward and fell in the process. I scrambled to my feet to find that the baron was hopping after me on one leg! I left my quarterstaff on the ground and backed off. I couldn't figure out how this was possible! Did the man feel no pain at all? Or was he really so insane that he had the impossible strength that you hear of berserkers having?

I didn't know, but I continued backing up, staying out of his way. Surely he couldn't keep this up for long! Yet he was attacking me at a remarkable speed, and had the advantage of being able to see where he was stepping, or rather hopping. I was keeping my eyes on the madman, and in the process I tripped over a tree root, again falling down. He swung at me and gave me a bad cut in the right calf. It hurt, but I didn't have much time to consider the pain. If I didn't fight him, he was going to kill me!

I had to run back and circle around the baron to get my quarterstaff, and the baron's men jeered me as I did it. Well, let them! They weren't trying to fight an armed and armored madman while they were completely defenseless and naked!

I got my staff and turned to find the baron only a few yards away. He had lost his great helm when his horse went down, and like most knights he wore an open-faced helmet under it. His face was red, his forehead was beaded with sweat and his eyes—there was no sanity in them!

He swung at me, but I slapped his sword aside with my quarterstaff. This is necessary, because you dare not use a wooden stick to fend off a steel edge. Rather you must slap the side of his blade and still make it go somewhere that you are not! No easy thing, but my life depended on it.

Before he could recover, I gave him a stop thrust to the solar plexus. I caught him square and hard, but it didn't stop him! I think it stopped his breathing, but the man didn't even bend over! He swung again, and again I was able to knock the blade aside. But this time, I was in position to swing a strong blow straight down on his head. It staggered him, and I could see blood run down his forehead where the edge of his helmet cut his skin, yet he was still on his feet, or rather his foot, for one was all that he had to stand on.

I waited a moment, surprised that I hadn't knocked him cold. Then his sword arm started to move, so I hit him again with all my might, this time a side blow to the neck.

He crumbled at my feet. I stood there, breathing hard, absolutely expecting him to get up and fight again.

Then a cheer went up from my fellow grunts, and Sir Conrad and Sir Vladimir were cheering with them! Soon the applause spread even to the baron's men, whether because they did not like him or because they truly admired my performance, I did not know.

But it felt good, and it felt better yet to be alive!

Sir Conrad and one of the baron's knights came out on the field and examined the baron. He was dead. My last blow had broken his neck.

"A very good fight," Sir Conrad said, getting out the medical kit he always carried. "Let's take care of that leg."

Can you believe that I had actually forgotten that I was wounded? There was a trail of my own blood from where I was cut to where I stood, yet I had forgotten about it!

It took fifteen stitches to close my wound, by which time the knights had loaded the baron, without his armor or surcoat, onto the back of one of the squire's horses. All present felt that the baron's arms and armor were mine by right of combat.

I never used them and I never sold them either,

though once a merchant offered me twenty-seven thousand pence for the set, mostly because of the solid gold fittings on the sword and helmet, and the spurs were solid gold, in the French style. It seems that the gold wash on the chain mail wasn't all that expensive at all, a mere five hundred pence, although it had to be renewed every year because it wore off.

No, I kept that armor and one day hung it on my wall, as a decoration and a memento of this day and all that happened because of it.

Sir Conrad asked two of Baron Stefan's senior knights to go with him to Okoitz, as witnesses as to what had taken place. Count Lambert's most powerful vassal had been killed, and a party would have to go and make explanation to him.

"Sir Conrad," I said, "am I in trouble for what I did this day?"

"Not as much as you were in a few minutes ago." He laughed. "But the fact remains that you have killed a man who vastly outranked you, and I'm not sure what Count Lambert will do. The duke would probably kill you on general principles, but I doubt if Count Lambert will. He never liked the baron, or his father either. Furthermore, the baron had no living relatives that I know of. He was the last of an old line. There will be no one powerful after your blood. I don't think that even his own vassals had much love for him, so it's likely that you're safe."

"Likely" is not a comforting word when the subject is one's own life.

Sir Conrad decided that it would be just as fast to complete the run as to go back, so soon the others left running. I returned with Sir Vladimir and the two of the baron's men who stayed behind. One of them, a Sir Xawery, was kind enough to lend me his horse, so that I didn't have to walk on my wounded leg. He led it by the bridle, so I had no difficulty with the animal. Baron Stefan's arms and armor were loaded on the back, and Sir

Vladimir promised to send someone out later for the saddle and lance.

Five of us went to Okoitz that day, Sir Vladimir, Sir Conrad, the baron's two knights, and myself. We were all in armor and I was riding Sir Gregor's war-horse, for my own had been given to Jozef Kulisiewicz almost a year ago. It was the first time that I had ridden a real charger, and the truth was that he scared me almost as much as the baron had that morning. A truly ferocious animal!

We stopped at Sir Miesko's on the way and he joined us, for all felt that it would be useful to have someone along who was versed in the law. Sir Miesko spent some time talking with Sir Xawery and then told me that I had little to worry about. I had been on my lord's lands and fought at his bidding, so I had done no wrong.

This relieved me considerably, and I was in a light-hearted mood as we rode past the new construction and into Okoitz.

Count Lambert was in the bailey, talking to his master carpenter, Vitold, when he saw us.

"Sir Conrad, don't tell me that you've gotten into more trouble!"

"Not I, my lord, but perhaps my squire has. Baron Stefan is dead."

I was thrilled that Sir Conrad had acknowledged me as his squire!

"Dog's blood! Next you're going to tell me that little Piotr has killed him!"

"I'm afraid so, my lord."

"Him! What did he use, poison?"

"No, my lord, he fought the baron at that man's insistence when he was naked and had only a stick, while the baron was fully armed, armored, and on horseback. These knights can all attest to that, for they were all witnesses."

"Dog's blood! They'd better, because right now I don't believe it! Gentlemen, this is best discussed in my chamber."

Some grooms came up and attended to our horses, and we were led to the count's chamber. A pretty wench served us the count's mead, of which he was inordinately proud, and in real glasses, the gift of Sir Conrad. It was remarkably good and had a flavor of rose hips.

Sir Xawery gave an accurate account of what happened and the three other knights attested to the truth of his statements. Sir Miesko discussed the legal aspects of the thing, most of which I could not follow, but the gist of which was that I was not at fault.

Count Lambert thought for a few moments.

"Well. It seems that Baron Stefan was crass enough to challenge a defenseless peasant and inept enough to lose the fight! Damn! And I'd always thought of him as one of the best fighters I had!"

"Crass he might have been, my lord, but my late lord was a great fighter! I tell you that he fought for a long while standing on one foot with a broken leg!" Sir Xawery said.

Count Lambert sighed. "As you will. But it doesn't solve what I am to do now! If a naked peasant can defeat one of my best knights, what am I to do? Some would say that Piotr should be hung as a public menace! Yet I must agree that he did no wrong if I am to believe you four, and how can I call four such honorable knights liars? Yet we can't have peasants killing full belted knights, can we? The whole social order would suffer!

"Much as it galls me to reward a man, especially this smart aleck, for killing one of my own vassals, I don't see anything for it but to knight the bastard!

"Piotr, kneel before me!"

I could scarcely believe my ears! Count Lambert himself was about to grant my fondest wish! Me! Sir Piotr! I quickly knelt before him as the count drew his sword.

"Wait, my lord," Sir Conrad said. "Piotr is my vassal and a student at my warrior school. The truth is that Baron Stefan picked him from among three dozen others because he looked to be the worst fighter of the bunch. And the baron picked right! Any one of the others could have done a better job than he did, and finished the matter quicker. I don't like the idea of one of my students being rewarded for dumb luck!"

My heart fell back into my knees. I was so close, yet I was being shot down by my own lord, whom I'd thought was my friend!

"Maybe they could have, Sir Conrad, but 'maybe' isn't doing it! You forget that I am your liege and I'll knight whom I damn well please! As to the others, knight them yourself if you want."

Count Lambert gave me the three traditional blows with the flat of his sword, the last of which nearly knocked me over. Thank God in Heaven that I was still in full armor, for I think the ring around my collar saved my life!

"I dub thee knight. Arise, Sir Piotr," Count Lambert said.

I did so and all the knights rushed over to congratulate me, and welcome me to their order. Yet Sir Conrad was somewhat distant.

"Count Lambert," Sir Conrad said. "What did you mean by saying that I should knight the others myself? I didn't think that a mere knight could do that."

"A mere knight can't. But there is a second matter created by today's doings. Baron Stefan had no heir, nor any relatives at all that I am aware of. Even his mother was an only child with both her parents dead. Therefore, all his property escheats to me. The bunch of you have seen fit to award his arms and armor to Sir Piotr, and I'll not dispute that, but all the rest is now mine.

"I'm minded to give it to you, Sir Conrad, and the baronage that goes with it, but we'll discuss the terms in private."

Sir Conrad was genuinely surprised. "Thank you, my lord. I don't know what else to say."

"Then don't say it. For now, supper will be served soon and I think Sir Piotr would like to tell his parents of his good fortune, or his 'dumb luck,' as you called it. Sir

Piotr, be sure to be back in time for supper. I'll try to work some knightly courtesy into you!"

"Be assured that I shall always be the most courteous of all your knights, my lord!" I said, for I truly meant it. At last, through the oddest of chances, I had attained my goal!

Chapter Twenty-one

▲▲▲▲▲▲▲▲▲▲▲▲▲▲▲▲▲▲▲▲▲▲▲▲▲▲▲

FROM THE DIARY OF CONRAD SCHWARTZ

I don't know which startled me more, Piotr being knighted or my being granted Baron Stefan's lands. That barony was huge and contained some of the best farm-land in Silesia. It was hopelessly backward now, since the baron and his father had refused to allow any of the new seeds or methods to be used, but I could have it in shape in a year or two. With that land, I could easily feed all my workers and wouldn't have to buy food anymore. I could expand the school system into the area and do a lot for the people who were living there. As to the baron's knights and squires, well, if they wanted to swear to me, they'd have to go through the Warrior school!

About Piotr getting knighted, well, I was happy for the kid, but it caused a fistful of problems. For one thing, an army can only hold together if it is essentially fair. If Piotr was knighted, I'd have to knight the rest of his class, probably at the graduation ceremony. I'd expected to have to knight my officers eventually, but these men were at the level of sergeants.

One of my long-term goals was to eliminate the gap that existed between the commoners and the nobility. At the base, it's an ugly thing. All men should be born equal. Now I was going to have to enlarge the nobility, rather than reducing it.

But maybe that was the way to remove the gap! If *everybody* was a knight, or could at least become one by dint of hard work, then there wouldn't be any nobility, at least in the old sense of the word. What's more, it was politically feasible. My knights would be the toughest fighters in the world and no one could doubt their right to the honor. I could knight any man who was good enough, whereas it would be just about impossible to "unknight" someone who was already knighted. He'd fight before he let that happen!

Maybe it would all work out for the best.

"Sir Conrad, just what was your objection to my knighting Piotr," Count Lambert said, once the others had gone.

"It will cause some problems, my lord. If Piotr is a knight, I'll have to knight the others in his class, and those who graduate from the Warrior's school in the future."

"I don't see the need for that, but if they're all as good at fighting as Piotr apparently is, why not? A good fighter ought to be knighted, and if you're right about the upcoming Mongol invasion, we'll need all the fighters we can get!"

"True, my lord, but I don't see how it will be possible to grant them all the privileges that your present knights enjoy. I don't think that they should have the right to peasant girls the way your present knights do."

"What?! Sir Conrad, rank hath its privileges! The right to dalliance with unmarried women is one of the biggest ones, and I won't let it be interfered with! Anyway, there are always plenty of eager wenches about."

"My lord, there are plenty of wenches about because at present not one man in a hundred is a knight. If my plans work out, I'll have every man in this part of the country in my army, at least on a temporary or standby basis. If we are going to knight them at the sergeant level, that will mean that one man in seven will be knighted. They'll be knights for the rest of their lives, whereas wenches stay unmarried for at most two years. If you do the arithmetic, you'll realize that knights will outnumber wenches by at least two to one!"

As matters sat, while a knight had the legal right to

force a young woman to have sex with him, in fact rape in the usual sense almost never happened. There were more volunteers than an ordinary man could handle! But with knights outnumbering unmarried wenches, the situation could get ugly.

"Sir Conrad, I don't feel like doing any arithmetic and I don't believe that even you can have every man in the country under arms. Anyway, if that many men are out there making the beast with two backs, there'll be a new crop of wenches coming out shortly."

"But my lord . . ."

"No 'buts' about it! I tell you that I won't have the privilege removed!"

"Yes, my lord. What would you think if I formed a special order of knighthood, for my own knights only. Then I could have certain rules of the order that would help alleviate the problem."

"Just what rules did you have in mind?"

"Well, for one, I would restrict the rights to wenches to those knights who are already married. That way they could get most of their sex from their wives and the wives would stop most serious abuses from occurring."

"I suppose that I could go along with that. Married men make better fighters, anyway. They're steadier."

"And I don't like this business of getting girls pregnant and then pawning them off on the peasants. I don't think it's fair to the girls. I think that the relationship should be a fairly permanent one, and with the wife's permission."

"That smacks of bigamy, Sir Conrad."

"Maybe so, my lord, but I think it would be far less cruel than the present system."

"Perhaps. Well, I won't bother forbidding it because the Church will do that for me. Set your order up any way you will, Sir Conrad. What I want to talk about is our arrangements on your new barony. I have been buying materials from you to build my new castle, and I am now considerably in your debt. I want that debt canceled."

"Done, my lord."

"And I want all future materials needed for it and for Eagle Nest to be given me free of charge."

"Very well, my lord."

"And that armor you're wearing. You gave the duke and his son each a set and now I even see Piotr wearing it. I want some for myself."

"You shall have it, my lord. Two sets, now that we have it in mass production. We can even make one set gold-plated if you want."

"Gold-plated? What's that?"

"My jeweler and I have come up with a method of putting a thin layer of gold over good steel, my lord. It looks like solid gold but it's as strong as steel. It doesn't rust, either."

"Then I'll take it! Lastly, my old arrangement with Baron Stefan had it that he was to provide me with twenty knights a year, each for three months. You should do the same."

"If you wish, my lord. But I had hoped to use those knights otherwise, at the Warrior's school. What say that in place of that service, I equip each of your knights with a set of plate armor. And in a year, we'll be set up to produce horse armor, and I'll give each of them a set of that as well."

"That seems generous, Sir Conrad. Throw in two sets of this horse armor for me, and one of them in this plate gold, and we'll call it done."

"Then done it is, my lord."

"Good. We'll swear our oaths at sunrise tomorrow. For now, I think supper should be ready."

FROM THE DIARY OF PIOTR KULCZYNSKI

My father was astounded at my good fortune, and soon took me around to all his friends in the town to show me off. My old playmates looked at me with awe, and two of the town bullies, who had once made my young life miserable now fairly groveled before me.

My mother, however, was much less than pleased. She much preferred me as an accountant than as a knight and cried for a long while as though I was going off immediately to die in battle. This got my parents into an argument and I was happy to have the excuse of the count's supper to get out of there. Already I was beginning to realize that these good people were now far below me.

Supper was served formally at the castle, with attractive wenches bringing our food and drink to us. Fortunately, this situation was well covered in the lessons that Lady Richeza taught us, so I committed no gaucherie.

All of the wenches, or more properly, "ladies-in-waiting" were anxious for my attention, all smiling and winking at me. Perhaps I should have expected this, for I had heard many stories of the vast privileges of one of Count Lambert's knights, yet I had somehow never dared dream of myself being the recipient of these feminine favors.

In truth, I didn't know how one went about accepting their offers, for it was a topic that Lady Richeza had never mentioned! But I had heard that when in doubt, it was always wise to ask direction from one's liege lord, so I asked Sir Conrad.

"Well, personally, I've always let the girls decide that for themselves, and so far I've never been disappointed. But if there's one that you particularly favor, you have but to ask her. In fact, you have the right to order any unmarried peasant woman in Count Lambert's domains to your bed, but I wouldn't do that sort of thing too often. It might cause hard feelings. You won't have to do any ordering, because you'll be hard enough pressed just taking care of the volunteers!"

I had of course been studying the serving girls who waited on us, and there was one blond girl who strongly resembled my love Krystyana. When next she came by, I softly said, "Tonight?"

"Thank you, Sir Piotr! I'd love to!"

From that point on, the meal went both too fast and too slow. On the one hand, I was most eager for the favors of my intended bed partner. On the other, well, the truth was that I was a virgin. I had only the foggiest of notions as to what precisely I was to do with the girl. Such was my love for Krystyana that I had never thought to pursue any other woman, and, of course, most of the women that I had met were either friends of hers or were waitresses at my lord's inns, who must needs retain their own virginity or lose their jobs.

I pondered the problem through the three removes of the feast, and decided that honesty was the only answer. I would confess my ignorance to the lady and trust to her courtesy to educate me as to what I should do.

With the meal over, another of the wenches showed me the way to the room given me for my own use. I sat down on a chest, suddenly very nervous. Was I supposed to go for her? Should I have brought a gift? Minutes seemed like hours, but in fact in what was really a very short time, she came.

"My lady, you see, I've never ... I mean ..."

She smiled and said calmly, "I know, my lord. They told me. There's nothing to worry about."

"But what should I do? I mean ..."

"Well, you might start by kissing me. Just put your arms around me ... that's better ... relax! Soften your lips, like this. That's better, *mmmm* ... much better. Now we have to get all this armor off you ..."

She was wonderful, as beautiful in mind as she was in body. Slowly, careful of my easily shattered confidence, she led me through a night of marvelous pleasure and wondrous delight. Her skin was so incredibly smooth and soft and yielding, yet there was a strength about her that seemed equal to my own. She was at once my earnest teacher and my willing slave.

I shall be forever grateful to that lady, yet after she kissed me good-bye in the gray dawn and had left, I realized that I had committed the greatest of wrongs to her. I had never asked her name.

When I joined the others, I was vastly tired, having gotten little sleep the night before. Yet there were oaths to be taken, Baron Conrad's to Count Lambert and my own as a knight to Baron Conrad. Then we had to return to Baron Conrad's lands, for much needed doing. Yet I asked my lord if I might have three days leave, on account of my wound, and he granted it, winking at me, for he knew my thoughts.

"Go to her, boy!"

At Three Walls, I spoke first to Yawalda at the stables, explaining to her my new knighthood and how I meant to use it. She agreed to take care of Krystyana's three children while I went to Krystyana!

Learning that she was in her room, I simply walked inside, delivered her children to Yawalda's waiting arms and barred the door behind us. Krystyana was so shocked by my behavior that it was a moment before she could speak.

"Piotr! What are you doing here? Get out of my room!" my love said to me.

"No, my love. I have a perfect right to be in your room. I am now a true belted knight, made so by Count Lambert himself only yesterday. You are an unmarried wench and not of the nobility. I have the right to take any such unmarried woman who attracts me. You attract me, you always will and you always have. Therefore, you now have the obligation to do as I please."

"Piotr! I am *not* your love and you will get out of here or I will scream!"

"Scream away, my love. It happens that just now I am the only true belted knight at Three Walls. There is no one here that would stop me from doing my duty." I strode forward and put my arms around her.

"*Duty!* Damn you, Piotr Kulczynski! Let go of me!"

"Never my love."

Krystyana let out a scream that could have curled the toenails on a war-horse. Yawalda must have gathered a crowd outside the door, because as soon as Krystyana ran out of breath we heard a round of applause from the hallway.

"Damn you! Damn you all! Is everyone against me?"

"No, my love. Everyone is for you. Every one of your friends want only what is best for you and so do I. And the thing that is best for you is me."

"God in heaven will damn you to hell forever!"

"God will do what he thinks best, and so will I, my love. Come, let's get this apron off you."

And so it went for hours. My courtesy, my gentle firmness and my love for her fell, it seemed, on barren soil. Yet I continued, for there was naught else I could do. I told her of the events of the past year, and she sneered at me. I told her of my fight with Baron Stefan and my victory over that valiant knight, and she called me a brute for harming a wounded man. I told her of my meeting with Count Lambert and of his knighting me, and she said that a pig with a crown was still a pig.

And every time she screamed, the applause from the hall got louder. Indeed, I found out later that there were more than three dozen well-wishers out there, and that they had sent to the kitchens for beer and popcorn to ease them while they waited us out. Even Father Thomas, the priest, had joined them.

By dint of the strength and dexterity I had gained in my warrior training, I eventually managed to get her undressed and abed. This brought on further complaints.

"Your armor is cold and scratchy, you oaf!"

"True, my love, but the fault is at least partly your own, for since my arrival here you have kept my hands so busy that I have not had the chance to doff it."

"You could always leave."

"Never, my love. But could I trust you to stay quiet while I remove it?"

"You might."

"Then I shall do so."

She was still while I took off sword and dagger, gauntlets and greaves, elbow cops and tasses. It was only as I was doffing my helm that she broke for the door. Of course, I was ready for that, caught her below the breasts with one arm and set her again on the bed.

"Be nice," I said.

"You bastard! Sir Conrad would never force a woman!"

"True, my love. But then he wouldn't marry one, either. Further, it's Baron Conrad now and if I'm truly a bastard, my mother would be surprised to hear of it.

Can't you give my suit even a little thoughtful considera-
tion?"

She was still struggling, and I found it best to simply
sit on her while I removed the rest of my armor, padding
and small clothes. She screamed some more and the
crowd cheered some more. Eventually, she desisted. I
threw my weapons to the far corner of the room, for my
love was in a truly fiesty mood and I feared she would be
tempted to sin with them, and in so sinning, add to my
wounds. In truth, my leg wound had opened a bit in the
struggle, but what's a little blood on the sheets on your
first night with a woman? Well, admittedly, it was the
wrong person's blood, but one can't have everything.

It was a long night, and the second in a row without
sleep. Nor was it nearly as pleasant as the one before,
for my love was not working at my pleasure as I was at
hers. Yet in the end I was successful, for in the early
dawn, I looked at my love and she looked back. And
smiled.

And that day we went to the priest and posted our
banns of matrimony.

And then I got some sleep.

Chapter Twenty-two

▲▲▲▲▲▲▲▲▲▲▲▲▲▲▲▲▲▲▲▲▲▲▲▲▲▲▲▲▲▲▲

FROM THE DIARY OF CONRAD SCHWARTZ

The big day had arrived. The first class of the Warrior's school was about to graduate. The three-dozen men would be the training instructors who would forge the army that would beat the Mongol horde, God willing.

Eleven months ago, there had been twelve dozen of them. Since that time, I had put them through the roughest program of basic training that I could imagine. Now two dozen of that original number were dead, killed on the training ground and on the obstacle course. Others were crippled for life and at least six men had been driven insane. But the core of the army was ready!

I'd invited a few dignitaries to observe the last day of training and the graduation ceremonies. Count Lambert, my liege lord, was there. His liege, Duke Henryk the Bearded, could not make it, but he had sent his son, Prince Henryk the Pious, to observe for him. Abbot Ignacy of the Franciscan monastery in Cracow had come at my invitation, as had some of his monks, including Friar Roman. Sir Miesko and Lady Richeza were of course in attendance, as were a few dozen of Count Lambert's other knights, mostly members of the more progressive faction.

There were a thousand others besides, because for this day only, the school was thrown open to the public. Many were there from Three Walls because word was out that all the men working for me would be going through the school, and they wanted to see what was in store for them.

And about four dozen young ladies from Count Lambert's cloth factory came, having heard that there would soon be three dozen new knights and most of them bachelors. It seemed that everyone but the men themselves knew that they would be knighted, but that's the way things usually go. I wanted to keep it from them so that they would get a greater emotional impact from the graduation ceremonies.

At dawn, a bugle sounded reveille and in a few minutes the men fell in on the concrete parade ground. A priest said a very short mass, without a sermon, and the band played Copland's "Fanfare for the Common Man." Then the thirty-six men, the four knights that had trained them and I recited the Warrior's Oath and the Warrior's Code before the assembled guests.

I announced the orders of the day myself.

"Gentlemen," I said, and got some smiles. Usually I was much less polite. "This will be your last day of training. You notice that we have visitors today. They are here to observe our training methods. Please go about the routines in the normal manner and as though no one was watching you, since I'd hate to have to wash you out at this point in the game. We'll make the morning run in full armor. After breakfast, we'll have an hour of pike-training and an hour of swords. After dinner there will be an hour of wagon-and-gunnery practice.

"You will then have the rest of the afternoon off, but be sure to go to Confession. You'll have to be in a state of grace to make it through this evening's ceremony. You see, gentlemen, tonight you are going to walk on fire. After that we will be up all night long, performing a vigil, so get some rest this afternoon. Be back here in a quarter hour in full armor. Fall out!"

That was more time than they usually got, our "hour" being twice as long as the modern one, but I wanted our visitors to have time to string themselves out along the obstacle course.

Count Lambert came up and said, "It's hard to believe that those men are the same ruffians I sent you a year ago."

"Yes, my lord, but it's true."

"That oath was touching," Prince Henryk said, "but what does this standing in neat lines have to do with defeating the Mongols."

"That's difficult to explain, my lord. It's all part of a program that makes these men the finest foot soldiers in the world. I've invited you here today to show you what these men can do. For now, let's mount up and find a good spot on the obstacle course."

I'd arranged for a dozen guides to take the bulk of the visitors around, but I wanted to escort the VIPs myself. It was not only necessary to build the finest army in the world, it was also necessary for the powers that be to know that it was as good as I said it was.

We stopped at the first major obstacle, a huge log suspended fifteen stories up between two big denuded pine trees. Four ropes went from the ground, up and over the log and then back down to the ground.

"They're not going to climb that thing, are they?" Count Lambert asked, proudly wearing his new gold armor.

"They'll climb it in full armor using their arms only, my lord. They'll go over the top and then back down the other side," I said.

"Have you done this yourself?" Prince Henryk asked.

"Of course, my lord. I've often led them through the course."

"I wonder if I could do that," Count Lambert said.

"I'm sure you could, my lord, if you had taken this training. But for today, I must ask you to observe only, and not participate."

"That verges on impertinence!" Count Lambert said.

"Perhaps, my lord, but we all know your abilities. This demonstration is to show you what the men can do."

Count Lambert started to make further objection, but Prince Henryk put his hand on the count's armored forearm.

"It shall be as you say, Baron Conrad," the prince said, and that ended the matter.

The troops came running in step up the trail, their armor clanging loudly. They were four files wide and ten ranks long, and singing the army song.

"That song sounds familiar," Prince Henryk said.

"The tune is an old Russian folk song called 'Meadowlands,' my lord. The words are by an English poet named Rudyard Kipling. I translated them and fit the two together."

The first rank went immediately to the four front ropes and went quickly up, their arms moving in unison and their legs hanging stiff below them. The troops behind did jumping jacks until the first four were halfway up, at which time the next four men started up as the others continued exercising.

"One of the rules of the course is that the men never stop moving. When they are waiting their turn, or waiting for the others to finish, they exercise in place," I said.

Abbot Ignacy made the sign of the cross as they scaled the dizzying height.

"That man on the left, near the top," Prince Henryk said. "That's Sir Vladimir, isn't it?"

"Yes, my lord. He and the three Banki brothers beside him have been largely responsible for the training."

"And that little one at the end who's jumping up and down, is that your accountant, Piotr Kulczynski?"

"Yes, my lord, only he isn't my accountant any longer. Once his training is over, I have another job for him."

"And what might that be?"

"I'm setting up a section of mapmakers, my lord, and Piotr will head it. By the time the Mongols invade, we'll have accurate maps of all of southern Poland."

"That will be of great use to my pilots!" Count Lambert said. "If I can ever get you to get to work on that engine you promised."

"I promised to work on an aircraft engine once your

people built a two-man glider that could stay up for hours, my lord."

"Then you'd best be thinking about it, because we're close, Baron Conrad, damn close!"

"Very good, my lord. For now, we'd best go to the next obstacle." I'd gone along with helping out with Eagle Nest, Count Lambert's flying school, because it looked to be a good way to set up an engineering institute at Count Lambert's expense. I never for a minute believed that those kids could build functioning aircraft in under twenty years. They were starting to build some decent gliders, though.

We got to an almost vertical cliff face fully thirty stories high only slightly ahead of the troops, who came clanking up behind us, still running in step. The first four started climbing immediately while the others did pushups.

"They move up like ants after a jar of honey!" Count Lambert said.

"Very deadly ants, my lord."

"But how is such a thing possible?" Abbot Ignacy asked.

"Training, Father, plus the fact that they have climbed this particular cliff so often that they know where most of the handholds are."

Soon, all of the men were on the cliff face and the front rank was nearing the top. Off to the right, a long slack rope went from a pole on the top of the cliff to another four hundred yards away on the ground. The arrangement was such that it was necessary to jump from the cliff in order to catch the rope. The first man up, Sir Vladimir, I was pleased to note, ran immediately toward the rope and flung himself off the edge as the crowd gasped in horror. But he caught the rope and slid down to the ground to be followed by the others.

"Doesn't that burn their hands?" Prince Henryk asked.

"No, my lord. If you'll notice, they're not holding it with their hands, but have caught the rope with the cuffs of their gauntlets. The rope is waxed and things don't get too warm."

"But what if they should slip and fall?"

"They generally die, my lord."

And so it went, as the men swung on ropes, ran across long bridges that were as narrow as your arm, climbed log piles, walked tightropes and everything else nasty that I could think up.

"When they're in full armor, we usually bypass the swimming events, since it takes a few days to dry out their gambezons," I said. "But rest assured that each of these men can swim a half mile in full armor—and six miles naked."

Despite the fact that we were on horseback, the men beat us back to the mess hall. The VIPs were invited inside and the rest of the crowd was fed outside.

Each of the men was doing in a breakfast that started with six eggs, a loaf of bread, and a slab of ham as thick as your finger, and went on from there. My own meal was almost as big.

"You certainly feed them well," Abbot Ignacy said.

"True, Father, but we burn it off them quickly enough. You won't find much fat on any of these men."

Pike practice came next, and the VIPs were treated to being charged by forty pikemen. At the last possible instant, Sir Vladimir shouted "Halt!" and they stopped with the sharp points a finger's breadth from our chests. Seeing that I didn't move, neither Count Lambert nor Prince Henryk flinched, but most of the others had moved back quickly.

"My lords, I'm sure that you felt the emotional impact of that charge. I ask you to imagine what it would be like if six thousand men charged you in that manner."

"Emotional impact? I was more worried about the physical one!" Count Lambert said.

"And I, too," Prince Henryk said. "But I see your point. That an enemy can be defeated without even touching him."

"That would be ideal, my lord. Once the enemy has broken, you usually lose very few men in the mop-up."

"The mop-up! You have a good turn for words, Baron Conrad," Count Lambert said.

Then the men were put to work on the dummies. These were full-weight straw figures of men on horseback, with a real lance held in place. They rolled down a long ramp and once they got to the level section they were going as fast as a horse can charge. In single practice, the object was to skewer the horse with a grounded pike without being run over or hit by the lance. When a single dummy was attacking a group of men, only the men in the center went for the horse. The others went after the rider.

"That's dastardly!" Prince Henryk said.

"What is, my lord?"

"They're deliberately trying to kill the horse!"

"Yes, my lord."

"That's unfair!"

"True, my lord. But was a horseman ever known to be *fair* with a footman?"

"Fair to a footman? I doubt if it ever crossed anyone's mind."

"Then why should a footman fight 'fair' with a horseman? If the horseman wanted to fight fair, he would get off his horse, at which time there would be no point in harming the animal. These men are not trained to fight fair, my lord, they're trained to win!"

"Well, I don't like it," Prince Henryk said.

"Will you like it when the Mongols start butchering your women and children, my lord?"

"Be damned, Baron Conrad."

"I think I will be, my lord."

Abbot Ignacy made the sign of the cross.

Count Lambert was worried about this altercation between his greatest vassal and his future liege lord, and tried to change the subject.

"Baron Conrad, this is all fine and well when practicing on dummies, but what of the real thing?"

"We've done it, my lord, at least to the extent of using live horses. We've never tried going for the rider of such a horse, for lack of a volunteer, but I myself have ridden an old horse into a mass of pikers."

"What happened?"

"I came down hard, my lord."

"And your horse?" Prince Henryk said.

"Dead, of course."

"You killed a dumb animal?" Prince Henryk asked.

"My lord, we *eat* dumb animals. I have lost two dozen men in the course of this training. What difference does a few animals make? This afternoon we'll be shooting four pigs to show you what our guns can do."

"At least you'll eat the pigs."

"My lord, we ate the dead horse, too."

The rest of the day went like that, half awestruck praise and half condemnation because I had no intention of losing men in order to conform with their ideas of a fair fight. Dammit, there *is* no such thing as a fair fight! You are either out there to kill the bastard or you shouldn't be fighting at all!

On the other hand, the reaction of the commoners was uniformly positive. They *liked* the idea of their enemies being dead and their own families being alive. But I couldn't shake the feeling that I wasn't going to get much help from the conventional knights. We were going to have to beat the Mongols on our own.

After the abbreviated day of training, the troops went back to the barracks to rest and we threw an afternoon party for our guests, with music and plenty of food, beer, and mead. The commoners were all buzzing about what they'd seen, and the girls from the cloth factory were literally jumping up and down, some of them, but the nobility was considerably more subdued.

Those knights who had come were mostly of the more progressive faction of Count Lambert's knights, and if *they* had reservations about what I was doing, I hated to think about the more reactionary knights. I suppose that I should have expected their reaction, but I really hadn't.

Most of them were eager to plant the new seeds and buy or make the new farm machinery. Quite a few had installed indoor plumbing in their manors, and many were setting up light industrial plants, with our help, to keep their peasants busy during the off-seasons. But they seemed to look on the army as a threat to their whole existence. By their lights, they were better than the commoners and had special privileges because they protected the land. It didn't take much in the way of brains for them to realize that my warriors were better fighters than they were. They felt they were being undercut, and I suppose they were.

I began to realize that the open house was a big mistake. I knew I'd never do it again, at least not with the nobility there, but there was nothing I could do now but brazen it out.

Chapter Twenty-three

^^^^^^^^^^^^^^^^^^^^^^^^^^^^^^^^^^

IT WAS getting dark when I called the crowd together and led them to a bowl in the hills that formed sort of an amphitheater. Once they were settled in, the troops marched up, barefoot and wearing tan linen fatigues and winter cloaks. An area in front, twelve yards to the side, was piled a yard deep with kindling wood, all carefully selected to be dry wood and free of knots.

There was a small brick wall, about two yards square, in front of it, with a few torches around. I stepped up to the front.

"You have seen these men traverse various obstacles in full armor. You have seen them prove their proficiency with various weapons, and today you have seen the first public demonstration of our guns. These men have the finest arms and armor in the world, but weapons are unimportant compared to the men wielding them. A true warrior is always deadly, even when he is alone and naked.

"Sir Vladimir, a demonstration, please."

Sir Vladimir was our best man at empty-handed fighting, much better than I was. Together, we had put together a decent system of self-defense, based on what little I knew about karate and a lot of trial-and-error. He put on a good demonstration, shouting as he smashed up boards and bricks with his bare hands and feet. Of course, the bricks maybe weren't baked all that well and the boards were light pine that splits easily along the grain, but the crowd *ooh*ed and *aah*ed at all the proper times.

"It is said that a true warrior can walk through walls, and in a sense, that's true. We have here a solid brick wall. Perhaps many of you looked at it as you came in," I said. "Sir Vladimir, walk through that wall."

Perhaps some of them expected him to do something magical, but what he did was give it a side thrust kick and it smashed nicely. Then he walked through the rubble. Okay, that wall had only been laid the day before and the mortar wasn't well set. Indeed, the mortar had been made with a dozen parts of sand to only one part of lime, but I hadn't made any promises.

"Any of these men could have done that. It's just that since we only had the one wall, and since Sir Vladimir is in charge of this installation, well, rank hath its privileges."

That got a small titter out of the crowd.

"A warrior can also walk through fire. More than that, he can walk over a bed of glowing coals, which as you know is much hotter. They are going to walk through this." I pointed at the big mat of wood. On cue, Sir Vladimir and the Banki brothers took the four torches to the four corners of the wood pile and simultaneously lit it afire. It went up with a huge *whoosh*! In moments, the fire was five stories high. The torches were thrown into the fire.

"There was nothing magic about that," I said. "We put some oil under the wood along with some of the black powder that we use in the guns. It also lights fires. I just wanted it all to start at once so that the whole fire would be burning evenly."

I then invited my noble guests to stand near the fire and had the cooks bring out some long skewers with thin slices of meat threaded on them. As the fire burned down to coals, the cooks set the meat over the fire and it soon broiled. This was offered to the nobles and what was left was given to the commoners, to show everybody that it really was hot. Mainly, it gave us something to do while the fire burned down to coals. During this time, there was no other light in the valley but the fire, and the human eye can acclimatize without a person's noticing it. Actually, the coals were becoming quite dim.

I asked the nobles to step back and we marched the troops up so that a dozen men were lined up in back and on each side of the fire. Sir Vladimir and the other instructors were in front of it, along with me. A few workers with long-handled rakes stirred the coals evenly, incidentally kicking up some spectacular sparks.

"You will observe that I am barefoot, as are all of my men. I'll be doing this first," I said. "As my liege lord Count Lambert is fond of proving, a leader must be able to do everything that his men can do. But while a warrior can walk through fire, often his clothes cannot."

I was wearing the same simple linen tunic and pants that my men were. I took off the tunic and threw it onto the bed of coals. It smoldered for a moment and then burst into a satisfying flame. Then I stripped off my pants and set them aside. I stood naked in front of the crowd. This was no big thing, because these people had never heard of a nudity tabu. Then I faced the fire.

Rationally, I was sure that this was safe.

It is the *amount* of heat that burns you, not just the temperature of the fire. If you touch a metal pot on a hot oven, you will be burned. If you merely put your hand in the air of a hot oven, you will not be hurt. The air in the oven is just as hot as the pot in it. Hotter, maybe, since the air heated the pot up. But air is a very poor conductor of heat compared to metal, and not enough heat gets into your hand to burn it. Charcoal is light, porous stuff, and quite a good insulator. Even when it's glowing hot, it takes a while to get enough heat into you to do any damage. For a few seconds, it won't hurt you at all. Of course, this doesn't apply to burning knots and hot rocks, but I had been as careful as possible to exclude such things. I hoped.

But all that was theory, and I'd never done it. I could feel the heat of those coals roasting my chest, but there was nothing for it.

"For God and Poland!" I cried and marched into the coals at a normal military quick-step. I was through in a few seconds, and I'd hardly felt a thing, but the cool, wet grass at the edge of the fire was refreshing.

When the crowd was finished *ooh*ing at me, I asked the instructors if they were in a state of grace. They all nodded yes.

"Then strip, but please don't throw your tunics into the fire. One demonstration was enough."

This sent a titter through the crowd. I was known to be a cheapskate about some things. When the men were ready, I nodded to them and they shouted the same war cry that I had. Originally, it was Sir Vladimir's, but I stole from everywhere.

"Forward, march!" And they did. And they did it without knowing the scientific reason making it safe to do. They went because they were warriors and their commander had ordered it.

FROM THE DIARY OF PIOTR KULCZYNSKI

The demonstrations that day were nothing much out of the ordinary. Indeed, we had run the obstacle course slower than usual, to give the crowd a chance to keep up with us. We had all practiced empty-handed fighting and had seen Sir Vladimir practicing his demonstration, so that was nothing special, either.

What *was* special was that I saw my love Krystyana in the crowd. She smiled and waved at me and though I did not dare to wave back, I risked a smile and a nod. How wonderful it was to show my prowess to my future bride!

But this walking on fire business was new, and we were all shocked by it. Shocked and frightened, for Baron Conrad had said that we would be doing it ourselves and never had he spoken an untruth to any of us.

We stood aghast as he walked naked through the burning coals. He walked calmly, even though that fire was hot enough to broil meat. Almost magically, you could see his footprints as he passed, black against the fiery red!

Then our instructors did it as well, with not a hint of

fear or hesitation, and we knew we were next!

"I believe in God, the Father Almighty, Creator of Heaven and Earth, and..." I heard the man beside me praying, trying not to move his lips or change his expression. In my mind, I prayed along with him.

My dozen was called to go first, and although we were all frightened, not one of us dared to flinch. We folded our clothes, gave our war cry and stepped as boldly as we could into what looked like certain death.

Yet God's hand was on us, and we were saved from the fire. Myself, I think it must have been that He cooled the fire below our feet, for after I had crossed and turned to face the fire again, I could see my own darkened footprints along with the others.

It was only with great difficulty that I did not fall to my knees and pray.

FROM THE DIARY OF CONRAD SCHWARTZ

I went through the same routine with the troops on each of the three sides of the fire and not a single man of them showed any fear at all. The crowd was awestruck, and so were the men who had just walked on fire.

Out of the corner of my eye, I saw Count Lambert doffing his cloak and looking determinedly at the bed of coals.

"My lord Count Lambert, are you truly in a state of grace? Have you said Confession and had Communion in the last few hours?"

"No, but—"

"Then I must forbid you to do this, for without God's help, you would surely be going to your death!"

"You *forbid* your own liege?"

"I am sworn to protect you, my liege."

This might have gotten nasty. If Count Lambert walked those coals, without having gone through the training school, it would take away much of the mystique that I was trying to build. Fortunately, Prince Henryk came to my rescue and restrained him. I addressed the crowd.

"That concludes the public portion of this ceremony. These men and I will be standing vigil tonight, and that is a private thing. My servants will escort you back to the barracks area, and provisions have been made for your comfort, or at least the best that we can do. The training school has already been expanded to take on the next, much larger class and there should be room for everyone."

I bowed and started to dress when Abbot Ignacy came to me.

"My son, that was an amazing demonstration. It reminded me of Shadrack in the furnace."

"Father, remember how I once asked you how it was possible for you to walk barefoot through the snow, and you told me that when your heart was truly pure, you really did have the strength of ten?" I asked.

"That was on the first day that we met. I remember it quite well. Perhaps fire has much in common with ice, my son. But you seem as troubled now as you were then. Would you allow me to stand this vigil with you?"

There was no way that I could refuse Abbot Ignacy, my confessor.

"Of course, Father."

"I too would like to stand this vigil," Prince Henryk said.

"As you wish, my lord. I will have some heavy cloaks sent up for the two of you."

Count Lambert and the other guests were already going back, so with the prince and the abbot, we went up to the hills.

It was near the summer solstice, and at these latitudes, the night is short. By the time we got to the ridge I had picked out, the night was more than half over. It was moonless and clear, and the stars were radiant. A good night for a vigil.

So far, the weather had been perfect for the graduation ceremony, but for a while I was worried that the valley below us would not be foggy enough for the optical effect that I wanted. At last it filled with fog while we were still in clear air. Perfect.

We spent the remainder of the night sitting or kneeling quietly on the dew-wet grass, our cloaks wrapped around us, each with his own private thoughts and prayers. As we waited, the full weight of my hypocrisy lowered onto me. The men about me all believed in me, had faith in me and what I was doing. In return, I was giving them lies and scientific stage tricks, and it rode heavy on my soul. Yet I had to make them believe that they were invincible, that they were capable of taking on the most disciplined, tough and deadly army the world had ever seen. Taking it on and beating it!

The Mongols had fifty years of uninterrupted victories behind them. They had regularly fought and beaten armies many times their size. They knew that their combination of tactics, strategy and speed had always won and would win again. They had conquered half the known world, more land and more people than Caesar, Alexander, and Napoleon put together.

One of their main weapons was terror. By building pyramids of the skulls of the people they murdered, by killing every man, woman, child, animal, and bird in the cities they hit, they created such a fear that it was said that men allowed themselves to be killed rather than annoy their own butchers! Stories circulated of whole companies of soldiers being killed by a single Mongol, dying without lifting a finger to help themselves.

My vassal Zoltan Varanian had spoken to a merchant who was stopped, along with the rest of his small caravan, by a single Mongol soldier. The Mongol had ordered all fourteen men in the caravan to dismount. Fearful of angering him, they immediately complied. He then ordered them to line up before him, to get on their knees and bow to him, and again they did as he ordered. Then he drew his sword and beheaded the first man in line. The other merchants made no move, and the Mongol proceeded to take the heads off three more men, for no reason except perhaps to practice his sword swing.

"This is crazy!" the narrator of the tale had said to his fellow merchants, "We outnumber him! We have weapons! No matter how good he is, he can't kill us all!"

"Quiet!" the man next to him said. "Do you want to make him mad?"

Yet another merchant was beheaded, and the narrator said, "Fools! He is already killing us! What more can he do?"

Shouting the name of Allah, he drew his sword and attacked the Mongol. They traded a dozen blows before the other merchants got their wits back. Seeing that it was an even fight and that the Mongol was not invincible, the other merchants drew their swords and joined in the affray. The Mongol was soon dead. Then they hastily buried the bodies of the dead along with the Mongol pony and all its equipage. And they fled from the lands of the Khan. Yet the fact remains that thirteen out of the fourteen armed men would have preferred to die rather than disobey the single murderer who was butchering them.

How do you defeat that kind of terror? The only way I could imagine was to build a counter mystique to fight it. And to do that, I had to lie to and hoodwink the very men who trusted me most, and to dirty my immortal soul in the process. I think that it never will be clean again. The thing had to be done, but in doing it, I have earned my place in Hell!

Dawn came up and with the sunrise, we recited our sunrise service, with the prince and the abbot standing silent.

I then arranged the men along the ridge where their shadows would soon be cast on the fog below us. I asked them to pray to God, to ask Him for some sign that what we were doing was right and just. We waited silently.

FROM THE DIARY OF PIOTR KULCZYNSKI

I think that I have never prayed as I prayed that night. God's hand had been upon me as I walked through the fire and it felt as though It stayed there through the night. I think that I was not alone in this, for many about me were on their knees, even my lord Conrad. It was hard to tell in the starlight, but I think I saw tears run down those noble cheeks.

The dawn came and we recited our vows. Then we were bid to continue our vigil, this time lined up and facing the foggy valley below. We prayed for a sign from God, to know that he blessed our efforts.

The sun rose slowly at our backs and the shadows came toward us from the hill beyond. Looking down, I saw my own shadow among the others on the fog below. But mine was different from the others.

Mine was surrounded by a holy halo! I stared, unable to believe what my eyes were seeing. I raised my hand and waved it to prove to myself that it was my own head that was so mystically adorned, and it was true!

Beyond all possible doubt, I had been personally, individually and radiantly blessed by God!

FROM THE DIARY OF CONRAD SCHWARTZ

Conditions were right. I looked down and saw beams of light radiating from the shadow of my own head. I waited a bit to be sure that the others had time to discover their own halos.

"Yes, brothers, it is real," I said. "Each of you has been given a halo that only you can see. When Moses went to the mountain and was given by God the Ten Commandments, he saw 'horns of light' coming from his head. What was given to him then is given to you now. Each of you has been blessed by God. Each of you has been made radiant. Our mission and our duty is clear. As a band of brothers, we must train the army that will rid God's world of the plague of Mongols that infests it.

"Will you stand with me, brothers? Will you join me in this great work? Shall we form the Invincible Order of Radiant Knights to accomplish this God-given task?"

They were stunned, shocked. Miracles were something that happened to someone else, long ago and far away. But these men had seen themselves walk through fire unharmed, and now they saw halos about their own heads.

Sir Vladimir was the first to recover.

"I will stand by you, my lord," he said, taking his place at my left side.

"And I," said Sir Piotr, his face streaked with tears.

All the others were soon with us, and there wasn't a dry eye among us, for even I was overwhelmed by the emotion of this thing that I myself had conjured up.

"Then so it shall be, brothers," I said. "On this holy ground, we shall form our order, and I shall knight you all on this spot."

I knighted the thirty-five students who had not been knighted before, and then Sir Piotr came up.

"My lord, I think it would be fitting if you knighted me this day."

"Perhaps it would be, Sir Piotr." I performed the simple ceremony on him. Sir Vladimir and the Banki brothers came up as well, with the same request. They, too, were reknighted.

Prince Henryk was standing back, undecided. Then suddenly he was on his knees before me.

"Is it possible, Baron Conrad? Am I worthy to join your order?" he asked as the tears streaked his face.

"Worthy, my lord? But it is I who serve you!"

"In status, yes, and that may not change. But you have been blessed by God, and this day so have I. If you think me worthy, I too would join your order, though my duties will never permit me to go through your school. Tell me, am I worthy?"

"My lord, you are the most worthy man I have ever met," I said, and I meant it. And so it was that I knighted my own prince.

"Would that I could join you, too," said Abbot Ignacy, "but my duties and my oath to the Church must forbid it. Yet I would do all in my power to aid you in God's work."

"This army will need chaplains, Father. Ordained priests who would go through our school, fight at our sides and pray for our souls. If you wished, you could find us such men."

"I will do so, my son and my lord. Somehow, I will do so."

Chapter Twenty-four

WE WERE silent as we headed back, but as we got to the barracks, I called them together and said, "Brothers, our order need not always be a solemn one. Tonight, we will be celebrating your graduation and quite a number of young ladies have accepted my invitation to help us do it. Get some rest now, and fall back in at six o'clock in full-dress uniform. Dismissed!"

We only had a few spare dress uniforms, but one of them was the right size to fit the prince, and he generally wore one from that time on, as did I. These were a lot like the uniform worn by the boys at Eagle Nest, except that the colors were reversed. The boys wore white pants and shirt, with a red jacket; we wore red pants and shirt with a white jacket. The brass buttons and epaulets were the same.

At six, I said, "Brothers! There are a few matters of business to be attended to before we can join the ladies.

"You have each almost a year's back pay coming. Those of you who were students were paid at a rate of a penny a day, so you will each draw over three hundred pence. As knights, your pay from this day on will be eight pence a day, paid monthly. The instructors will draw their back pay at this rate. From this day on, the Banki brothers will be promoted to knight bannerett, at sixteen pence per day, and Sir Vladimir will be your captain at thirty-two.

"After the festivities, you will have three weeks leave. I've arranged for each of you to have a horse during your vacation. Please take good care of it. Go home and enjoy yourselves! And when you come back, try to bring a dozen new recruits with you! We'll need them for the next class.

"One last item! You are all invited to Sir Piotr's wedding tomorrow at Okoitz, so don't get *too* drunk tonight! Fall out!"

It was a good party, and I had the feeling that most of my new knights would be married in the near future, or they would if the girls had anything to say about it, and they generally do.

FROM THE DIARY OF PIOTR KULCZYNSKI

My love was at my side as the party got under way. I was introducing her to my classmates and in the process saying good-bye to them. Baron Conrad was assigning me to head up a section of mapmakers while they would be back here training new troops. We would meet again, but not soon and not often. It was hard, for we had gone through Hell and Heaven together, and in the doing of it, we had become close.

I had attended to half of them when a surprise occurred. Coming toward us through the crowd was the lady I had had on the night of my knighting! Suddenly, I felt very awkward, for how does one introduce a lady that one has taken in pleasure to another lady that one is about to marry? Worse yet, I *couldn't* introduce them, for I still did not know the first lady's name!

Yet again, she saved me, for she was a gem of courtesy.

"Piotr Kulczynski, surely you remember little Mary Ponanski that used to live four doors from your father in Okoitz!"

So at last I knew her name! "Of course I remember the little girl that we used to chase away from the big boys' games! But can it be that that skinny little girl is the charming lady I see before me? Oh ho! A duckling has turned into a swan! But then you must know Krystyana, my bride to be," I said, introducing them.

We chatted for a while and Mary pouted a bit because she had recognized me and I had not returned the favor.

"But you are not fair," I said. "Girls change more than boys do, and more pleasantly. But why are you wasting your time with someone who is almost an old married man, when there are so many eligible young knights around?"

"To find out which one I should be chasing, of course! You know all of these men, Piotr. Tell me, which one is the best?"

"The best? Well, that's a complicated question! If you mean 'Who is the best mathematician?' you are out of luck, because that's me and I'm already taken. If you mean 'Who has the best taste in women?' well, that's me, too, since I'm getting Krystyana and they are not! But the best man for you? Let me think. Maybe August Poinowski over there. What do you think, Krystyana? Is August handsome enough for our little Mary? I can testify to his character, but it takes a woman to tell if he is good to look at."

My love said that he was a fine-looking man, so we made the introductions. And you know? Not three weeks went by before Mary and August posted banns to marry in the church!

It was in this manner that I returned to Mary Ponanski the great favor that she had done for me!

FROM THE DIARY OF CONRAD SCHWARTZ

Sir Piotr's wedding was well attended, and the weather was so fine that they held the reception outside. While talking to Count Lambert, he suggested that I look up at the sky. I looked. A large, two-place sailplane was circling overhead. The pilot must have found a good thermal above the town, because he kept on circling for hours. So now, in addition to everything else, I had to build an aircraft engine!

FROM THE DIARY OF PIOTR KULCZYNSKI

And so it was that on a beautiful spring day in the year 1237 I married my love Krystyana, and we lived happily ever after, or reasonably so.

Interlude Four

THE TAPE wound to a stop.

"Good God, what a training program!" I said. "Conrad should have been a practical psychologist instead of being an engineer! And that graduation ceremony! I can't help wondering why armies in the twentieth century didn't use the same techniques."

"It wouldn't have worked," Tom said. "You must bear in mind that Conrad was working with some very uneducated and naive troops. With a modern education, it takes a pretty weak mind to fall for things like that firewalking stunt. A good modern soldier is a very well educated and superbly well-trained specialist. You don't want stupid troops, not when they have to operate some remarkably sophisticated equipment. But given his situation, cousin Conrad did the right thing. I'm proud of the boy."

"Another thing is that weights and measures system he came up with. I got to working it out during some of the slow parts on the tape."

"Yeah, I saw you playing with the calculator. Did it myself, the first time I sat through the thing."

"Well, it's flat amazing how many numbers work out right! The way his mile works out at 1728 of his yards, and his pound comes out at one 1728th of a ton, and even his volt and his pint come out right! All at accuracies better than could be measured with medieval instruments! That's almost too many 'gosh numbers' to believe."

"Well, it wasn't all luck. Conrad was using a base

twelve numbering system. It's one of the three natural systems, along with base eight and base sixteen. The ancient Indo-Europeans, our ancestors, used that same base twelve system for many thousands of years, and used it for their own systems of measurements, until some dull person started to count on his fingers and invented the decimal system in the process. A lot of what Conrad was doing was just setting things back to the old, sensible way of doing things.

"But enough of this. Supper is getting cold, and the girls tell me that they have something special planned for tonight's entertainment. Let's close it up!"

Weights and Measures

**ARMY ARITHMETIC IS BASED ON A
DUODECIMAL SYSTEM,
I.E., BASE 12.
ALL ARMY WEIGHTS AND MEASURES
ARE BASE 12.
CONVENTIONAL UNITS ARE IN BASE 10.**

TIME

ARMY UNIT	CONVENTIONAL UNIT	NOTES
Day	Day	Local time starts at daybreak, zero being when the sun is a half circle on the horizon. Navigation time is set with the third hour happening at high noon at Three Walls.
Hour	120 minutes	
Dozminute	10 minutes	
Minute	50 seconds	
Twelminute	4.167 seconds	If the clock at the right were set to navigational time, the time would be 6:23:33 A.M.
Dozsecond	.347 seconds	
Second	.0289 seconds	
Twelsecond	2.41 milliseconds	

Weights and Measures

ARMY CLOCK

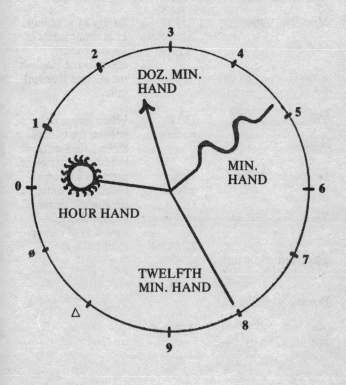

THE TIME IS:
Ø248

Weights and Measures

DISTANCE

ARMY UNIT	ENGLISH EQUIV.	METRIC EQUIV.	NOTES
Mile	mile	1.61 kilometers	Purely by accident, 1728 army yards is almost exactly equal to the English (or ancient Roman) mile.
Twelmile	440 ft.	134.0 meters	When larger or smaller units than those listed were required, a series of prefixes was used identical to those of the metric system, except that kilo- meant 1728 rather than 1000, etc.
Dozyard	36.7 ft.	11.2 meters	
Yard	36.7 in.	.931 meter	
		7.76 cm.	
Twelyard	3.06 in.		
		6.47 mm.	
Dozmil	0.255 in.		
		.539 mm.	
Mil	0.0212 in.		

Weights and Measures

AREA

ARMY UNIT	ENGLISH EQUIV.	METRIC EQUIV.	NOTES
Sq. Mile	Sq. mile	2.59 sq. km.	
Sq. Twelmile	4.44 acres	1.80 hectares	
Sq. Dozyard	1344 sq. ft.	124.9 sq. meters	Rarely used.
Sq. Yard	9.34 sq. ft.	.867 sq. meters	
Sq. Twelyard	9.34 sq. in.	60.2 sq. cm.	
Sq. Dozmil	.065 sq. in.	.418 sq. cm.	
Sq. Mil	.0005 sq. in.	.290 sq. mm.	

WEIGHTS

ARMY UNIT	ENGLISH EQUIV.	METRIC EQUIC	NOTES
Ton	1780.9 pounds	807.8 kg.	The "ton" is a cubic yard of cold (4°C.) water.
Twelton	148.4 pounds	67.3 kg.	It should be noted that these "weights" are units of mass (as in the metric system) and not units of force (as in the English system). It should also be noted that everyone except scientists and engineers uses units of force and mass interchangeably, and that even the above two groups confuse them more often than not.
Dozpound	12.37 pounds	5.61 kg.	
Pound	1.031 pounds	.467 kg.	
Twelpound	1.37 ounces	38.96 grams	
Dozcarat	0.115 ounces	3.25 grams	
Carat	0.0095 ounces	0.2705 grams	

Weights and Measures

VOLUMES

ARMY UNIT	ENGLISH EQUIV.	METRIC EQUIV.
Volton	1.057 cu. yd.	.808 cu. meters
Twelvolton	17.78 gallons	67.32 liters
Dozpint	1.48 gallons	5.61 liters
Pint	.988 pint	.467 liters
Twelpint	1.317 fl. oz.	38.96 cu. cm.
Dozdram	.1098 fl. oz.	3.25 cu. cm.
Dram	.0091 fl. oz.	.271 cu. cm.

Weights and Measures

ANGULAR MEASUREMENT

ARMY UNIT	CONVENTIONAL UNIT	NOTES
Angday	360°	Angular measurements are based on the army-clock shown on the "time" chart. Angles are read clockwise from the horizontal as opposed to the conventional counter clockwise.
Anghour	30°	
Angdozmin	2.5°	
Angmin	12.5 min.	
Angtwelmin	1.04 min.	

In practice, the names of angular units are rarely used. An army engineer would read an angle of 45 degrees as "ang one six oh oh".

NAVIGATION

Army navigators state their longitude in accordance with the time of day (Three Walls time) that the sun is at high noon. The longitude of Three Walls is therefore 3000.

Latitude is also based on the army clock. The latitude of the equator is 6000. The south pole is at 3000; the north pole at 9000. The left side of the clock is not used.

South, of course, is at the top of an army map.

Weights and Measures

TEMPERATURE

The army thermometer was an absolute scale, like the modern kelvin and rankine scales. Zero was at absolute zero, 459.67 degrees below zero fahrenheit. The melting point of water was set at 1000 (base 12, or 1728 base 10). Thus, the degree used was about a quarter of the size of the fahrenheit degree and a sixth that of the celsius degree. In practice, though, most people ignored the thousand numbers it took to get to the freezing point of water and would call a pleasant room temperature "eleventy one degrees."

Listed below are some commonly encountered temperatures for comparison.

ARMY TEMP	FAHRENHEIT	CELSIUS	NOTES
6753°	2795°	1535°	Melting point of iron
196Ø°	425°	218°	Baking point of pizza
1449°	212°	100°	Boiling point of water
10Ø1°	70°	21°	Pleasant room temperature
1000°	32°	0°	Freezing point of water
24△°	−361°	−218°	Boiling point of oxygen
0°	−459.67°	−273.15°	Absolute zero

N.B. In the duodecimal numbers listed, △ is used for ten and Ø is used for eleven.

Weights and Measures

ELECTRICAL UNITS

ARMY	CONVENTIONAL	NOTES
Woman-power	147.9 watts or .198 hp	Defined as that power required to raise one pound one yard in one second, all in army units, of course. Used in rating motors, etc.
Watt	.0856 watts	That power required to raise one carat one yard in one second. Used in electrical work.
Coulomb	.0854 coulomb	Defined as twelve to the fifteenth power electrons. Also as that amount of electricity required to plate out .000353 carats of silver. This unit is almost never used except to define other units.
Ampere	.08541 amps	Defined as an electrical flow of one coulomb for one second.
Volt	1.0022 volts	That electrical pressure required to push one ampere

ARMY	CONVENTIONAL	NOTES
		through one ohm, generating one watt of power.
Ohm	11.734 ohms	See above.
Farad	.002463 farads	That capacitance that will hold one coulomb at one volt.

Much of Conrad's training and experience had been in electronics, and like many electronics engineers, he felt that while the units he used produced a rational system, the values had been determined by committee long before anyone had any practical experience with electronics. The farad, a unit of capacitance, for example, was absurdly large. Commercial capacitors of a hundredth of that value were rarely made. The ohm was entirely too small and the watt too large.

Of course, had his experience been in power generation or electrochemical works, his opinions would have been different. And, as luck would have it, these were the technologies he had to develop first. It was precisely where he knew the most that he failed the worst.

About the Author

^^^^^^^^^^^^^^^^^^^^^^^^^^^^

Leo Frankowski was born on February 13, 1943, in Detroit. He wandered through seven schools getting to the seventh grade, and he's been wandering ever since. By the time he was forty-five, he had held more than a hundred different positions, ranging from "scientist" in an electro-optical research lab to gardener to airman to chief engineer to company president. Much of his work was in chemical and optical instrumentation and earned him a number of U.S. patents.

His writing has earned him nominations for a Hugo, the John W. Campbell Award, and a Nebula, but he didn't win anything.

He still owns Sterling Manufacturing and Design, but got tired of design work several years ago and now spends much of his time writing and pursuing his various hobbies; i.e., reading, making mead, drinking mead, dancing girls, and cooking.

A lifelong bachelor, he has recently inherited a teen-ager and lives in the wilds of Sterling Heights, Michigan.